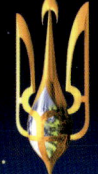

ATLANTIS MOTHERLAND

Authors
Flying Eagle & Whispering Wind

© Tetra XII inc. 2003
The entire contents of this book are protected according to United States and International Copyright laws and regulations.

Printed in Korea; Amica International Inc.

Publisher: COSMIC VORTEX
P.O. Box 880502, Pukalani, Maui, HI 96768
http://www.atlantis-motherland.com

Library of Congress Control Number: 2004091463
ISBN 0-9719580-0-9

The Artist
ERNIST NELSON
(Black Stallion)

Noted worldwide, for his magnificent sculptures and paintings, his multifaceted creativity grants him a broad range of art forms and insights into natural reality. His genetic memory and foresight gives birth to the endlessness of his artistic creations. His original techniques and media lend a depth to creations that stimulate the intellectual and emotional aspects of the viewer.

Flying Eagle & Whispering Wind

Flying Eagle, great grandson of the famous American Indian Chieftain, Quanah Parker, is a dynamic lecturer, a philosopher, a geologist, an artist, an astrologer and an ad-lib piano composer. Whispering Wind is an artist, counselor, a dancer, an actress and an adventurer. These two inseparable scientists have extensively researched throughout the entire Earth, to finally solve the worlds greatest mystery; The location of the ancient civilization of ATLANTIS. This 28-year research has opened doors into the innumerable quandaries of almost every field of science. Their research has created a demand for seminars and lectures. They are formulating the nucleus of a worldwide cultural superstructure; The Cosmic Vortex family. This rapidly expanding multinational family is composed of dedicated persons who possess a strong desire to find their true identity and purpose, to facilitate the harmonious rejuvenation of our cultural heritage and to restore balance to beautiful Earth and ATLANTIS-MOTHERLAND.

Dawn of a New Age

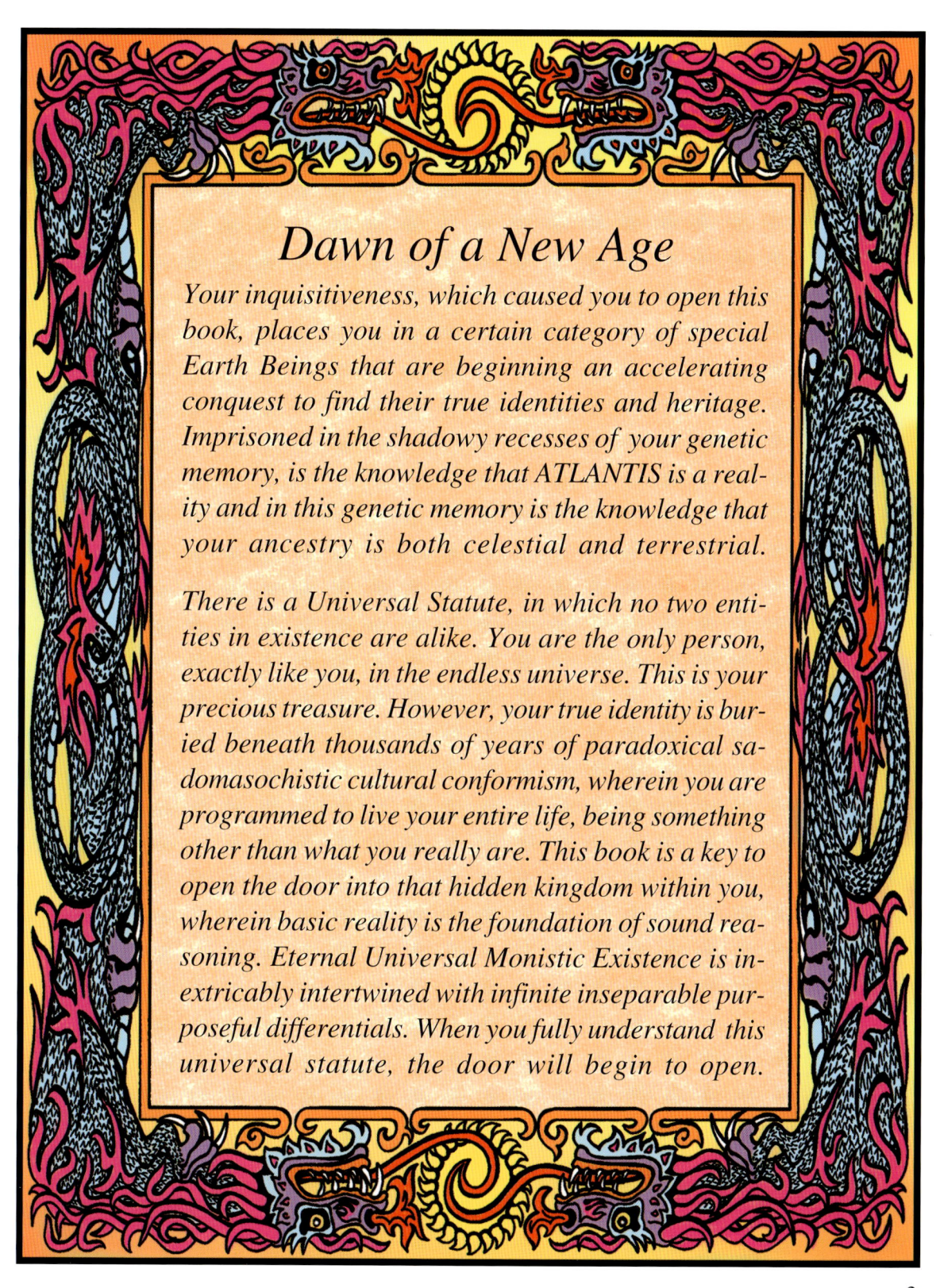

Your inquisitiveness, which caused you to open this book, places you in a certain category of special Earth Beings that are beginning an accelerating conquest to find their true identities and heritage. Imprisoned in the shadowy recesses of your genetic memory, is the knowledge that ATLANTIS is a reality and in this genetic memory is the knowledge that your ancestry is both celestial and terrestrial.

There is a Universal Statute, in which no two entities in existence are alike. You are the only person, exactly like you, in the endless universe. This is your precious treasure. However, your true identity is buried beneath thousands of years of paradoxical sadomasochistic cultural conformism, wherein you are programmed to live your entire life, being something other than what you really are. This book is a key to open the door into that hidden kingdom within you, wherein basic reality is the foundation of sound reasoning. Eternal Universal Monistic Existence is inextricably intertwined with infinite inseparable purposeful differentials. When you fully understand this universal statute, the door will begin to open.

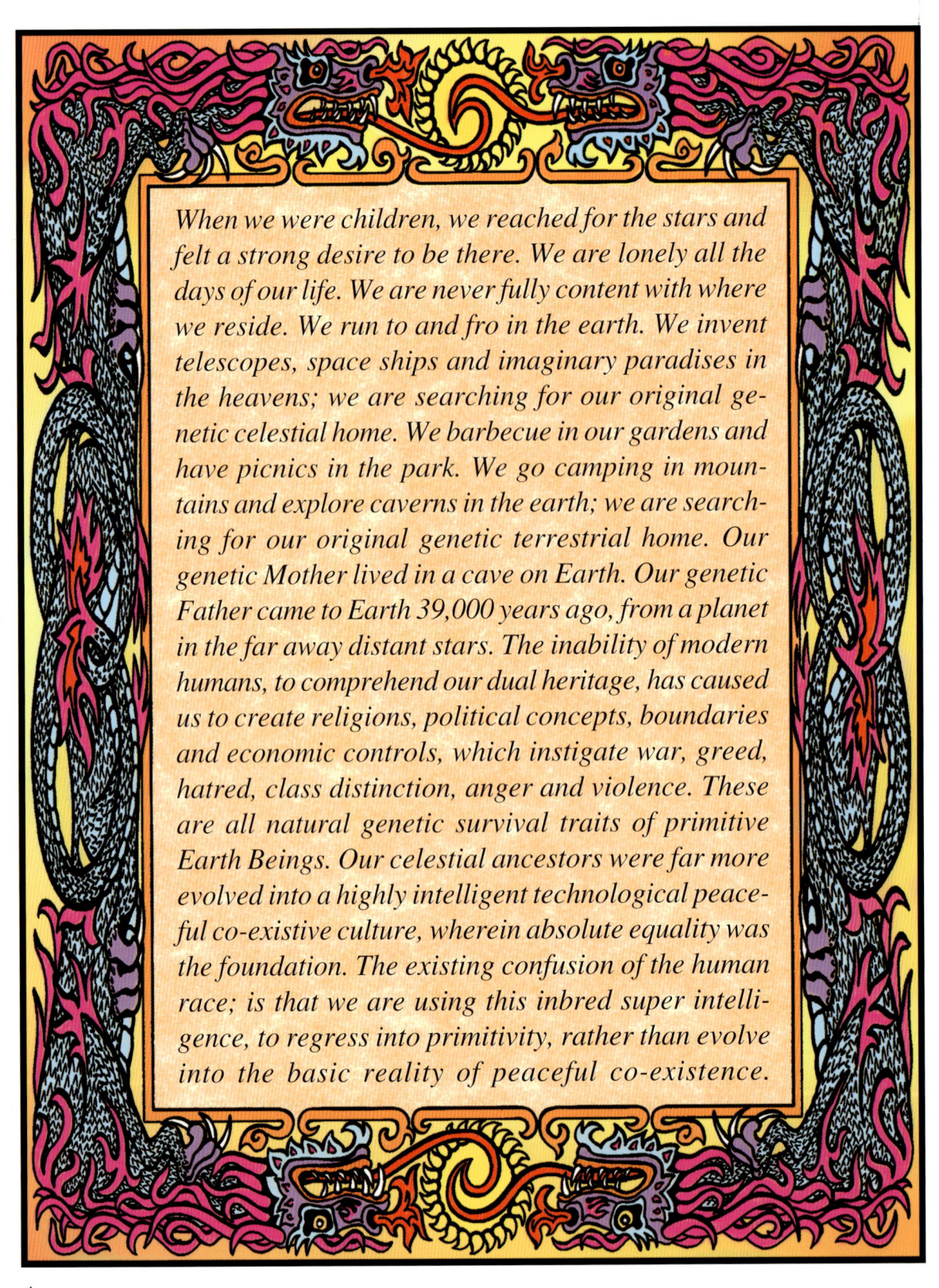

When we were children, we reached for the stars and felt a strong desire to be there. We are lonely all the days of our life. We are never fully content with where we reside. We run to and fro in the earth. We invent telescopes, space ships and imaginary paradises in the heavens; we are searching for our original genetic celestial home. We barbecue in our gardens and have picnics in the park. We go camping in mountains and explore caverns in the earth; we are searching for our original genetic terrestrial home. Our genetic Mother lived in a cave on Earth. Our genetic Father came to Earth 39,000 years ago, from a planet in the far away distant stars. The inability of modern humans, to comprehend our dual heritage, has caused us to create religions, political concepts, boundaries and economic controls, which instigate war, greed, hatred, class distinction, anger and violence. These are all natural genetic survival traits of primitive Earth Beings. Our celestial ancestors were far more evolved into a highly intelligent technological peaceful co-existive culture, wherein absolute equality was the foundation. The existing confusion of the human race; is that we are using this inbred super intelligence, to regress into primitivity, rather than evolve into the basic reality of peaceful co-existence.

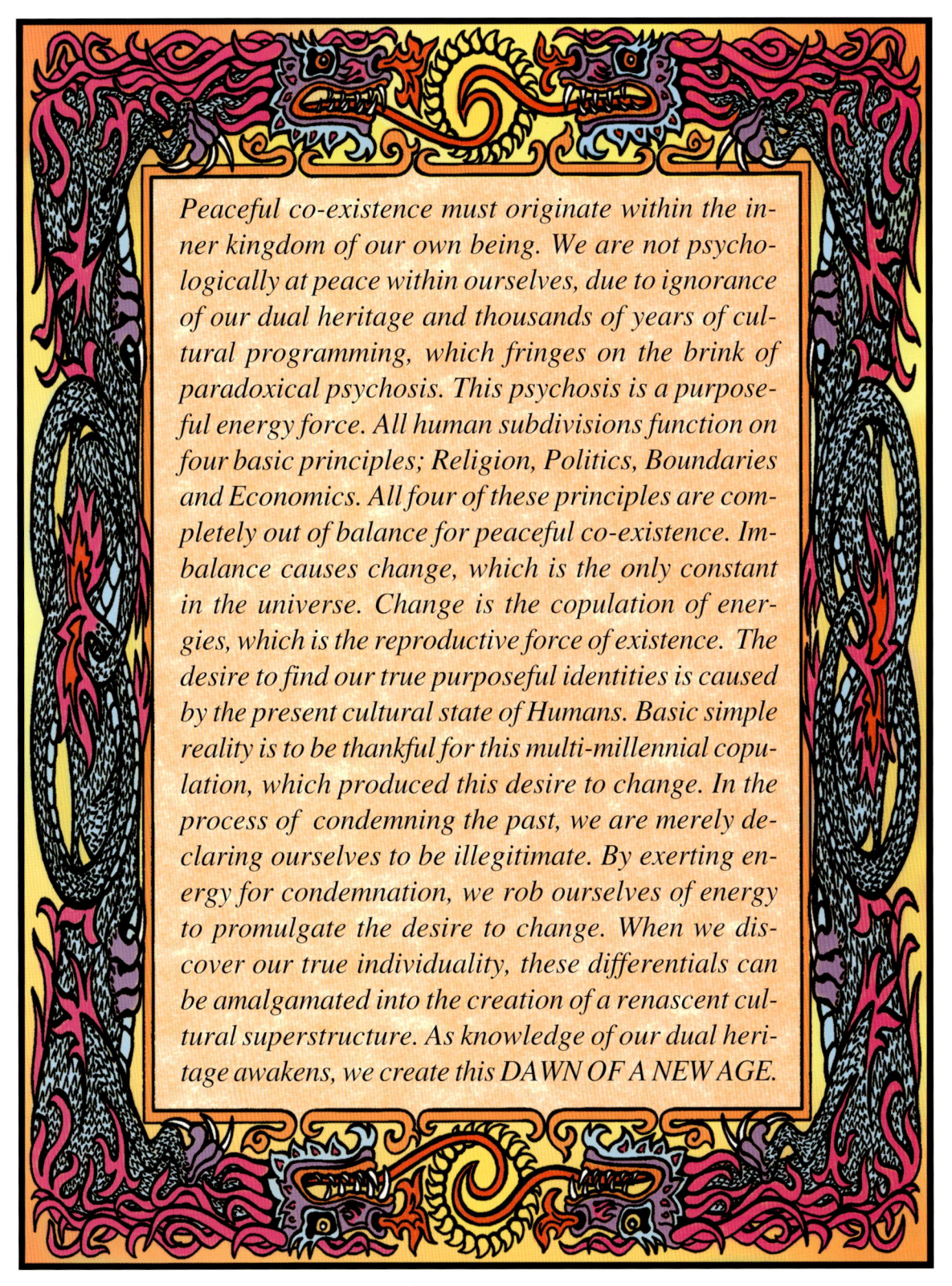

Peaceful co-existence must originate within the inner kingdom of our own being. We are not psychologically at peace within ourselves, due to ignorance of our dual heritage and thousands of years of cultural programming, which fringes on the brink of paradoxical psychosis. This psychosis is a purposeful energy force. All human subdivisions function on four basic principles; Religion, Politics, Boundaries and Economics. All four of these principles are completely out of balance for peaceful co-existence. Imbalance causes change, which is the only constant in the universe. Change is the copulation of energies, which is the reproductive force of existence. The desire to find our true purposeful identities is caused by the present cultural state of Humans. Basic simple reality is to be thankful for this multi-millennial copulation, which produced this desire to change. In the process of condemning the past, we are merely declaring ourselves to be illegitimate. By exerting energy for condemnation, we rob ourselves of energy to promulgate the desire to change. When we discover our true individuality, these differentials can be amalgamated into the creation of a renascent cultural superstructure. As knowledge of our dual heritage awakens, we create this DAWN OF A NEW AGE.

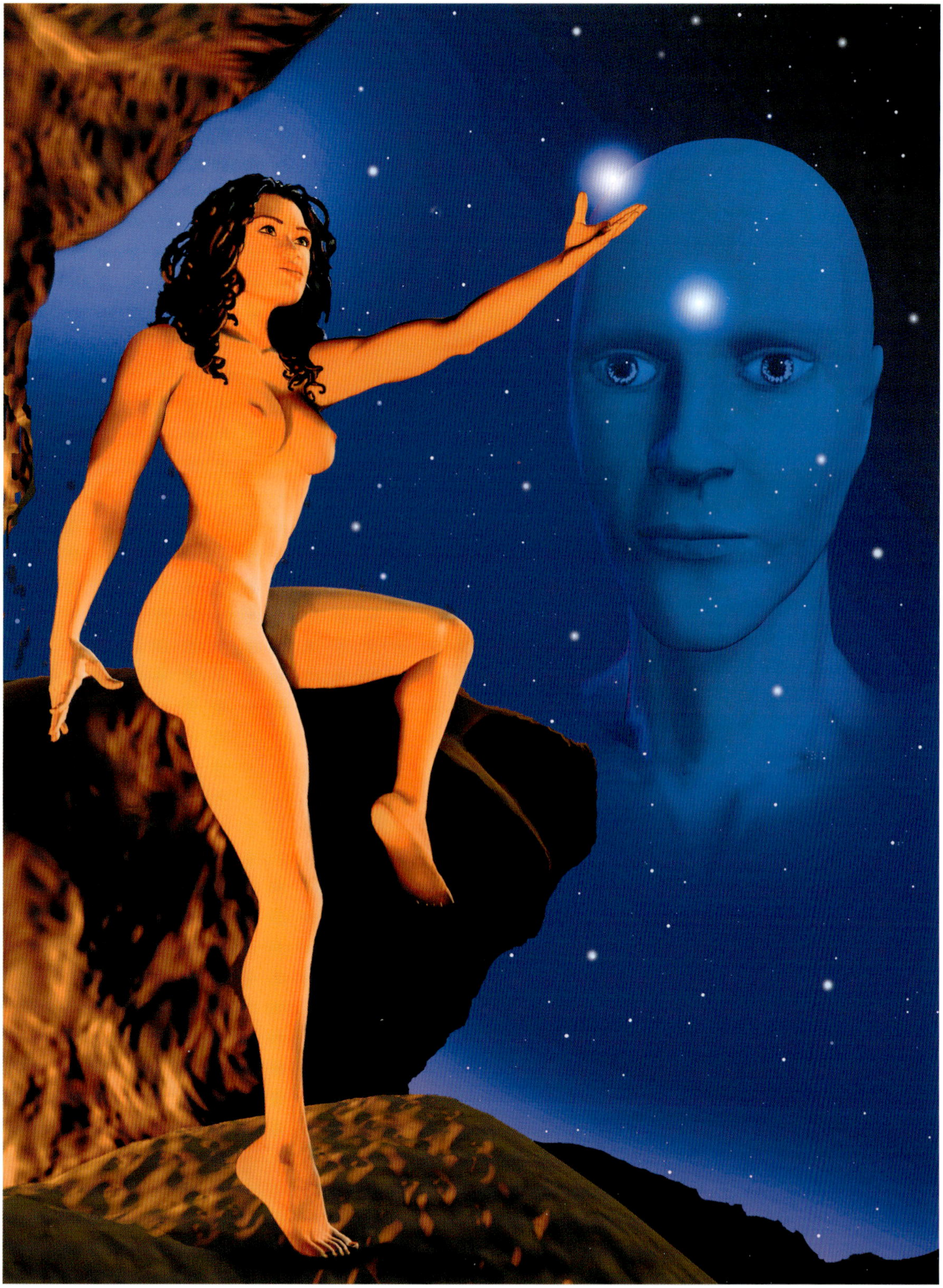

37,000 BC

Her name is Tua, the primitive sound for Bird. She is a primitive maiden, three years past puberty. She lives with her Mother and Father in a cave near the top of a high hill. Her Father is Dai, the primitive sound for Mighty One. He is the leader of a large tribe of primitive beings who dwell in the plain surrounding the hill. Her Mother is Tai, the primitive sound for Wise One. She is a strong primitive female who is very protective of her only daughter. She will violently attack any male that approaches Tua.

Tua is always alone and shuns the rest of the tribe. When males try to mate with her, she fights like a tiger. She growls and bites like a wild animal and chases them away with a spear. The entire tribe has a fearful respectful reverence for Tua. These primitive beings are aware of the natural tradition wherein the strongest rule. Tua's Father is the strongest male and her Mother is the wisest Female. Tua is destined to mate with the next leader of the tribe. The males challenge each other to be the one Tua selects to mate with.

Tua gazes at the brightest star in the night sky. She reaches for the star, as if beckoning for it to come to her. She feels a powerful reproductive force coming from this star. She removes her body coverings and sings a low musical chant. She is repeating E TUA, E TUA over and over. This is the primitive sound for BIG BIRD, BIG BIRD.

An intelligent force, in the far away heavens is calling to Tua. This reproductive energy force is transmitted from a planet, eight light years distant, by a being from a species, many millions of years more evolved than Tua. This highly advanced civilization has searched the universe to find a species which is chromosomally compatible to reproduce with and a planet compatible to their life sustenance. These scientific explorers and universal adventurers have explored many energy sources and know that the speed of light is not the fastest frequency for transmission in the universe. Their radionuclidic metrological control, of the one trillionth of a nano second decay of the alpha particle in the nucleus of an atom, uses the straight line ray of the Alpha Particle decay, as a conductor to transmit various frequencies, including thought waves. Many probes have shown Tua's emotional and glandular functions are compatible to breed with and the beautiful Blue Planet, where Tua dwells, is very hospitable to their species.

The receptivity of Tua is amazing to the Being who is transmitting thought frequencies to her: "Tua. Your Father and Mother will soon die. You must find a mate to lead your people. Your species will vanish if they do not have a strong leader. I will come to you soon. Together we can prevent your species from becoming extinct. You and I will become the future leaders of your large tribe. I will mate with you. We will begin a new tribe with countless numbers. I will come to your planet the next time the moon is big. Watch for the "Big Bird" in the meadow. Others will come with me. You will know me. I am Xoah."

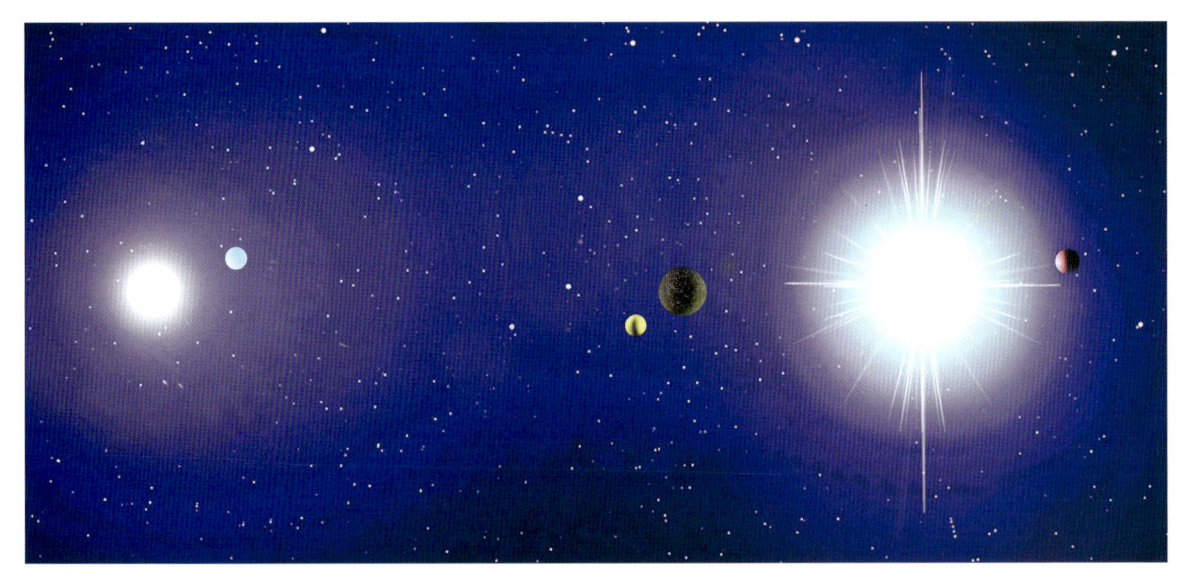

SIRIUS STAR COMPLEX IN CANUS MAJOR

Xoah dwells on a planet in the Sirius Star complex in the constellation, Canis Major. Earth astronomers have been mystified as they watch this star move about the heavens. This brightest star in the sky is not one star. It is a trinary star complex composed of a blue-green giant star, named Sirius A, a white dwarf star, named Sirius B and a burned out black dwarf star, named Sirius C. The black dwarf star is the center of gravity, which holds the white dwarf star and the blue-green giant star in orbits around this center of gravity. These two stars are always at 180° opposition to each other as they orbit the black dwarf, approximately once every fifty years. The apparent motion of Sirius, is the white dwarf and the blue-green giant moving in their orbits. They are so close to each other they appear as one star when viewed from Earth.

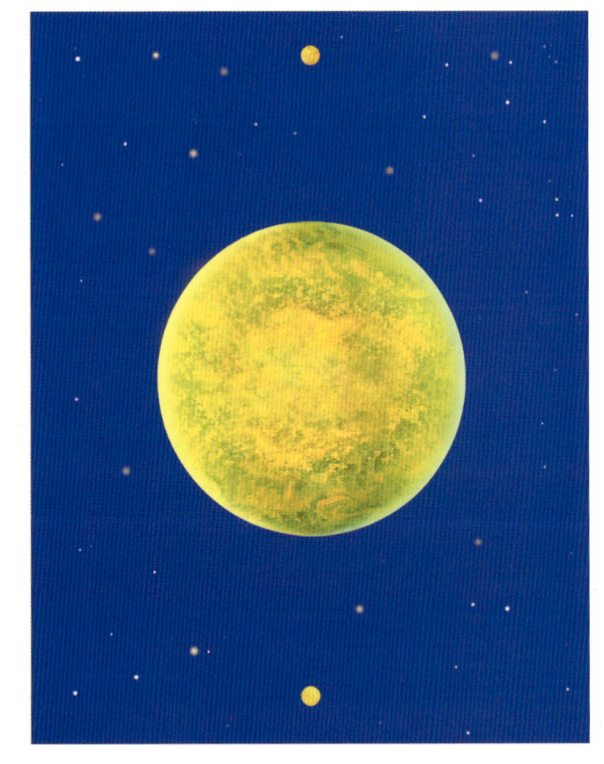

The planet Xoah dwells on is Xylanthia. This planet also orbits the black dwarf star approximately every 50 years. Xylanthia is stationary with respect to Sirius A and Sirius B. It has 1 axial rotation every 24 hours. This configuration creates a simultaneous sunrise and sunset every 12 hours. There is no night on Xylanthia. This planet has two moons, which are stationary above the two Polar Regions. These moons are always full due to the reflection of Sirius A and Sirius B. The brilliance of Sirius A is created by a terrific atomic fission. The hot Sirius B is in a disintegrating atomic fission.

Sirius C, the oldest star in this trinary complex, was originally an exploding fissionable mass. The only planet that did not fall back into Sirius C during its billions of years of contraction, was Xylanthia which was originally formed from Sirius C. Sirius B has only one planet. This white dwarf star had other planets, which have plunged into this fiery hot star during billions of years. The giant, Sirius A, is in the early process of hurling matter outward, which will form planets in its future.

The surface temperature of Sirius A and Sirius B are approximately the same. Each successive Xylanthian day has an even temperature which is slightly cooler at the simultaneous sunrises and sunsets. The temperature fluctuates from 70 to 80 degrees.

Xylanthia is billions of years older than the Earth. The black dwarf star, Sirius C, is many billions of years older than Earth's sun. This star burned out before the Earth sun came into existence. The magnetic forces of Sirius A and Sirius B, prevented Xylanthia from falling into Sirius C during its contraction. These same forces hold Xylanthia in its present configuration. This planet is only one half the size of Earth.

The planet of Xylanthia has no oceans. Its water cycle is vastly different from the

SIRIUS STAR COMPLEX; ORBITAL CONFIGURATION

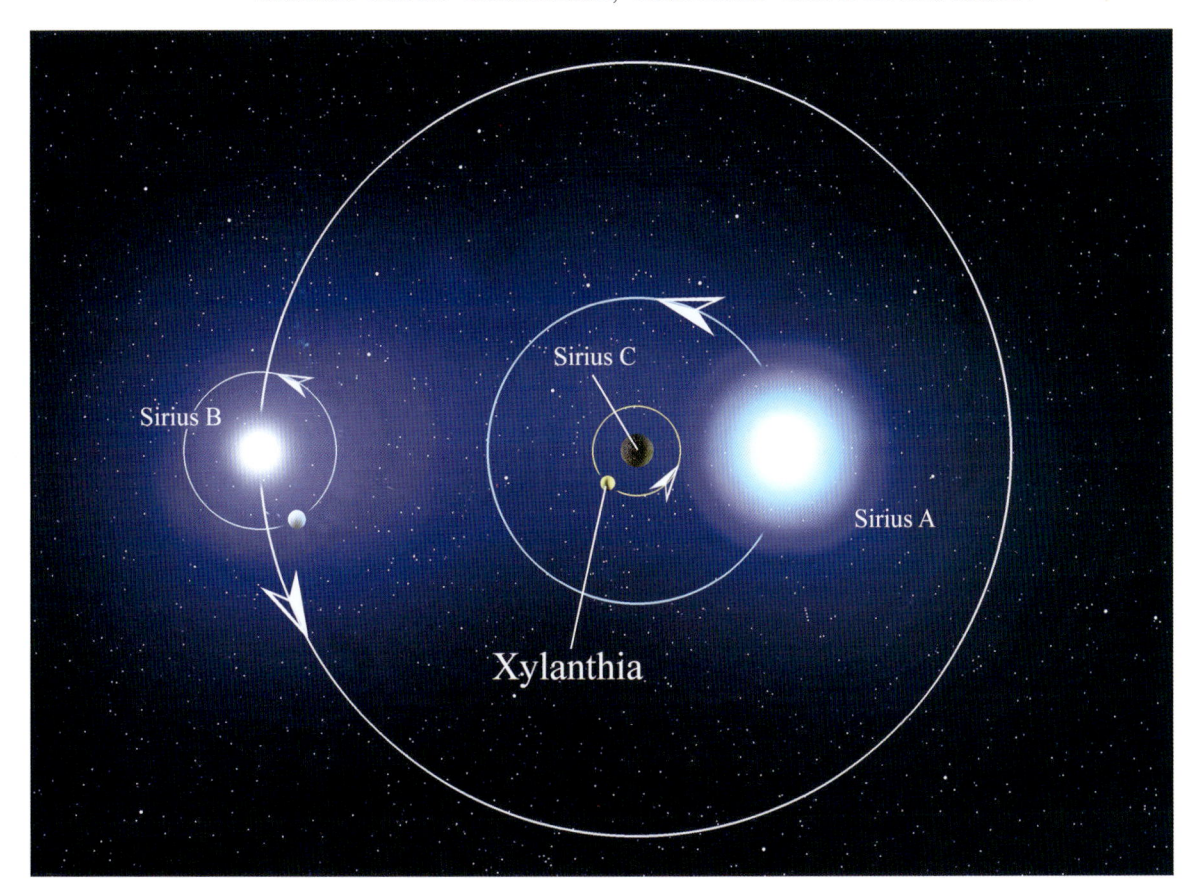

Earth. Controlled sulfur dioxide emissions from the planet, sodium content in the atmosphere and thermal differentials, cause a surface condensation during twilight times. This condensation generates a mist that rises from the planet's surface every 12 hours. This process produces only the quantity of water needed for the subsistence of the inhabitants and the exotic vegetation and fauna. The majority of flora and fauna exist in the lower elevations. The higher elevations are used for advanced technology and scientific research installations, many of which are below the surface. There are no clouds, storms or high winds. Thermal differentials create a constant gentle breeze. As one star is setting on one horizon and the other star is rising on the other horizon; a spectacular vivid rainbow appears on both horizons, due to the condensation mists rising from the planet's surface.

The cosmic influence of these two suns created a biological androgyny in all fauna, including the Xylanthians; all species on Xylanthia are both male and female. This stellar configuration also created a gynaecandrous or androgynous function in all flora on Xylanthia; the staminate and pistillate position in all flower clusters had either the male or female flowers uppermost.

The Xylanthians are the result of a 3 million-year evolution from an androgynous flying serpent-like creature into a large flying-reptile creature, which stood seven feet tall on two, six toed feet. These creatures' bodies and wings were covered with hairless and featherless leather-like membrane. They had a 16-foot wingspread and a long tail, which they used for balance and as a weapon in battle. These creatures were solitary. They were carnivorous and cannibalistic. They fatally battled after a dual breeding process. They produced two offspring; the stronger of the two would kill and eat the weaker one, during their early life. Asexual reproduction rarely occurred.

These androgynous flying reptiles evolved into a bi-pedal lizard. Their wings transformed into two arms with six fingered hands. Their tails gradually disappeared. These lizardlike beings remained carnivorous and cannibalistic. They formed breeding pairs. It was not uncommon for both breeding partners to conceive. As these upright creatures evolved, they began to form tribal groups, which battled against each other for territory. These small groups lived in caverns, which were plentiful in the higher elevations on Xylanthia. These strict carnivores gradually became omnivores.

As these primitive creatures evolved, they migrated from high plateau regions to lush green valley regions at lower elevations. These valleys had become fertile areas with ample water and a rich variety of flora and fauna for their sustenance.

As their evolution progressed, these creatures began to make tools. Their communication skills became more advanced, they developed farming and began bartering among tribes. They started building primitive shelters aboveground so they could live near their crops, to care for and protect them. They began creating weapons for hunting and to protect themselves and their crops from predators and rival tribes. As food production increased these tribes became larger and basic societal rules began to be created and enforced.

During the next two hundred thousand years, these beings of Xylanthia developed into their present biological form. The Xylanthians are androgynous beings. They are over 6 feet tall and slender with narrow hips and small shapely buttocks. They have no hair on their body, no eyelashes or brows. Their soft naked skin is almost translucent, light blue white. Their eyes are large almond shaped and very blue with large pupils. They have thin lips and a delicate small chin. Their nose is straight and not large. Their small ears are close to the head, slightly pointed on top with no lobes. They have 6 fingers and 6 toes. The Xylanthians have hemispherical breasts with pink protruding nipples. The vulva is prominent. There is no scrotum or external testis. Their penis is pointed and lies inside the vagina and protrudes 8 to 10 inches at erection. The testis and ovaries are two glands, which perform separate functions. One gland produces eggs and one produces sperm, they are located back in the vagina at the base of the penis. The egg producing gland is attached to the uterus with a small fallopian opening.

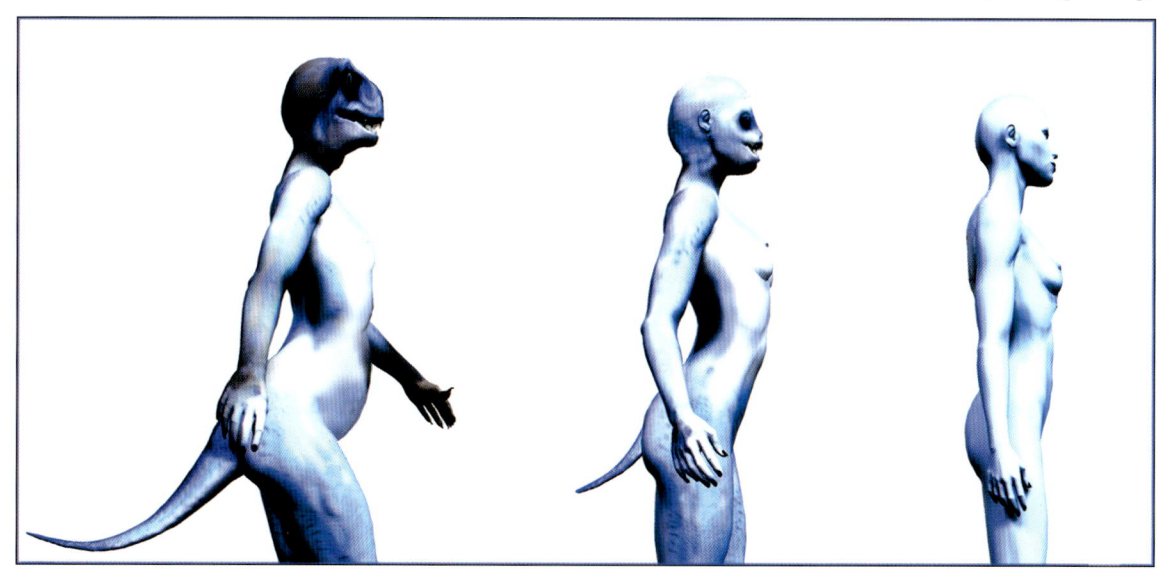

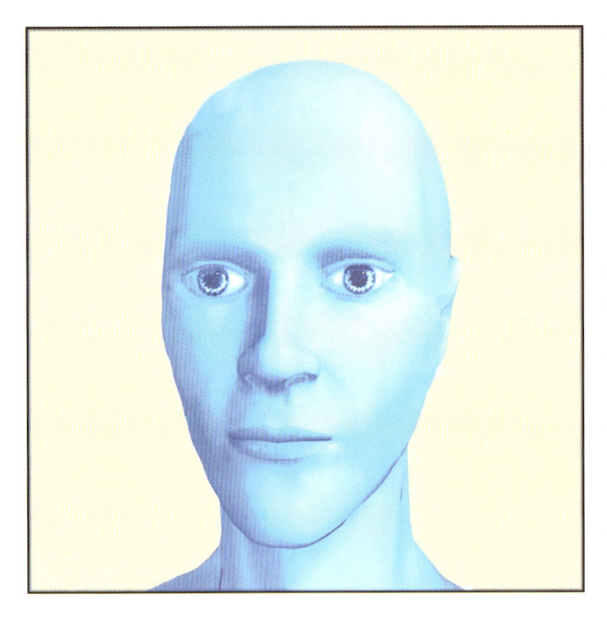

As Xylanthian weapons became more sophisticated and deadly, tribal wars dominated their existence. After many generations of endless battles, one tribe finally gained supremacy over all others. A powerful aristocratic government was formed that maintained strict governmental control over all functions of society. These aristocratic Xylanthians maintained their power by class separation. Members of the government and military were honored and given every luxury available, while the rest of the populace struggled to maintain bare existence. The inequality, discrimination, hypocrisy and injustice of this system lead to a completely polarized and corrupt society. Political conspiracies within the justice, economic, and social functions of society were rampant. The populace abused mind altering chemical substances and developed religious fanaticism as ways to cope with their oppression. The greed of the aristocracy was boundless; the more they had, the more they wanted. As their knowledge of science and technology increased the aristocracy became obsessed with the possibilities of unlimited power through control of the processes of nuclear fission and deoxyribonucleic acid alteration. The government created secret scientific research laboratories, which were isolated from the populace. The aristocracy was also obsessed with increasing their knowledge of quantum physics and the laws of relativity. This quest to create eternal life and gain unlimited power and wealth was more addictive than the drugs that were used to keep the lower class subdued.

A small group of scientists became aware of the way the aristocracy was using these new technologies. They knew this misuse of power would eventually destroy all life on Xylanthia. These few scientists found a way to secretly isolate themselves in a series of massive underground caverns. For ten years, they conducted research for ways to use their advanced technology to create a better society. As their studies were reaching completion, their underground complex was discovered by a secret government agency which dropped a nuclear device on their laboratory, killing all the scientists and destroying their entire research records. One scientist named Xypha had been isolated at another location on the planet. For the subsequent 10 years this scientist remained in hiding, continuing the research of the massacred scientists. During these 10 years the government became increasingly oppressive. A massive revolution of the populace began. Over 3 million Xylanthians were slaughtered and another 3 million inhabitants were enslaved and assigned to various slave labor positions. During the chaos of war and government confusion while re-classifying the citizenry and assigning them to labor functions, Xypha was able to re-enter society as a scientist, and was enslaved to the DNA research laboratory for botanical research.

The revolution caused a complete segregation of Xylanthians. The commander of the military became the absolute monarch. The entire working class, including all scientists, was forced to live in poverty. Food was rationed. They lived in crowded compounds. Curfews were established. All beings worked a 10 hour day with only one day off each month to attend government lectures on new rules, punishments and assignments. Clothing consisted of a simple uniform, which by law, was worn by all worker class citizens. Forced surgical sterilization was performed to control population growth. The military police strictly enforced the laws and continually monitored all workers. There were no prisons or courts. Any member of the military police could pass judgment and punishment at-the-spot of any incident. The only punishment was death. The workers were not permitted to possess any tasty food or beverage. The complete crop of every farm complex was tabulated and sent to government controlled processing plants. If any farmer or processing compound worker were found with any fresh produce, they were killed. If a baker, or any associates, were found to have any sweets, they were killed. Listening devices and hidden cameras were everywhere. Stool and urine samples were randomly taken and analyzed, throughout the entire work force. Sterilization, of both males and females, was enforced to prevent over population. This slavery existed for 10 years after the revolution.

Xypha, the scientist who had escaped the massacre, was assigned to DNA alteration of fruits and vegetables to increase the natural yield and improve the taste. Xypha secretly used this time at the laboratory to continue the work of designing a way to improve the culture and daily lives of Xylanthians, realizing that greed, hatred, jealousy and fear were the enemies of a harmonious culture. These emotions were not only taught by society but were caused by chemical processes within their brains. Xypha experimented with chemical processes that would naturally curb aggressive behavior and promote feelings of love, contentment and compassion. Xypha discovered that mixtures of carbon, hydrogen and oxygen would produce crystalline phenolic resins of numerous types of cannabinols which would alter emotional and mental processes without physical harm. The entire ruling class selfishly enjoyed an exotic fruit which Xypha DNA altered with cannabinol C_{21}-H_{25}-$O(OH)$. The aristocrats behavior began to change; they began to become aware of philosophical reality.

Within one-year, the harsh controls and restrictions of the enslaved population were modified. The military began to mingle and reason with the workers who were allowed to work fewer hours and have time for recreation. The on-the-spot judgment and killings stopped. The two classes began to interact with sharing of luxuries, including Xypha's exotic fruit, which eliminated anger and revenge in the working class. Sensual relations were exchanged. Joyful ceremonies with music, feasts, theatre and dance became common, with both groups attending. Pleasant living facilities were erected for the working class.

As this commingling of these two groups continued, the Xylanthians gathered into intellectual groups and began reasoning together. The various scientists in different categories discussed ways to more peacefully coexist and evolve into a harmonious society. The Monarch and all government advisors joined in these discussions. The Xylanthians built a gigantic facility for research to improve upon their existing electronic and nuclear intelligence. The first priority of the scientists' research was neutralizing radiation caused by atomic wars in various parts of their planet. Their next mission was to design political, economic, sociological and cultural systems wherein everyone could live in ultimate contentment. Meanwhile the exotic fruit reproduced itself twice annually and the entire 20 million beings on the planet Xylanthia enjoyed the prized special fruit.

Xypha became the leader of the scientific community with full cooperation from the monarchy. The scientists and the government formed a coalition, combining their knowledge and efforts to achieve technological alteration of their planet, which the wars had devastated. Within 5 years the great mass of the military was transformed into a civil construction unit. The same beings that used to indiscriminately kill their fellow citizens were now wholly concerned with improving conditions for everyone.

Years of extended debate, dialogue and reason established the design structure of an Alpha Processor. In the following 150 years, a master Alpha Processor was constructed and linked, by a bio-contact, with each Xylanthian. The Alpha Processor was magnificent in size and beauty. The function of the government was replaced by this Alpha Processor, which analyzed each Xylanthians needs and desires and transmitted this information to the entities talented to fulfill such requirements. This interchange of energy between each being and the Alpha Processor ensured that all Xylanthians had equal access to knowledge and everyone knew that they were an intricate participant in the vitality of the their monistic species. Any being can communicate with anyone at any time, by bio thought process through the Alpha Processor.

This expansive evolution of technological and sociological sciences instigated a radical change in the behavior of all Xylanthians. DNA enhancement determined each one's individual talents, interests and expertise. They highly respected each other's differences. The Xylanthians had, by this time, eliminated hunger, poverty and sickness. War had been abandoned. They no longer felt fear, hatred, jealousy or prejudice towards each other. Religions were abandoned due to their paradoxical psychotic nature. Anyone in this advanced society could lie under a sensor and the entire physical and psychological system could be scanned in seconds, the sensor would automatically fragment the cells that were malfunctioning and reconstruct them immediately.

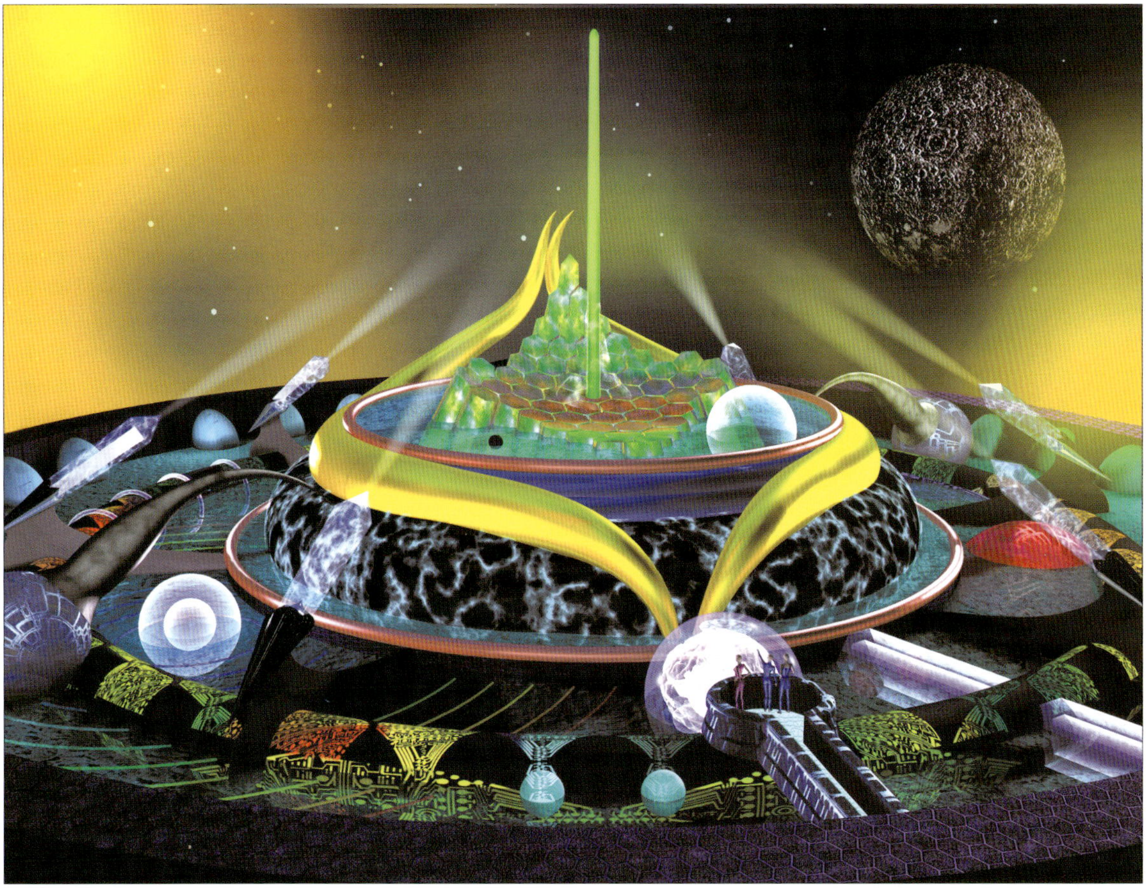

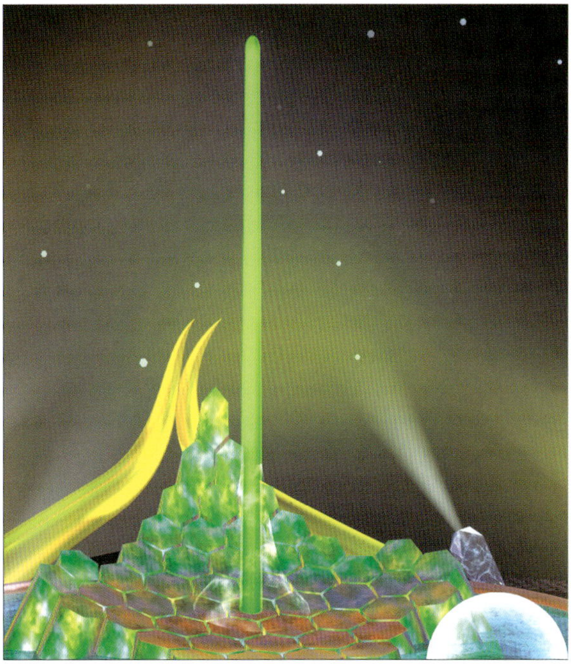

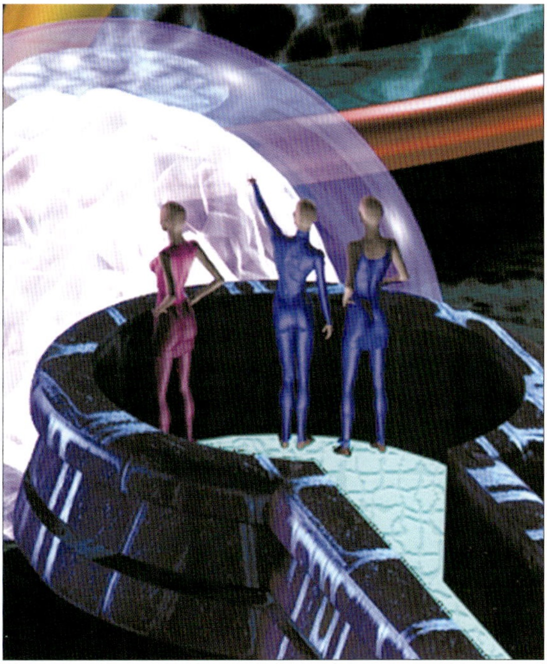

Advanced DNA enhancement initiated a neuro-psychological function creating a natural desire for peaceful coexistence. The Xylanthians began to live for the pleasure of their work, which was to care for their planet and species. These Xylanthians enjoyed beauty of all kinds. They were zealous environmentalists and altered all flora and fauna which was dangerous or poisonous, nurtured the most beautiful of birds and animals and cultivated exotic flowering plants and trees. The Xylanthians delighted in song, music, dance and theatre and liked adventure and debate. They exhibited themselves for sensual pleasure and did not discriminate against any part of their body. Clothing was worn only as needed for protection, technical purposes or special ornamentation.

The Xylanthian sensual and affectionate emotions are not selective. There are no marriages or family structures. Each being in this monistic society loves and respects everyone equally. This eliminates possessiveness, jealousy, insecurity and monotonous familiarity.

There was no personal desire to procreate. The common concern of Xylanthians was the creation of the best offspring to advance their culture. Their offspring were genetically designed with qualities and talents as were needed in their society. Xylanthians maintained a fertile sperm production by an anovulatory cycle in which eggs were not released. The control of fertility did not alter the pleasure of copulation. The Alpha Processor regulated conception for population equilibrium. If a selective breeding was desirable it was possible for one beings sperm and ovulation activation to be simultaneous, thereby causing an asexual reproduction. However, if a complex breeding was desired; one beings sperm was de-activated and their ovulation was activated during sexual relations with the chosen partner. This created a unique Xylanthian with a new combination of genetic factors.

Xylanthian offspring have no special emotional attachments to their parent or parents. Gestation is 190 days. They are suckled for 3 days and were then placed in special facilities designed to stimulate their development. Each Infant is born with a bio-receptor-transmitter linked to the Alpha Processor, which instructs them according to their kinetic talents. They become ambulatory in 6 months. At 3 years of age they are divided into talent groups. Adulthood is reached at 10 years of age, when these young scientists begin their pleasureful, adventurous and explorative professions in this highly technological society.

The Xylanthian technological complex demands a tremendous power consumption. This power demand is fulfilled by cosmic receptors which collect cosmic energy from Sirius A and Sirius B. Receptors are located at the Polar Regions. These locations provide continual contact with both stars. Energy is transferred from the receptors to cosmic separators which select components that are fusional with planet resources. All Xylanthian transmissions are by remote function.

The foundation, of all Xylanthian technological precepts, is based on the principle of an INFINITE AMALGAMATING MONISTIC UNIVERSE (IAMU). Scientists discovered that perceived voids in astral existence and presupposed empty space in atomic structure, were completely filled with energy functions composed of particles which were infinitely divisible. Xylanthian society was patterned from their scientific discovery that all

Xylanthian Subterranean Cosmic Particle Receptor.

entities in existence have no individuality, separate from monistic universality; each entity is an infinitely divisible energy design which has a purpose and is directly relative to and is dependent upon the function of the whole. IAMU research also revealed there is no pure basic unit in existence; all entities, regardless of how small or large, contained a quantity of something other than its major content. Positively or negatively charged particles each possess a minor quality of the other. THEIR RESEARCH PROVED ASTRAL EXISTENCE AND MICRO EXISTENCE TO BE ONE MONISTIC INFINITE INSEPARABLE WHOLE.

IAMU IS THE LIFE FORCE THAT PERMEATES ALL THAT EXISTS. EXISTENCE HAS NO BOUNDARY. BOUNDARIES ONLY SURROUND THAT WHICH IS COMPREHENSIBLE IN AN INCOMPREHENSIBLE INFINITE WHOLE. TRUE PRIMORDIAL REALITY IS INCOMPREHENSIBLE INFINITY.

Xylanthian scientists conquered the knowledge of POLARITY WITHIN A WHOLE; every entity in the monistic whole, has a polarized function. IAMU existence possesses a will to be nonexistent. This will creates a desire, in all entities, to be something other than what they are. This desire initiates

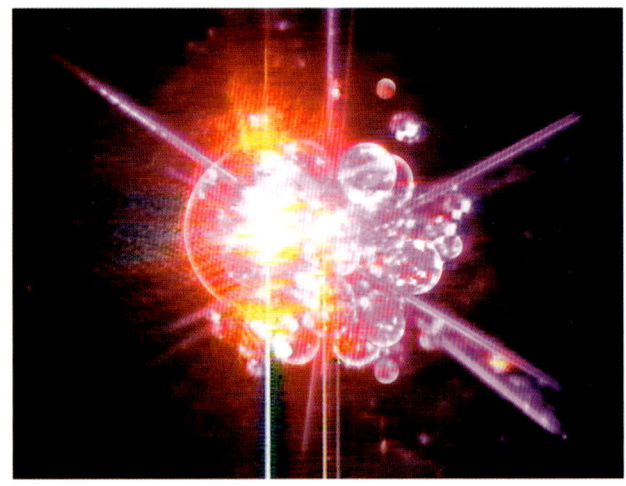

Xylanthian Cosmic Particle Separator and internal components.

a powerful force called procreation (change). The only way nonexistence can be attained is to change from what is, to something else; once any entity changes, its former existence becomes nonexistent. No entity can be changed back to its original state. Change is motion, the bloodstream of existence.

IAMU is perpetual change in boundless Existence. Two forces regulate change; the receptive force and the creative force. Their diastolic and systolic motion is the breath of existence. These two forces are inseparable. When the receptive force contracts, the creative force automatically expands and penetrates the receptive force. This influences the receptive force to expand into procreation (change), thereby becoming the creative force. This change subdues the creative force into a systolic state, causing it to become the receptive force.

Xylanthians discovered the bio-transmitter, in their brains, creates an energy frequency with a speed of transmission, faster than any previously known energy force. They found this energy frequency was not a concentric emission from a given point as most energy transmissions are; but a straight line controlled directive frequency. Computation of the Alpha Processor disclosed that thoughts, emotions, dreams and imagination, are energy forces that can be generated by the semi-bio brain of the Alpha Processor.

The process of atomic sub-particle fragmentation was used to change any entity in existence into any desired infinitesimally small state of sub-energy. By using thought frequency as a conductor, this sub-energy could be transported anywhere and reconstructed to an almost original state of existence. This entire procedure only consumes one trillionth of a nano second per light year of distance, thereby minimizing the degree of change. Fragmentation was attained by templating the sub-atomic structure of any object or frequency and reducing this structure to the state of nirvana, wherein the changing diastolic and systolic forces of the creative and receptive forces reach a point of balance. The speed at passing point of balance is the ultimate motion in existence, infringing on the state of incomprehensible non-existence.

The omega particle in an atom, exists for thirteen hundred-billionths of a second, before it changes to non-existence and becomes something other than what it was during its brief existence. Its androgynous purpose is to be primarily receptive to its minor creative component, entice it to penetrate its receptivity and give birth to another energy source, thereby changing into another particle with a major creative component. All of this function takes thirteen hundred-billionths of a second; Xylanthian scientists regard this as a basic motion, light speed is archaic. As Xylanthian scientists probed into the Alpha particle, they found a universe of galaxies, novas and star systems. They probed the sub-atomic substance of a planet in one of these minute star systems and found they were fragmenting particles of emotion and thought. They also found they had discovered the universal constant: incomprehensible Infinity.

The Alpha Processor was designed to process 1 billion independent links simultaneously, without interrupting its continual link with each of Xylanthia's 12 million inhabitants. It is also linked to other processors in advanced societies at various places in astral existence. They extensively researched to find a probable unknown Universal Processor.

"Blue Planet Contacted, Being Responding"

There is no classified information on the planet. Anyone can access the Central Processing Unit and all data at anytime. When new data is uploaded, it is available to the entire populace.

Xoah uploads a message that creates a tumultuous joyful uproar of the entire populace, "BLUE PLANET CONTACTED, BEING RESPONDING". Everyone accesses the probe that Xoah has originated. The Alpha Processor immediately applies IAMU frequency and everyone sees this Blue Planet Being. They all know that she can see Xoah who is using thought frequency to maintain contact with her. The Xylanthians are sensual beings. They see her beautiful nude body. They hear her musical chant. They see her hand reaching toward them and they want to touch her. They can feel her strong desire to breed. Their exuberance increases for hours as they feast, dance, make music, and copulate in the gardens outside the complexes. They tease Xoah because he doesn't break his thought contact with Tua until the morning sun on the Blue Planet causes her to cease contact. An exuberant joy is felt throughout Xylanthia. Everyone immediately requests access to the Blue Planet files. The Alpha Processor has received this inquiry and automatically opens, BLUE PLANET database.

Database listed fifty thousand probes on Blue Planet, which showed a five million year evolution of the present Blue Planet beings. The original beings were primarily aquatic animals with a diet of small marine animals; however their relaxation and breeding was on shore land where they occasionally ate flightless birds. These original creatures had two front flippers and two rear flippers, which were used for their excellent swimming abilities and aquatic food gathering. On shore land they were quadruped on their four flippers, although some shore land movements were bipedal on the rear flippers. Their bodies were four feet in length and covered with silky hair.

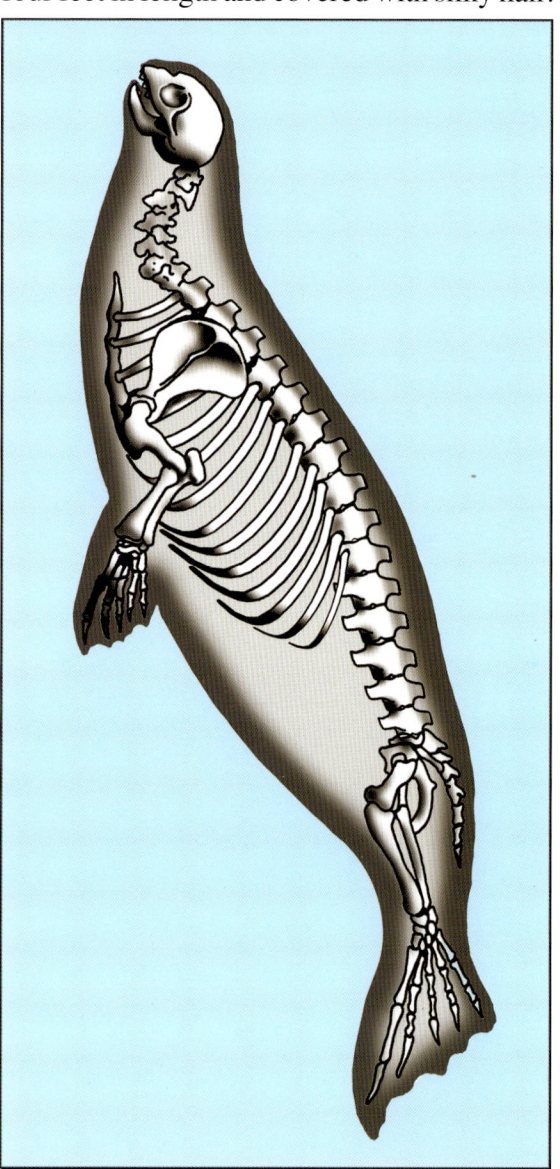

Medical science is mystified by the coccyx (tailbone) at the lower end of the human spine. The coccyx is the evolutionary remnant of the combined tailbone structures of the primitive Xylanthian creature and the aquatic Earth creature.

PRIMITIVE HUMANOID SPECIES

During one million years of evolution, Tua's aquatic ancestors became bipedal land animals. Their front flippers evolved into arms with five fingers and their rear flippers became legs with five toes. Their silky hair grew longer and coarser, to cope with weather conditions. These upright creatures were omnivorous. Their diet was insects, small rodents and fruit. They became nomadic; where there was water, they subsisted on fish. Their genetics made them excellent swimmers. Fish could be caught with hands or mouths. They roamed over vast areas in pairs, producing one off spring annually. The offspring was deserted in one year to find a mate from another parentage.

During the following million years these upright beings began to form groups and establish territorial boundaries. They dwelled in caves instead of their nomadic temporary nesting habit. As their brain capacity evolved they made clothing, tools and primitive weapons. They hunted large animals in groups. The increase of small populations instigated territorial wars. Intertribal breeding increased. Cannibalism existed when food was scarce.

Tua's ancestors, the Pinnipedia family, branched into several species. The Phocidae (seal-like creatures) had no external ears. The Otariidae, Tua's seal-like ancestors had external ears. The Otariidae branched into the primitive Humanoid species, at the same time the Pongidae came forth from the sea and evolved into Anthropoid apes, gorillas, chimpanzees, orangutans, gibbons and other genus.

Xylanthians observed the evolution of another creature on Blue Planet, similar to their ancestors, a winged reptile (pterodactyl) that became extinct 50 million years before Tua's ancestors came out of the sea.

This extinction was due to drastic extended arid climate conditions on Blue Planet, which prevented these creatures from evolving into a similar species like the Xylanthians. Instead they evolved into a dwarfed species, the sguamata family. This evolution branched into the lacertilia and iguanidae species, creating the lizards, chameleons, geckos and various snakelike genus.

The Xylanthians also discovered similar creatures, on planets in other galaxies, that evolved into beings like themselves, who eventually communicated with the Xylanthians via the Alpha Processor.

Direction of Migrations

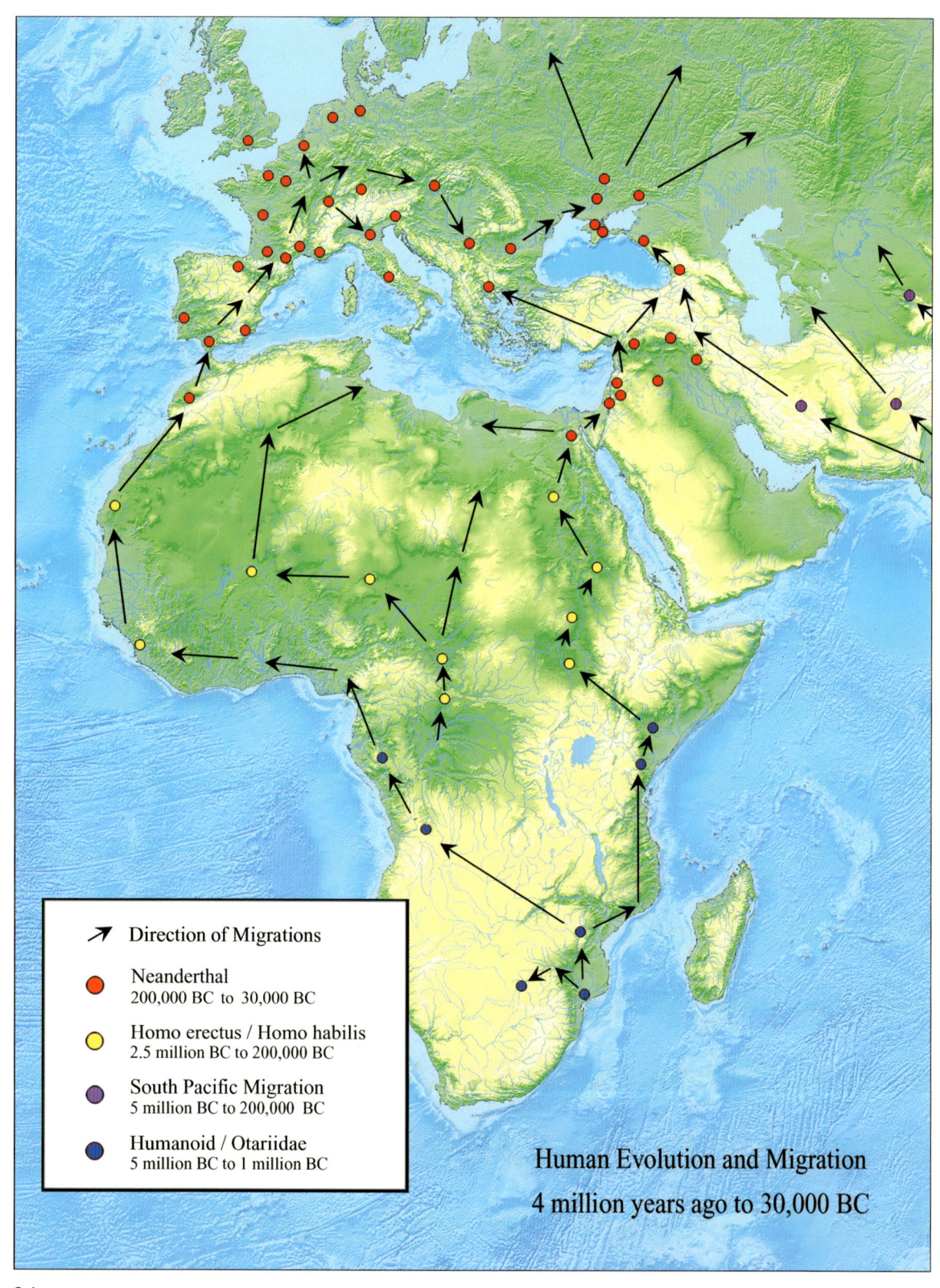

- **Neanderthal** 200,000 BC to 30,000 BC
- **Homo erectus / Homo habilis** 2.5 million BC to 200,000 BC
- **South Pacific Migration** 5 million BC to 200,000 BC
- **Humanoid / Otariidae** 5 million BC to 1 million BC

Human Evolution and Migration
4 million years ago to 30,000 BC

Severe climatic changes and food depletions instigated migrations, of Tua's primitive ancestors to various locations on the Blue Planet. During these lengthy migrations, tribes began to intermingle and breed with two similar natured tribes of beings, which were chromosomically compatible for interbreeding. These three different natures evolved from the same aquatic-to-land process at different locations on Blue Planet at slightly different time periods. There were two evolutions from South Africa and one from the South Pacific island region. The African migrations were northward to Europe. The Pacific migration was into continental Asia (Peking Man).

The mixture of genes, between three types of these primitive species, increased their brain capacity. All Blue Planet beings were born with bio-transmitter-receptors in their brains. The function of their bio-transmitter-receptors was limited to inner-body necessities. As their brain capacity progressively enlarged, they began to reason outside their primitive needs for basic survival. They created more sophisticated tools, weapons, traps and utensils. They began to reason beyond basic survival and use their creative imagination to create art forms. They started contemplating the behavior of other species. An awareness of heavenly bodies became more prevalent. They saw the stars at night, as nearby and very close to them, slightly above the clouds. They developed basic language systems. Their Petroglyphs originated written language.

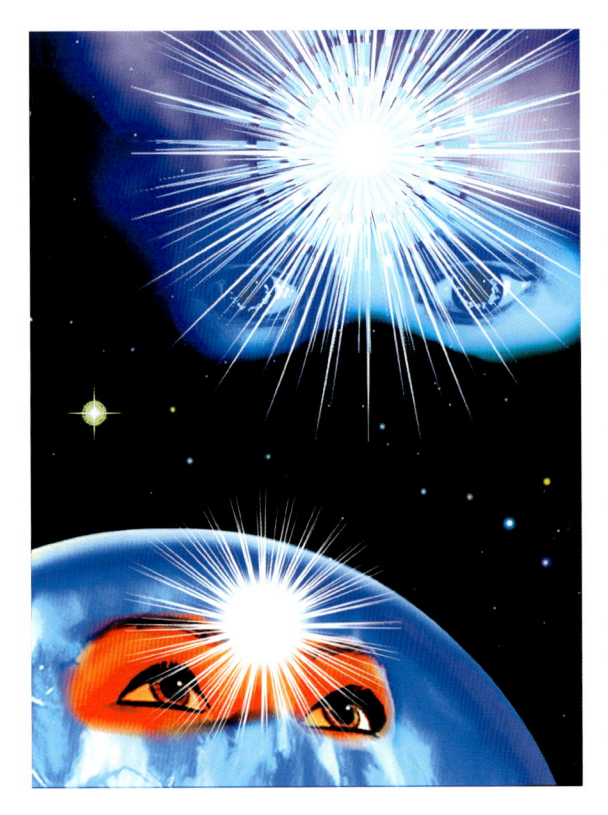

Tua was a stargazer. Her bio-transmitter-receptor had developed far past any other Blue Planet being. Xylanthian scientists knew the Blue Planet was compatible for their existence. They had made thousands of probes, in as many years, to contact a being that had developed the ability to respond and communicate with them. For 15 years, Xoah had repeatedly probed and watched Tua grow from a beautiful baby girl. Xoah knew she was attracted to this brightest star. Xoah's continual probes into her brain finally stimulated her bio-transmitter-receptor into a conductive communicating factor. Once this conductor is established, two-way communication is possible.

The pleasure outbreak on Xylanthia reached a maximum, Xoah's desire to transport to Blue Planet, changed the planetary emotion to an explorative adventure mode.

Xylanthians have space traveled for thousands of years. They have colonized planets in distant galaxies. These adventurers rarely return to Xylanthia. When explorers leave the planet, the Alpha Processor stimulates fertilization to replace them and preserve population equilibrium. Xylanthians only expire at their own will, as one expires one is replaced.

Travel ships are common. When one leaves the planet, everyone accesses the processor and experiences the same emotions as the travelers. The travel ships are large crafts designed for various speeds. The fastest speed is the IAMU fragmentation process which is one trillionth of a nanosecond per one light year of distance. The next slower travel is used for traveling on a controlled light beam at one hundred eighty thousand miles per second; this speed is used for inner stellar travel to nearby star systems. Both of these speeds require IAMU fragmentation process controlled by the Alpha Processor.

The next slower speed of twenty five thousand miles per hour is manually controlled, after re-materialization, for inner planetary travel outside atmospheric resistance. The crafts slowest manually controlled speed is zero to twenty five hundred miles per hour, for inner atmosphere maneuvering. These later two speeds use electro-magnetic gravitational components to regulate maneuverability.

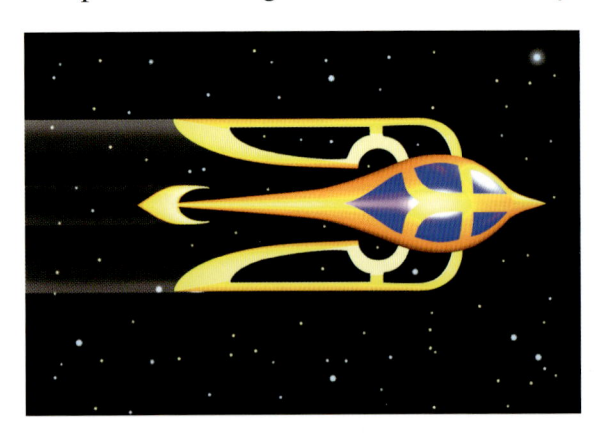

| XAAH | XOAH | XONA |

| XIZA | XOTH | XETI |

6 SCIENTISTS WERE SELECTED TO TRANSPORT TO BLUE PLANET

XAAH (Greek name Hera) is a Psychologist who probes the innumerable processes of mating, child rearing and sociology on thousands of planets.

XOAH (Greek name Poseidon), is a scientist of animal husbandry and DNA evolution. Xoah is eager to meet Tua and to study the myriad of fauna on Blue Planet.

XONA ((Greek name Hestia), is an obstetrician and gynecologist. Studying Earth's heterosexual functions is novel and exciting, compared to Xylanthian androgynous function.

XIZA (Greek name Demeter), is a botanist who has probed more than a billion botanical species in the universe. Xiza is excited for the opportunity to experiment with Earth flora.

XOTH (Greek name Zeus) is a Meteorologist and enjoys observing weather conditions and thermal reactions throughout the known universe. Xoth is also a tactical engineer.

XETI (Greek name Hades), is a Geologist who enjoys probing the cores of planets and discovering treasures of minerals of countless numbers.

The entire planet of Xylanthia links into common consciousness, as the craft is loaded with laboratory supplies, survival equipment, a transmitting and receiving IAMU processor, a 12 foot long tapered pure emerald antenna and the six scientists.

The entire populace cheered hilariously as the big ship lifted off the planet surface, rose to a high altitude, fragmented and rematerialized in the star system of the Blue Planet almost immediately. The craft was in inner planetary speed mode at materialization.

The ship lowered its inter-planetary speed to atmospheric speed to prevent burn out. It circled the Earth at low altitude, crossed slowly over a large body of water and settled gently in the center of a beautiful green meadow, surrounded by exotic vegetation. It is a warm sunny late afternoon.

As the ship settles gently to the ground,

an entire tribe of primitive beings scatter into the nearby woods and hide like frightened animals. Xoth activates the Emerald Rod to link with the Alpha Processor on Xylanthia. A low oscillating humming sound breaks the quiet stillness, as contact is established with Xylanthia. The vivid colors and intoxicating air are gloriously sensual. Every Xylanthian is preparing to take this first step into an unknown new world.

As the primitive Beings watch from their hiding places, they see six tall, thin, white skinned, semi-nude beings descend from this horrible thing that has disrupted their placid afternoon behavior. What are these strange creatures that have come out of the belly of this monster?

The Xylanthians are standing in the green grass near the ship, they deeply breathe in this novel, stimulating and invigorating air. It has much higher nitrogen content than Xylanthian air. The beautiful azure sky is a unique delight. The sky on their planet is yellow, due to sodium content in the atmosphere. They know from their scientific probes that this air they are breathing contains Argon instead of Sodium. This new environment captivates each scientist.

29

Enjoyment changes to expectancy, as a loud clear sound interrupts the stillness that has quieted the entire environment. The Xylanthians know that the reverberating sound is coming from a high hill on the far side of valley. They see Tua running toward them at the speed of a deer. As she runs down the slope of the hill, she is screaming at the maximum of her voice: E-TUA, E-TUA, E-TUA, over and over. The "Big Bird" has finally landed, she runs so fast toward them, she looses her animal skin clothing and continues running nude.

Tua crosses the valley, screaming all the way. She runs toward the group of six scientists, who are almost identical in physical appearance. She runs directly into Xoah. She jumps and locks her legs around Xoah's thin waist. Her arms are tightly wrapped around Xoah's neck as she throws back her head, still screaming loudly.

30

Xoah's arms reach tenderly around Tua's body, caressing her tenderly and holding her close. Feeling the gentle touch, she stops screaming and utters a low musical sound. Xoah gently stands Tua on the ground, holding her two hands and keeping her nude body close. She feels Xaoh's hands and is inquisitively intrigued by the six fingers. She gently touches and begins to explore the rest of Xoah's body. Making primitive musical sounds as she investigates. She compares her dark skin to Xoah's blue-white translucent skin, as she places her arm next to Xoah's arm and points to one and then the other. She caresses Xoah's hairless head. Xoah is combing six fingered hands through her long black wavy hair. Tua points to the metal breast cups on Xoah and removes one, pointing first to Xoah's pink nipples and then to her own black breast nipples.

These Primitive beings and the Xylanthians are uninhibited about nudity. It is natural. Tua points to her vulva, which is hidden with black kinky hair. Then she points to Xoah's genital area, which is covered with a protective guard. Xoah drops the guard on the ground. Tua sees the hairless vulva and begins to caress it, which causes an immediate erection as Xoah's penis extrudes outside the vulva.

Xoah knows the biological functions of these primitive people. The physical touching of her breasts, her shapely buttocks and finding the vaginal opening in the mass of hair causes extreme sensual pleasure. The magical moment of intense sensuality during this first contact is interrupted when Xoah perceives a group of Primitive Beings approaching.

The Primitive Beings in the woods are observing Tua's encounter with Xoah and their fears are beginning to subside. They cautiously begin to move, out of the forest, toward the Xylanthians and Tua. Each one waits, for another to go first. The females and children stay in the rear and let the males go ahead.

There are about 50 members in the tribe. One large male called E-Gu, which is the primitive sound for "Big One", leads the group as they slowly make their way to the ship. E-Gu has challenged all the males in the tribe for the right to breed with Tua. E-Gu wants to become their next leader, however, Tua has not accepted him.

Xoah knows the tradition of the tribe for the Alpha rights to lead. He knows E-Gu will challenge him. The Xylanthians never resort to physical violence, but Xoah respects their tradition. E-Gu is approaching Xoah with a spear in one hand and an ax in the other. The other males form a large semicircle a short distance away. They enjoy a good fight. Tua growls and snarls, like the tigress she is. She would like to attack E-Gu herself, as she has many times when he has tried to mate with her. Tribal tradition prevents females from interfering with male combat. She steps away from Xoah as E-Gu moves closer.

E-Gu lunges at Xoah with his spear. Xoah's hand calmly raises and transmits an energy force that sends E-Gu tumbling and rolling through the grass, all the way to the surrounding males. The males jump up and down with excitement. E-Gu loses his spear as he tumbles. He rushes again toward Xoah with his ax raised, uttering a loud roar. Xoah's raised hand again sends E-Gu tumbling back into the men. E-Gu slowly stands upright, walks a few steps toward Xoah and lays his axe on the ground; the tribal symbol of surrender.

The entire tribe begins jumping, dancing and yelling. Then suddenly all is quiet. Everyone turns around and looks toward the Hill. Tua's parents, Dai and Tai, are walking toward the large gathering. A dead silence prevails as Dai, with spear and ax in hand, walks toward Xoah. Dai is the mightiest of the primitive males. Everyone knows that Dai could have easily defeated E-Gu, however they all wonder if he can defeat this strange being. Dai, with no fear, walks directly up to Xoah. He kneels down and places his ax and spear on the ground. Dai then slowly stands up and places his powerful hands on Xoah's hands.

33

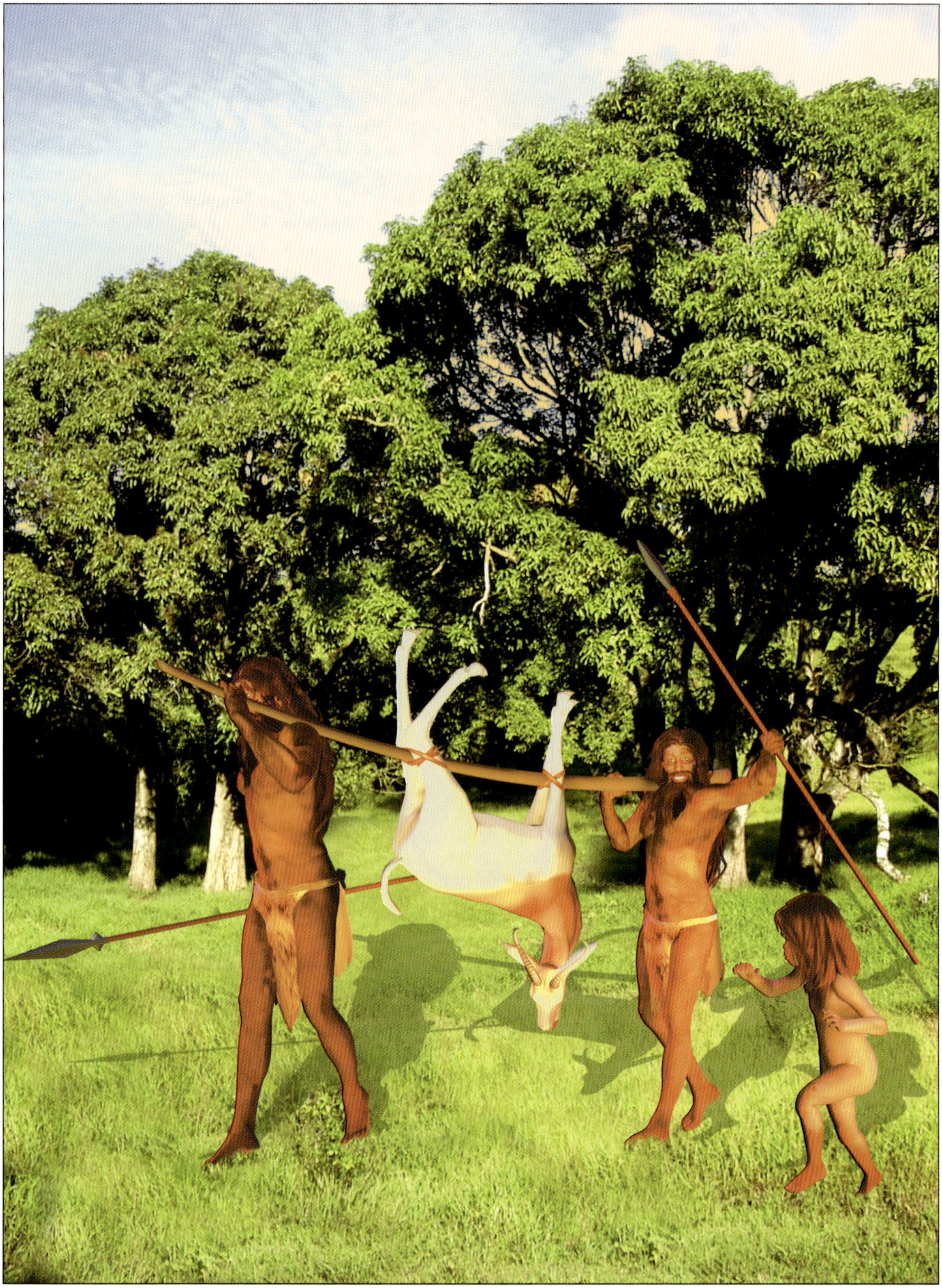

A loud tumultuous roar rises from the entire tribe. E-Gu jumps for joy, after all there are other females available. They now have a new leader. The tribe disappears again into the forest, where their mammoth tusk and hide huts are. Soon they return to the meadow, the females bring fire pots and baskets of exotic fruits. The males bring meat, nuts and firewood. They want a feast to honor their new leader. It is late afternoon as the feast is being prepared, some dance around the fires. The Xylanthians are coaxing the primitive beings to not be afraid of them. The Xylanthians are exotic dancers; the Primitive ones want to learn their dance. The primitive ones honor the Xylanthians by playing music. They use Mammoth skulls for drums and play melodious tunes on bird-bone flutes. A simultaneous sunset and full moon rise is a rare treat for the Xylanthians. There is no night on Xylanthia. This spectacular gathering of beings from two worlds, eight light years apart, creates a hypnotic atmosphere. Tua and Xoah are clinging to each other like childhood sweethearts.

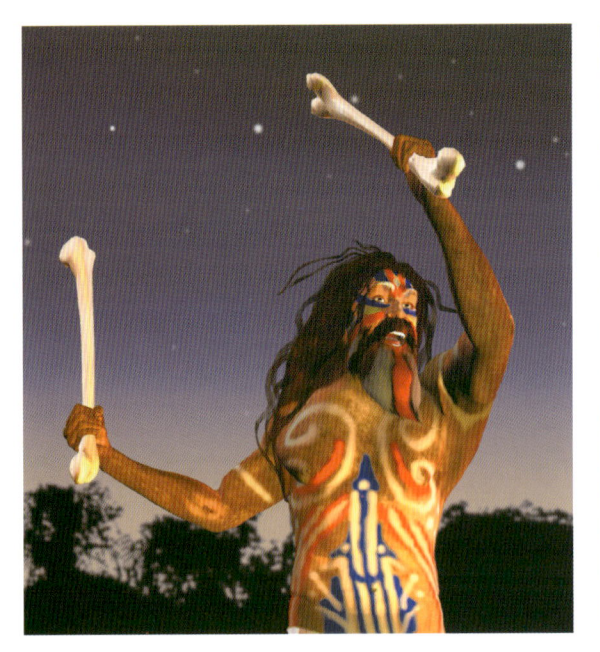

The dancing and feasting continues into the night. The Xylanthians diet is vegetarian. They enjoy tasting roasted meat for the first time. Xoah particularly loves the taste of a fish, which Tua roasted over the fire. Everyone is eager to please these great and powerful new beings, especially their new leader, Xoah. The tribe is gradually losing their fear of the Xylanthians. An interchange of touching begins as several members of the tribe begin inquisitively touching the Xylanthians. The Primitive beings are curious about the lack of hair, the very soft translucent skin, the six fingers and six toes and the androgyny of the Xylanthians. The Xylanthians are curious about the hairy bodies and heterosexual differences of the Primitive beings. Neither of these two species is inhibited about any part of their bodies. The primitive beings copulate for reproduction, during fertility only. The Xylanthians copulate for pleasure anytime.

Xona and E-Gu have been very affectionate toward each other since late afternoon when E-Gu gave a rare and valuable gift to his new leader. When E-Gu approached the Xylanthians, they noticed his eyes and hands were red and swollen. E-Gu stretched out his swollen hands and offered his tribute to Xoah. Xoah opened the leather pouch and Tua reached with delight into the golden treasure and tenderly gave a taste of this ambrosia to Xoah. It was honey! Xylanthians had never tasted this delightful substance. Xoah showed his appreciation by giving E-Gu back his ax. By tribal tradition, this makes E-Gu Xoah's trusted warrior. Xona was touched by E-Gu's generous gift.

Feeling his pain, Xona slowly reached out to E-Gu. E-Gu looked to Xoah, who reassured him that it was all right. Xona's long fingers clasped the back of E-Gu's neck. E-Gu felt all the pain of the bee stings subside and the swelling in his face and hands immediately began to go down. E-Gu clasped Xona's hand, which was quite warm from radiating healing energy. He held it gently and caressed Xona's smooth hairless head. These two beings immediately developed a strong attraction to each other.

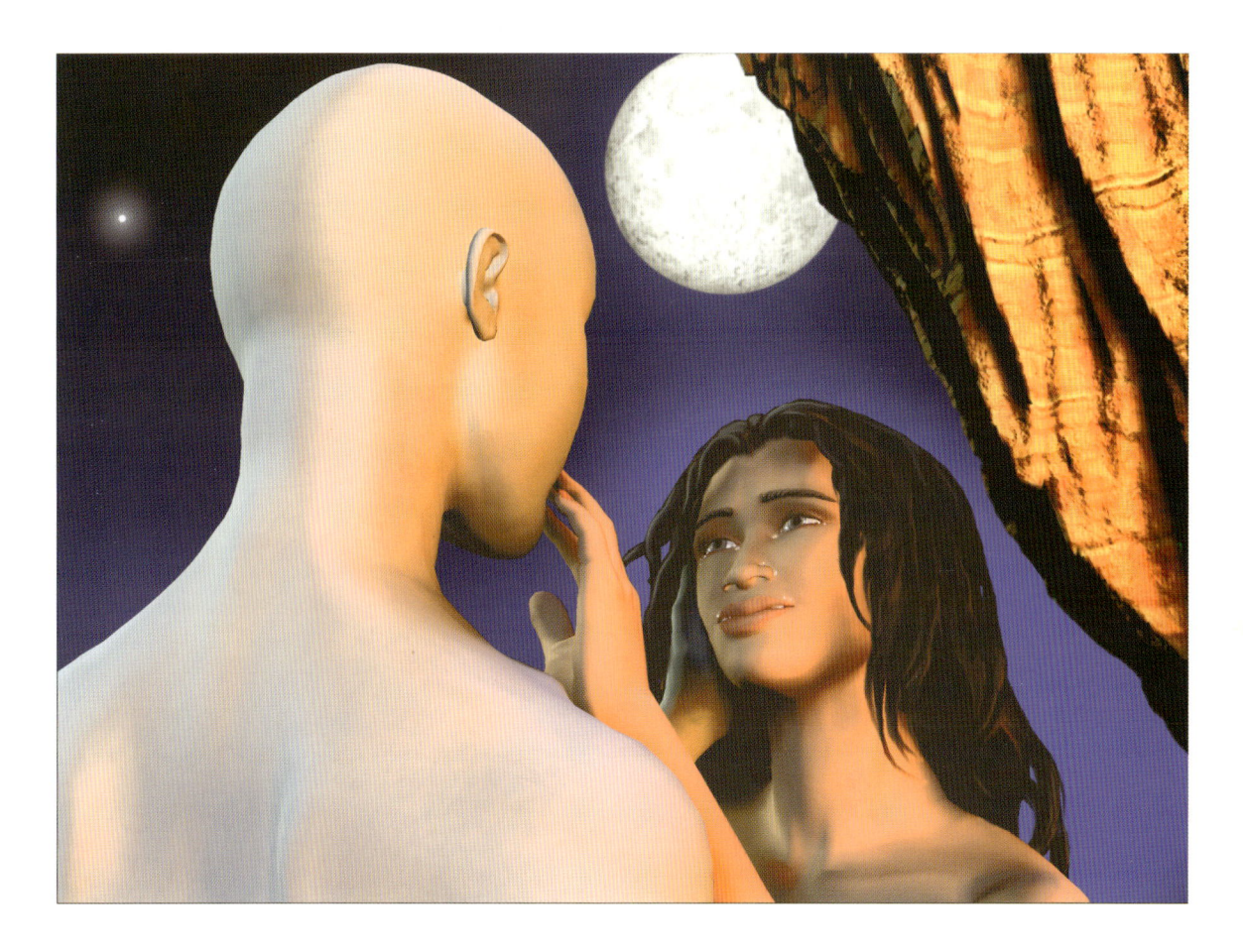

The feast is ending, the tribe goes back to their dwellings in the forest. Dai and Tai also go into the forest. E-Gu gives them his mammoth bone hut, as he has great respect for this mighty warrior who has defeated him in battle many times. Tradition transfers the cave on the high hill, to the new leader. Tua leads Xoah toward the cave. Tua and Xoah have been inseparable since their first encounter, except during E-Gu's challenge and the brief transfer of leadership from Dai. The 5 scientists retire into their craft.

It is bright moonlight, as Tua and Xoah reach the cave. They stand at the entrance to the cave. Tua points to the bright star. Xoah looks at Tua's beautiful face as large tears trickle down over her full lips. They turn and look at each other. Tua gently brushes a tear off Xoah's cheek and caresses Xoah's thin lips. Xoah touches her lips with gentle fingers, holds her head and tenderly kisses her lips. Tua makes a musical sound as they seem to blend into one being. Primitive beings never kissed. This was the first kiss on Blue Planet. Tai had made a pallet of soft animal skins. The full moon lighted the cave. Tua was fertile. A new species originated on Blue Planet.

For the next 8 hours, 12 million Xylanthians are "online" participating in the most energetic celebration in the planets history. The Alpha Processor is increasing its capacity to prevent "lock up". The Alpha Processor is now sending the following upload to all Xylanthian receptors: Blue Planet mission consummated.

37

The next morning, the primitive beings awaken at dawn. They are exuberant from the energy of last evening's events. They go to the meadow and begin "cleaning house after the party" and "eating the leftovers." The 5 scientists descend from the ship, marveling at the glorious sunrise while the full moon is simultaneously setting. E-Gu and Xona manage to find each other very soon. Xiza begins inspecting the plants and trees. Xaah is busy observing the primitive males lounging in the grass, while the females are doing all the cleanup work. Xeti is intensely testing the rich soil and various stones. Xoth stands in amazement at the beautiful cloud colors in the sunrise, a magnificent spectacle compared to the yellow cloudless sky of Xylanthia.

Two hours later, Xoah and Tua come down the hill, walking slowly, with their arms around each other. As the crowd sees them, a mummer of approval creates a harmonic musical sound, echoing throughout the meadowland, it sounds like a grand symphony.

The Xylanthians have the ability to "tune in" to the neuro-receptors of other species. In speaking Xylanthian language, any species "hears" their own language. This ability makes it possible to communicate with ANY SPECIES through the master processor. The primitive beings cannot reason why these new creatures "know" their language. The primitive beings have a very limited vocabulary. Most of their communication is by gestures and facial expression, however, they fully understand what is transmitted by the Alpha Processor.

The Xylanthians do not have leaders, each one has a talent that enhances other talents to accomplish the current purpose. Xoth, being the tactical engineer, suggests to Xoah, to care for the sick and feeble. Xylanthians are always tuned in to each other. Xaah and Xona begin unloading and setting up scanning constituents outside the craft. This equipment is in remote contact with the on board processor which is linked to the Alpha Processor on Xylanthia. Inside the spacecraft is a 12 foot long tapered emerald rod which serves as an antennae to link the processor on the craft to the master processor on Xylanthia. This is the purpose of landing the craft, nose toward the ground.

Xoah sees one male that has his right hand shriveled badly with two fingers missing, from some previous battle. Xoah gently leads him to the scanner. As all are watching, Xoah persuades the frightened male to lie down on the table under the scanner. Xaah's mind makes a remote connection and an entire new hand is formed in three seconds. Everyone screams a loud "AH". When the male sees his hand he screams loudly and runs away into the woods, like a wild animal. Everyone curiously wonders why he was reacting so strangely, they think he has suffered great pain. They all move away from the scanner in fear. They can hear the male yelling loudly in the forest. The yells become louder as he comes back out of the forest with his axe. He runs toward the crowd, who think he has gone mad. As he runs he knocks down limbs of trees and pounds the ground. He runs straight up to Xoah and lays his axe upon the ground in front of Xoah and sits down in genuflect. Everyone jumps up and down, yelling a tumultuous "AH"! Xoah gently touches the male's head. The excited and curious crowd want to touch his new hand. Xoah is pleased to see a new emotion originate in this tribe, a single tear rolls down the males cheek.

Their two basic primitive sounds, a lion's roar to get immediate attention and AH, an expression of approval, joy or amazement.

"Go into the forest bring all the sick ones and the old ones."

Xoah makes the sound of a lion's roar and everyone sits down. Xoah speaks: "Go into the forest and bring all the sick ones and the old ones."' The primitive beings quickly rise up and run into the forest. Within minutes they begin to bring twenty-three tribal members to the scanner; crippled beings, old males and females near death, infants and children with fever and disease, and young children who had been defaced by wild animal attacks. Within three hours everyone is completely miraculously healed. The elderly are as active as they were in their youth. Mothers see their children healed. Hunters see their favorite disabled hunting partners able to hunt again. These primitive people have only shed tears from severe pain until now. A new emotion originated on the Blue Planet, tears of joy.

"This land is a delta region in a vast plain"

It is now noon. The scanner is placed back in the craft and the protective shield is activated. Everyone goes into the forest. Fruit is plentiful. The Xylanthians are primarily vegetarians. The tribe seems to enjoy showing the scientists where the different fruits are. They forage for several hours, as they walk for many miles. This land is a delta region in a vast plain where several rivers come in from the surrounding mountains. It is three hundred miles from south to north and 400 miles from east to west. The hill where Xoah and Tua live is in the center of this vast delta region, on the southern edge. This plain is spider-webbed with hundreds of small islands separated by small streams. They wade across these streams as they forage. The primitive males catch fish with their hands and share them, eating them raw. The scientists taste them but they prefer fruit, berries and greens. The Xylanthians are enjoying experiencing the feeling of the water as they playfully splash, jump, and immerse themselves in this invigorating environment. They are also intensely studying its properties, life forms and functions. This walk seems to be a new world to the ones that were healed and had been imprisoned to their small area.

As they walk, Xoah and Tua are never apart. The other couples see this and begin to stay close to each other. The lone males and females start friendships. Three females have attached themselves to Xoth. Xaah and Xeti, each have found females. The primitive males who generally fight for females, are content to see these friendships develop. Xona and E-Gu frequently disappear into the forest, during the afternoon. Bu, a large warrior and friend of E-Gu, is being very friendly with Xiza. Evening is approaching. Everyone is exhausted. No feast tonight. Xoah perceives that the 5 scientists are going to spend the night in the forest. Xoah takes Tua into the craft for the night. Tua is eager to see the inside of "Big Bird". Xoah is pleased to not climb the hill to cave. Xoah is exhausted. A highly sensual night is transpiring. Xoth is having great pleasure with three primitive females. The four other scientists and their partners are awake all night.

The Alpha Processor reveals that the interbreeding of androgynous and heterosexual beings is inevitable on Blue Planet. Xylanthian research has proven that the offspring of this interbreeding will possess physical and emotional changes. The Xylanthians copulate for pleasure at their leisure. The primitive beings copulate only during menstrual cycles. The primitive females only ovulate at menstruation. The Xylanthians are only fertile by Alpha Processor influence. Research calculates that the mixture of genes in this future genus will cause ovation in the females to be between the menstrual cycles. This will create a desire to copulate spasmodically, since there will be no obvious physical indication of ovulation. Future males will also experience a hormonal change during a comparative cycle of the female. This spasmodic copulation to reproduce, mixed with the copulative pleasure syndrome of the Xylanthians and the various balances of physical appendages and chromosome differentials, will evolve into an erratic eroticism which will cause prejudicial cultural conflicts for fifty thousand Blue Planet years, until natural reality and genetics are understood. The recessive genes of the Xylanthians will be obvious in this new species. The black hair and eyes of the primitive beings will change to blue and green eyes. The body hair will change to blond, red and shades of brown. Some of the future offspring will be hairless or partially hairless. The dark skin color of the primitive being will change to various lighter colors. The height of the offspring will increase during this evolution.

The Alpha Processor further notes that the X and Y chromosomes of the Xylanthians are evenly balanced, due to their androgyny. The interbreeding with the heterosexual primitive beings will cause various differentials in the XY chromosome constituency and different degrees sexual behavior. As this genus evolves the genital appendages will be altered inconsistently. Some beings with male organs will have female tendencies and desires. Some beings with female organs will have male tendencies and desires. Other beings will be hermaphrodite and either bisexual or heterosexual. Some will be bisexual regardless of their genital design. The inability to understand this reality will create many ignorant cultural conflicts.

It is Day 3 on Blue Planet. An excited expectancy is prevalent as everyone gathers in the meadow in the early morning light. The primitive beings marvel at the affection between Xoah and Tua. These primitive males are not affectionate toward their females. Observing this closeness, the males maneuver around in the crowd to find their females. They slowly reach for their females' hands. A murmur of "AH" sounds through the tribe. The females with infants place their babies hands in the hands of the males; the first time any male has touched an infant. Some of the males hold an infant in their arms for the first time. The five scientists observe this novel experience and know it is the first stepping-stone to male-female equality, which will take thousands of years to evolve. They realize their cohabitation with these primitive people will be regressive. The Xylanthian androgyny is puzzling to these heterosexual beings; as males and females are sensually attracted to them.

The primitive beings do not have the intelligence to realize they are self destructing, moreover a way to prevent it. This lack of intelligence and the benevolent syndrome of the Xylanthians, is the prompting factor of Blue Planet Mission. The primitive beings have a strong will to survive. The Alpha Processor uses this will, as a basic energy source, to design a method for their survival. The only way to attain this is to alter their genetics by interbreeding with the Xylanthians.

The five Xylanthian scientists have both male and female organs in a fertile mode. Xoah's desire is for male fertility only. The five scientists will breed with males, females and themselves. As time passes, this breeding pattern will automatically link each offspring's neuro-receptor to the Alpha Processor. This technical intelligence will take forty thousand years of genetic evolution to mature, in the Blue Planet being's brain functions. To accelerate this evolutionary process, it is necessary to gather all the tribes in the area, into one large tribe, to live together in peace and multiply, to ensure the survival of this new hybrid Blue Planet species that will be created.

Xoah instructs E-Gu: Select five of the strongest warriors. Go to each of the 21 tribes that you have defeated in battles. They all have seen the Big Bird before it landed. Tell them all that has happened in the last two days. Take no food with you. They will honor you when they hear your message. Let them know that I will welcome them to this large area where food is abundant. Have them bring their sick, their old ones, and their crippled ones to be healed. Assure them that our tribe will not battle with them. Instruct them to leave their heavy belongings. We will share our fire and other needs with them. Tell them to gather here in the plain when the next big moon appears.

A miniature encoding processor, which is linked to the Alpha Processor, is encased in the beautiful pendant that Xoah gives to E-Gu. All Xylanthian spectacular gold jewelry has encased processors used for specific functions. Each precious stone is selected for a predesignated technical purpose.

Xoah hangs a decorative encoding device on E-Gu's neck. E-Gu you are my great warrior. Do not remove this from your neck until you come back. This gives you the power to speak your own words and each tribe will know what you speak. E-Gu casts a longing glance toward Xona, who assures him that they will be together again when he returns. E-Gu is pleased and very proud to perform this mission for his powerful leader. He selects five of his most trusted hunters and leaves immediately. The entire gathering gives them a farewell gesture, which is placing their right hand on their left shoulder and moving their hand outward in a semicircular motion around to the right. This is their good hunting and safe return gesture. As the six primitive emissaries disappear into the forest a musical harmonious "AH" reverberates through the meadow.

During the next twenty-eight days, a massive schooling process was organized, with fifty dedicated students. Xoth designed the curriculum and is coordinating the schooling process. Xiza is teaching them how to plant seeds in the ground to grow plants and trees. The first farmers on Blue Planet. Xoah is teaching them how to capture baby animals, domesticate them and breed them with each other for food consumption. Xona is instructing the women about feminine hygiene and showing them how to better care for their infants. Another lesson is how to make carrying devices to take their infants with them, when gathering fruit and other chores, rather than leave them alone for wild animal prey. Xaah is teaching males to respect their females, instead of physically harming them. Xeti shows the tribe how to build stone huts, to prevent wild animals, serpents and rodents from entering, as they do in their caves and flimsy shelters.

Xeti has a device that uses a beam of Alpha particle straight-line energy, which will slice or bore through solid rock. It is possible to program this device to cut stone to any size or shape. After the stone is cut, it can be templated, fragmented and levitated. The tribe is awed at Xeti's ability. With ten males to assist, Xeti builds 125 stone dwellings, some very small and some large, in 25 days. They are scattered some distance apart in one of the many meadows. The first village on Blue Planet. The white limestone is quarried from the hill where Tua's cave is. Over 500 beings are expected soon. They will all have ample dwelling space. Stone houses will be constructed in the forest for Xoah's tribe. A special house will be built for Dai and Tai to honor them for their many years of wise leadership.

E-Gu and his five hunters return from their mission. They find Xoah and kneel down. Xoah tells them to stand up. Xoah informs them about equality. "No one is greater or lesser in the tribe, each one has a talent and all work together to survive. " The six messengers are pleased to hear Xoah's words. They stand up and feel very proud. E-Gu eagerly begins telling Xoah about their adventure. "The other tribes were afraid when we came into their territory but I told them that we did not come to battle. I gained their confidence with the ability to speak their language. They did not understand how I could do this. I told them just as you instructed. They are afraid but very inquisitive. All 21 tribes agreed that they would come to the meadows when the moon is big." Then E-Gu carefully removes the ornamental encoding devise and offers it back to Xoah with some hesitation. E-Gu enjoyed the power of speaking all languages. Xoah holds up one hand with a gesture of refusal and tells E-Gu to keep it. "You will need it when the other tribes arrive. You and your five partners will organize the tribes to help in a great and wonderful work that we will be doing. You are my good friend and partner."

Xoah notices that E-Gu is looking all around the area for something. Xoah tells E-Gu, "Xona is in the forest with the females." No one has ever seen E-Gu run so fast. Instead of running around the shrubs, he is jumping like an antelope and soon disappears into the forest. Bu, one of E-Gu's partners, is nervously wandering around. Xoah tells Bu that Xiza is at the rock quarry on the hill. Bu is very bashful. He starts slowly walking toward the hill. Xoah observes Bu walking faster and faster. When Bu thinks he is out of sight of Xoah, he begins to run up the hill. The other four partners of E-Gu start helping the tribe carry supplies to the new stone village.

The moon is nearly full. Twenty one tribes of primitive beings are beginning to come into the far away meadows from every direction. Xoah instructs E-Gu and his partners; Meet each tribe separately as they come near. Talk to the leader of each tribe as they come. Warn them not to fight with other tribes. They will listen to your words. They will respect you. Ease the fear of the leader and the tribe will follow him. Take one tribe at a time near Big Bird and warn them not to get too close. Let them see you touching the Xylanthians. Xaah and Xona will set up the bio-neuro scanner. First they will heal all in the tribe that need healing. Then take the tribe to the stone village, which you saw in the meadow, when you returned from your journey. Share our fire with them and give them food. Our tribe has gathered a bountiful supply of fruit, nuts, meat and firewood while you were on your important mission. Use as many of our tribe as you need for helpers. They will be happy to work with you and your partners. Divide the stone dwellings so that everyone is satisfied.

Within three days all of the tribes are in the village. They are in complete awe of what they have experienced. They are marveling at the magic healing of over 150 of their members. Babies that were near death are vibrant, crippled ones are running, the very old are active and the sick are well. It is evening. They are all roasting antelope meat over their fires. They are hungry for antelope, after their long journey without fire. Each tribe is still uneasy and concerned about being so near to tribes they have battled with for years.

Xoth suggests that Xoah bring everyone together and speak to them. Xoah calls E-Gu and asks him to go to the village, while they are eating. Tell them I have invited all the leaders to bring their tribes to a meeting in the morning, in the meadow below Tua's cave. Invite our own tribe also.

Early the next morning, a tumultuous din awakens Tua and Xoah. Xoah hands Tua a gift for this special occasion. Tua unfolds what appears to be a small piece of cloth. It opens into two large pieces of the most beautiful hot pink thin fabric. Tua ties one around her waist for a skirt and the other over her shoulders. Quite a contrast to animal hides. Her shapely body is partly visible through the gorgeous material. Xoah places a beautiful pendant around Tua's neck. Its encased micro function will "zap" any being that will attempt to harm Tua. Tua is extremely happy. Her eyes sparkle, as giant tears flow down her checks. Xoah gently kisses her. A jeweled encoder ornament hangs on Xoah's neck. Hand in hand, they walk to the cave opening.

As they stand in the entrance, the loud noise outside immediately changes to an eerie silence. Tua is startled at first. Xoah puts an arm around her waist, which makes her feel secure. Xoah appears to be slightly surprised at the size of the gathering. A short distance down the slope are the 5 scientists. Further down the hillside, the local tribe is standing together, shoulder to shoulder, suggestive of guards for the scientists.

At the foot of the hill in the meadow, all twenty-one tribes are gathered, some distance apart from each other. These primitive beings are never separated from their weapons, which are a crude stone-ax and a spear. Years of fighting each other for food and territory, dictates tremendous tension in the entire area.

Xoah knows these primitive beings have a neuro-receptor in their brain function. The encoder force will translate Xylanthian language into the separate dialects of each tribe. The five scientists are very expectant, as the

Tua's Protective Gift

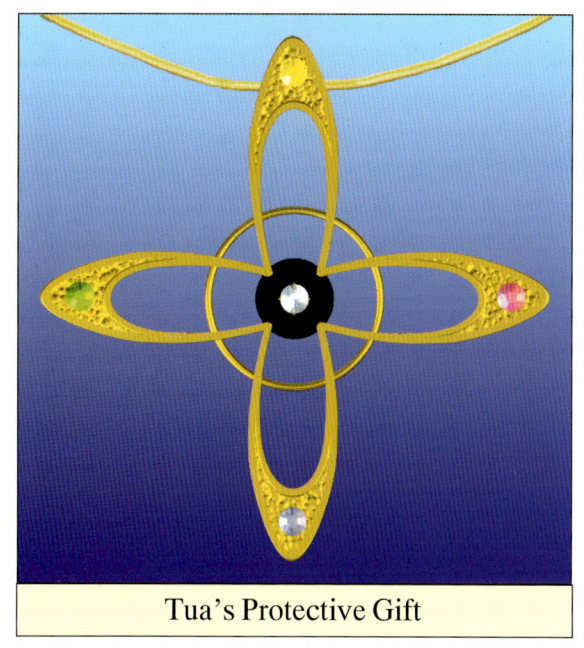

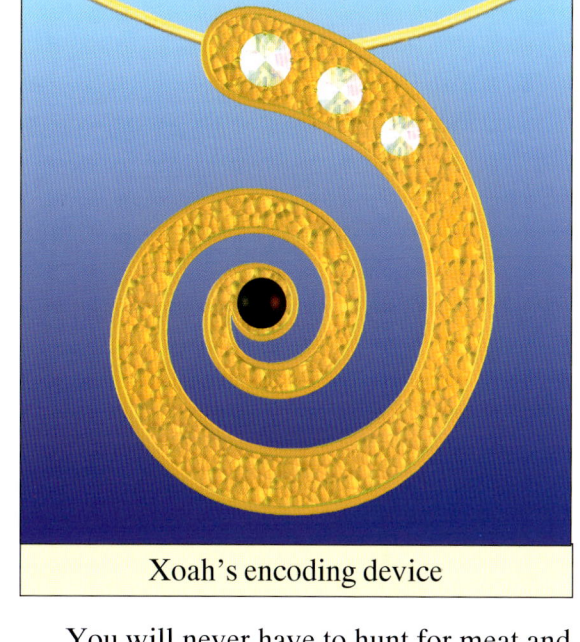

Xoah's encoding device

Alpha Processor transmits a surge of confidence to Xoah. This is a primary experience for Xoah. Everyone feels the increasing energy as if a massive battle was about to begin.

Xoah sends forth the mightiest lion's roar that has ever been heard by these beings. Antelope five miles away, dart for cover. Like a lightening bolt struck, immediately everyone in the area drops to the ground in a sitting position, including Tua who sits down near the cave opening. Xoah sits down on the stone which Tua had sat upon to communicate with Xoah on Xylanthia.

Xoah speaks with such volume it causes the five scientists to look at Xoah in wonderment. Their quiet love sick friend has been transformed by the Alpha Processor energy boost. Xoah speaks: We came here from a far away place in the sky. We want to be your friends. Many moons ago your tribes were much larger. Several have died. Your babies are dying, disease is killing your young hunters. Let us help you, or your tribes will be smaller and smaller until you will be no more.

You will never have to hunt for meat and food again. We will show you how to tame the wild animals and grow food. We will show you how to live side by side and never fight. We will share everything equally. Together we will become one tribe with numbers like the stars in the sky. Our offspring will spread across all the lands that exist. We will all live together in peace. Leaders, continue to care for your tribes. We will often meet together to attain equality and communication. You sit here in this open meadow like frightened wild animals, afraid to come close to each other. Stand up. Move closer to each other and trade weapons. Xoah has won their confidence. Weapon trading is a rare primitive ceremony. Cautiously the different tribes begin to mingle and trade weapons. Tribal leaders trade weapons. The local tribe intermingles. The leaders are very eager to trade weapons with E-Gu and Dai. Trust and friendship begin. Females become friendly with each other. Xoah, Tua and the five scientists join the ceremony in the meadow. Now they are all one large tribe.

"The first village on Blue Planet"

E-Gu brings the leaders of each tribe to a shady place by a stream near a meadow, for a meeting with Xoah. The leaders are overly submissive to Xoah who explains the value of equality; That each one has a different duty to perform but no one is greater or lesser. "I am no greater than any of you. My duty is be a friend to you. Together we can satisfy the needs of all of our people. We will never need to fight and wound each other."

Xoah places an encoder on each leader. Each one is encased in a different attractive jeweled pendant. The leaders are extremely appreciative and proud. Xoah explains the purpose of the encoders. "Try them." An extraordinary emotional occurrence is pleasing to Xoah and E-Gu. As one former enemy speaks to another former enemy, they are shocked to learn that their hatred for each other was merely the inability to communicate with each other. None of them truly wanted tribal wars which wounded their tribal hunters. Their hatred, fears and suspicions of each other begins to diminish with this new ability to communicate. They begin slapping each other on the shoulders and jumping up and down like happy children. True friendships are developing as they each want to communicate with every leader.

Xoah and E-Gu look at each other with a certain unspoken understanding, that this new friendship ceremony will continue for the entire day. E-Gu starts walking toward the forest where Xona is with the females. Xoah starts walking up the hill to Tua's cave. They both turn and wave, a gesture of approval, to each other. Xoah tells E-Gu to bring the leaders together again the following morning.

A completely different energy among the twenty-two tribal leaders is a contrast to the preceding days meeting. They are sitting closer together, occasionally patting each other on the back in a gesture of friendliness.

They are very attentive as Xoah begins to speak: "The purpose of forming this large tribe, is to create a society wherein everyone is content to use their individual talent to survive. Which is more valuable, the one who makes a good spear or the one who uses the spear, to get meat? Both the spear maker and the hunter eat the meat. They share the meat with the ones who cook the meat, and the ones who make the axes to break the wood that makes the fire to cook the meat. Without any one of these, there would be no meat."

"Now we must work together to prepare for survival of our children and their children for many generations in the future. Many tribes in many far away lands, will be coming here, when they receive word of our progress. Some will be friendly and will join us. Others will want to destroy us. We must prepare for the future. We will build a large beautiful city with high walls to protect us. We will make farm lands to tame wild animals and grow food. We must look far into many tomorrows and know that our children's children will survive in a peaceful society."

The five other Xylanthians join the meeting. Xoah tells the tribal leaders: "Do not be frightened of our little boxes. They will not harm you. We will show you their purposes."

Xiza, the botanist, has been experimenting with local food bearing plants. Xiza gathers the leaders in a circle around a bush which has tiny berries that the primitive beings enjoy eating. Xiza places a micro apparatus near the bush. In seconds the green tiny berries turn a bright red and quickly grow to ten times their normal size. Xiza eats one and motions to the leaders to taste them. In seconds the bush is bare. Some of the leaders hand the six scientists and E-Gu some berries. The scientists look at one another. The first time primitive males have shared their food. Xoah, who is a scientist in animal husbandry, points a micro device at a far away antelope, as the leaders are watching, the antelope comes close enough to Xoah to get its ears scratched. Xona, a gynecologist, displays an erect penis protruding from Xona's vagina. Xona sends a micro impulse, from a finger ring, to one of the semi-nude leaders who gets an immediate erection. Xona knows that their inquisitiveness and lack of inhibitions will be helpful to the future interbreeding process. Xaah, the psychologist, uses a micro devise to put one of the leaders into a sound sleep and then awakens him. The leaders marvel at this. Xoth, the meteorologist, places a tiny box next to the nearby stream. A dense cloud of mist envelopes the group and then moves away. Xeti, the geologist, has a larger more sophisticated box which Xeti tuned in to a very large round boulder by the side of the stream. A small puff of dust and a perfect cube of stone appeared. He asks the fearless E-Gu to sit upon it. Xeti then pushes a control and E-Gu and the stone raise high into the air and set down in the midst of the group. The leaders shake their heads in disbelief as they try to lift the huge stone cube. Xeti then tunes into a large dead tree, the kind the primitive beings break up with stone axes for fire wood. In 3 seconds the entire tree is a neat pile of perfectively cut firewood.

The five scientists return to their projects. Xoah and E-Gu give each other a look of approval. The leaders are anxious to tell their tribes what they have seen. There is a strong feeling of trust and unity as each one leaves.

Six Blue Planet full moons have passed since Big Bird settled down in the meadow. Xoth has been busy coordinating Alpha Processor technical engineering, with the actual construction of the early stages of a magnificent metropolis that will baffle Blue Planet scientists for forty thousand years. E-Gu and the leaders of the tribes have selected Primitive Males from each tribe to perform various tasks according to their talents. The Primitive Males are eager to please Xoah and the other leaders. They are proud of their new abilities to use the scientists powerful small boxes.

Xona informed Tua that she will give birth to twin boys in three moons. Xoah treats Tua like a delicate tender flower blossom. Xoah never leaves her alone, day or night. Xoah likes Blue Planet water. Xoah takes Tua to a quiet pool in the woods, where warm mineral water flows down Tua's hill from a hot spring geyser on top of the hill. Everyday they swim together for an hour. In the daytime they lounge together on the grass and watch the beginning of this great Empire, the Motherland of Tua.

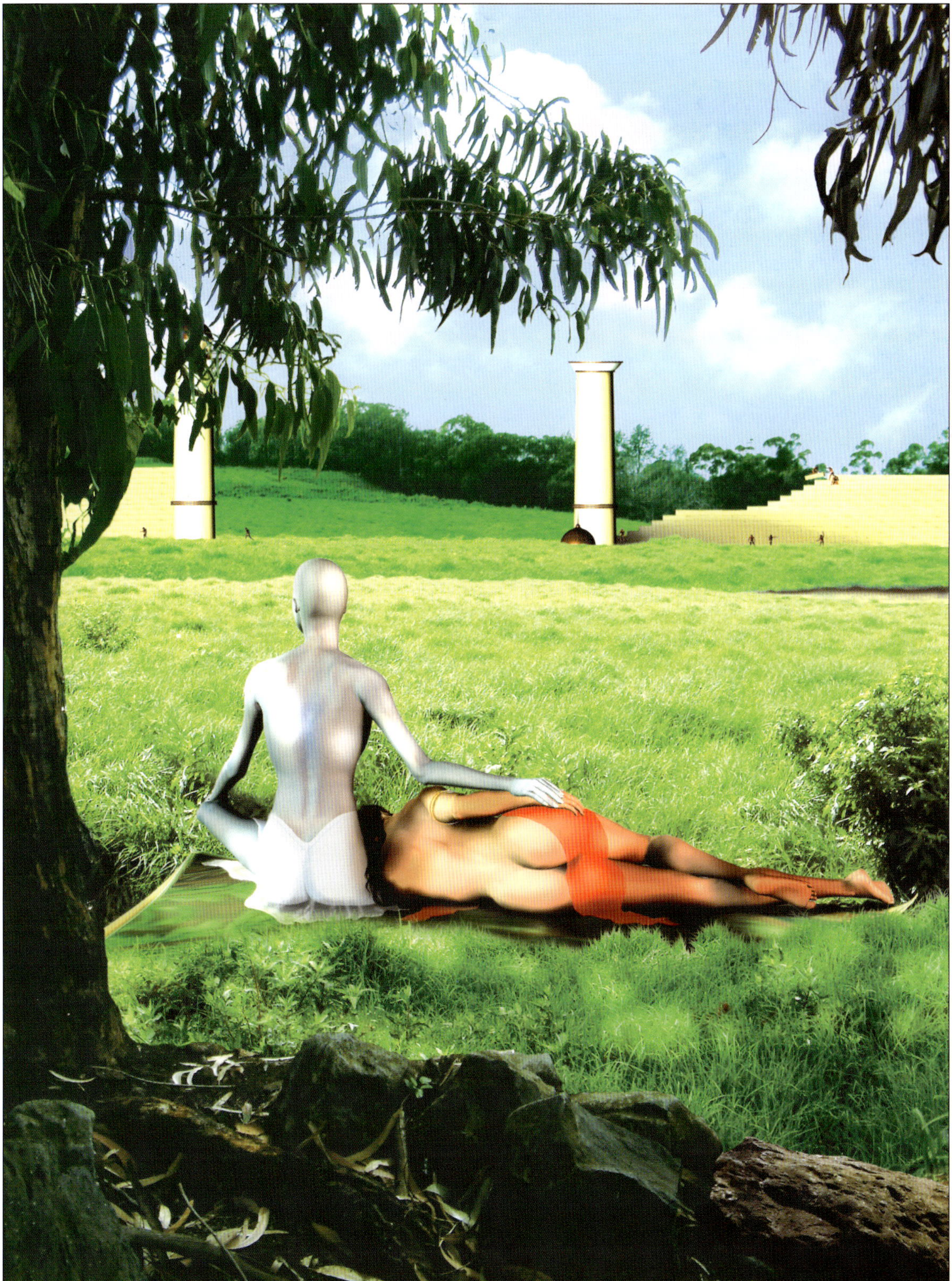

Top priority is given to the construction of Tua's and Xoah's private temple on the top of Tua's hill. Her cave is lower down on the side of the hill. Xeti, with the Alpha Particle beam and two hundred strong primitive males, easily finish the temple, thirty sunrises before Tua's birthing time.

Xeti bores deep into the hill and brings up a cold bubbling artesian water supply. A natural geyser on top of the hill, provides a bountiful supply of hot water. A portion of water, from these two massive fountains, is transferred to the temple.

Xona monitors Tua daily. Females from the village bring Tua the choicest of food everyday. They treat Tua like the Queen she is destined to be. Tua is healthy and vibrant, however Xona asks Xaah, the psychologist, to council Xoah who is excited like a wild bird in the meadow, with a flock of babies. Xiza, the botanist, creates a fabulous garden, of various trees and shrubs, surrounding the temple. Water from the fountains is carried in small aqueducts. Xiza's advanced technology grows a large tree in just a few days.

Thirty sunrises later, a giant full moon is setting on the distant horizon, as the morning sun peeks over the opposite horizon. The stillness of the night changes to a glorious stupendous rhythmic symphony which reverberates across the vast area. An unusual dynamic energy force seems to encompass every living entity for miles around. The vegetation is swaying gently to and fro, in a gentle breeze, like a choreographed dance. Thousands of birds of every color and size leave the forests and circle around and around Tua's hill. Their various songs blend together melodiously. All the females from the village, are in the meadow at the foot of the hill. They are making bird sounds that create harmonics with the bird's songs. Each Drummer from twenty-two tribes carry their mammoth skull drums, to the meadow and beat them with all the vigor they possess. Their unison rhythm vibrates the ground and sounds like the entire heartbeat of all life.

These beautiful primitive beings have keen natural senses. They know when a storm is coming, days before it arrives. They know when danger is near, before they hear or see it. Now they know something grand is about to take place in the temple on the hill.

Xoah is inside the temple with Tua and Xona. The five Scientists have gathered outside the temple. They are more concerned about Xoah, than they are about Tua. They know Xona's expertise. Xoth sends a request to the Alpha Processor and Xoah is slightly tranquilized. Xona transmits a "thank you" to the 5 scientists.

With gentle massage from Xona, Tua easily releases her two male babies, with contractions and no labor pain whatsoever. Xona removes and disintegrates the placentas, cleanses the infants, cauterizes the umbilical cords and gently places the infants near Tua's enlarged breasts. As Tua places an arm around each baby her customary large happy tears flow down the sides of her checks, like two crystal rivers of life. Xoah gently touches each baby as they begin to suckle. Xoah's lengthy kiss to Tua, is interrupted by Xona who tenderly brushes tears from Xoah's face and motions toward the door. Xoah does not want to leave. Xona emphasizes, Tua must rest and you also. I will call you when they awaken.

As Xoah comes out to the scientists, the tranquilizer ceases and Xoah seems to transform into one of the primitive beings. Xoah runs to the scientists and jumps up and down wildly, yelling loudly. Xoah is actually jumping high above the scientists heads. Xoah's friends are amused. Xoah finally sits down, exhausted and finds reality again.

Tua and the babies are sleeping. Xona is contemplating the novel experience, examining the sleeping infants' anatomy and vital signs. This is a novel experience for Xona who had only cared for Xylanthian births. Xona senses someone's presence. Looking toward the door, Xona sees Dai and Tai timidly peeking in. Xona motions for them to come in and be quiet. Tua's Mother and Father see Tua and their two grandsons. They stand side by side near Tua, with their arms around each other. Xona takes their hands and places them on the babies. Their faces lighten as if a powerful beam of light is shining on them. They stand there silently for a long time Tai places a rare flower and a small pouch of honey, near Tua. Dai gives Xona his favorite natural crystal stone. They gently caress Xona and leave.

Xoah asks Xoth to speak to the tribe. Xoth goes to the rock by Tua's cave. The drums stop. The singing stops. The birds fly back into the forest. All is quiet as Xoth speaks; TWO FUTURE LEADERS ARE BORN, THE BABIES AND TUA ARE ALIVE AND WELL. A resonate AH can be heard as far as a distant meadow where wild horses raise their heads in astonishment. Xoth continues; Xoah and Tua will bring the babies to the village in a few sunrises. Tua was happy to hear your sounds. You are great and wonderful beings. You are working and living together without fear. The sun is not high. Let us all prepare a feast and celebrate our two future leaders.

As the sun is setting, 550 primitive beings are dancing around and among 22 fires, where mammoth, horse and antelope meat is roasting. The sound of 22 drums and melodious chants can easily he heard by Tua and Xoah, resting with their babies in the temple.

Ecstatic erotic revelry on Xylanthia, is reaching the maximum capacity of the Alpha Processor, as they celebrate this successful creation of a new hybrid species on Blue Planet.

The five Xylanthians come down the hill from the temple and join the feast which continues until sunrise. The females with small infants and pregnant females leave early in the evening. The older children eventually fall asleep near the fires. This is the first time the tribes have totally mixed. The males and females are intermingling. A full moon lights the meadow with a golden glow. The difference in languages, is no deterrent to the sensual communication of couples, as they form intertribal pairs, during the night.

The UNIVERSAL REPRODUCTION FORCE HAS A UNIVERSAL COMMON LANGUAGE. The Xylanthians discovered one hundred thousand years past, that reproduction energy is the key to longevity. The energy created by copulation climax, releases an enzymic catalyst to the hormones that regulate the time clock of longevity. The prolific sensual activities of the Xylanthians accounts for their agelessness. The Xylanthians are stimulated by the novelty of these Primitive Beings.

Many primitive females are nearing birthing time from Xylanthian impregnation. None of the Xylanthians have conceived from intercourse with primitive males. Xona discovers most primitive males are sterile, however their sterility does not prevent their desire and performance. Their sterility is the result of their strenuous physical exertion from chasing wild animals and fighting tribal wars.

Time ceases the next day. Those who are not sleeping are casually lounging and developing a basic intertribal communication. A common language is beginning to form, especially among the children. A secure tranquility is felt by everyone, including Xoah on top of the hill with Tua and the twins. Tua has seen many primitive black eyes, dark skin, black hair babies. She is delighted to see these two blue eyed, white-skinned, blond haired treasures. The first beings on Blue Planet with RECESSIVE GENES.

As the seasons pass, the volume of births is increasing. A portion of Xeti's crew has proudly constructed a stone nursery building in the meadowland. It is useful and sanitary. Xona is teaching female assistants. Xona's reward is observing the females acquiring a feeling of self confidence, rather than their submissive introverted customary culture. Xiza teaches the females how to use certain roots of plants as soap, to wash their animal skins and their babies. The new mothers see Xona as a Goddess, their babies are all born alive and healthy. The former live birth expectancy was ten out of one hundred births. A clatter of inquisitive females and some males, is a common occurrence, when recessive genetic twins are born to a female which is impregnated by a Xylanthian. There is no envy between mothers, when the blue-eyed, light skin twins are born. Xona is wise, by letting one twin suckle another mother when a twins's mother has insufficient breast milk. Xona teaches the mothers the Xylanthian principle of child raising, wherein no child is attached to one specific parent. This creates an independence, which increases advancement to adulthood.

The twins are generally one male and one female with heterosexual genitals. Occasionally, both twins are androgenous. The ratio of X-Y chromosomes and hormones vary in heterosexual beings. The Xylanthians know the mystery of the pituitary and hormonal functions can be artificially altered. They also know this mystery can never be solved, due to infinite deoxyribonucleic acid presence in psychological and physiological components.

Xylanthians pioneer research revealed that prejudice and discrimination among children was directly related to parental influence. When children were raised with all their necessities equally distributed, prejudice and discrimination ceased.

An accelerating renaissance of changing culture, is prevalent in this unique tribe. The primitive beings have a very large brain. Their learning capacity exceeds the expectations of the scientists. The influence of this abrupt change in their living conditions, stimulates their desire to learn. The females are learning to spin thread and weave cloth. Xiza explains the making of dye from plants. They are learning the art of pottery. They are sun drying fruit for winter months and making oil lamps with fish and animal fat. Xona has taught them hygienical principals to prevent diseases. Xaah introduces them to child psychology, to encourage children's self esteem.

The primitive males are building stone corrals to enclose captured wild horses, cattle, the elephants and antelope. Xoah teaches them the art of animal husbandry. Xoah instructs them to stop killing the mammoth or there would be no more. The males have competitive sport in domesticating the horse and attempting to ride the bulls. An occasional broken leg or arm does not alter their enthusiasm. The elephants domesticate easily, with gentle persuasion and tender care.

Xoth teaches the primitive males how to make various new tools to enhance their cultural change. Xiza introduces them to the intricate facets of farming; tilling the soil, fertilizing the soil with animal waste, planting, cultivating, harvesting, grinding grains for bread and food storage. Xeti, the master architect, is their favorite teacher. They learn stone cutting, irrigation, canal construction, wood, stone and ivory carving, the melting of sand to make glass, the extraction of metals from stone, the use of metals for tools, needles, spearheads and knives, how to make shoes from animal skins and bridling the horse.

Tua gives birth to another set of twin boys. Xona and the primitive females care for Tua and her babies, they treat her like the Royal Queen that she is. Tua's two year old twins are in the collective environment with other two year old children.

The children from Xylanthian breeding have a different psychogenetic intelligence, than the primitive children. Many thousand years will lapse before Blue Planet scientists are capable of comprehending psychogenetics. The recessive genetic composition, of the Xylanthians, contains DNA formulas for both physical and psychological systems. These composites differ from Blue Planet Beings.

The psychological and physiological systems of all Blue Planet animals, are inextricably intertwined. This complexity is confounding by assuming that genetics dictate the physiological properties and not the psychological components. Certain birds will fly seven thousand miles to hatch their young. They abandon their chicks who later fly to the exact habitat of their parents. This is simply psychogenetic memory. The concept that Humanoids have no pre-birth memory is absurd.

In the complexity of DNA substructure, it may eventually be understood that anything in infinite monistic universal existence, contains some form of the knowledge of its origin. This knowledge is hidden in the subatomic residue which everything acquires during the process of change. To substantiate this reasoning, the law of holism must be applied. "Nothing can be changed back to its original state, without residue." Pure Gold? Never, only .999 Gold and .001 residue. Pure Xylanthian? No, don't forget the lizard. Pure primitive Humanoid? No, the Otariidae.

This intermixture of recessive and dominant genes is constructive to the development of the Xylanthians and Primitives Beings. The Xylanthian offspring learn to utilize their sixth sense syndrome, without the necessity of the Alpha Processor, wherein they are aware of eminent danger, poisonous foods and forthcoming weather. The Primitive Beings learn artistry, mechanics, association and equality. Together, they develop an appreciation of each others difference, without prejudice. There is no discrimination between sexes. Nudity is normal. The reproductive force is joyfully stimulated, not dampened by cultural or parental dominance. They learn that each of their body parts has a purpose and no part is more or less significant. When the children reach ten years of age, they are adult and skilled according to their individual talents.

Evolution of Art

Xiza, with many students creates luxurious gardens surrounding Tua and Xoah's temple. The Temple is now sufficiently expansive for its various functions.

It has been twenty-five years since Big Bird landed in the meadow. Tua has given birth to five sets of twin male children, who are destined to be leaders in one of the most fabulous empires to ever be created on Blue Planet. The Alpha Processor blocks Xoah's reproductive glands. This does not prevent Tua and Xoah from having their sensual pleasures. Their attraction to each other confounds the other five scientists, due to the normal absence of a mating process of Xylanthians. The five scientists have all bred with each other and produced many sets of androgenous twins. They have also bred with primitive males and females creating some twin births and some single births. When Xylanthian breeds with Xylanthian, the gestation is six moons. When Xylanthian breeds with a primitive female the gestation is nine moons. When a primitive male breeds with a Xylanthian, the gestation is seven moons. This variation in gestation length will become inconsistent in future generations as the cross breeding process varies. Xona has discovered that the ovation cycle of some females who have partial Xylanthian genes, is not at menstruation period as it is with primitive females. Primitive beings copulate during menstruation to reproduce. Xylanthians copulate for pleasure. The intermixture of genetics, combined with the irregularity of the ovation cycle, stimulates a spasmodic copulation outburst which generates a population explosion that will eventually overpopulate the entire surface of Blue Planet.

During the next fifty years, the population has increased to thousands. Xoah, Xiza and Xeti organize a work force wherein leaders and their helpers form groups to perform different functions suited to their talents. Tua's and Xoah's expanded temple and gardens serve as the main meeting location for the six scientists and the major leaders of the massive work force. The intermixture of genes stimulates a new society of highly skilled beings who are talented in every category, necessary to cope with the survival needs of the populace and the massive construction of this Utopian metropolis. Thousands of workers, elephants, horses and the technological genius of the Xylanthians creates a harmonious energy force that impregnates Tua's hill, which gives birth to one of the greatest wonders Blue Planet will ever know. The artistry and grandeur will never be surpassed. It will set a template in time for Blue Planet Beings to copy for tens of thousands of years into the future.

The technical equipment is all removed from Big Bird and installed in an obscure room in Tua's and Xoah's Temple. The twelve foot emerald antennae, which glows in the dark, and the super sensitive equipment is placed in an area which is off limits to anyone except the six highly skilled Xylanthian scientists.

Xoth prepares to transport Big Bird, back to Xylanthia, to be used in other missions on other unknown planets in the distant universe. Xoah consoles Tua's flood of tears and sadness as thousands watch Big Bird rise gently from the ground, circle Tua's Hill three times, raise to a high altitude and disappear. Xoah knows Xoth will be back to Blue Planet without Big Bird.

Tua is now ninety years of age and very beautiful. Xoah has coaxed an artesian to make a small replica of Big Bird and place it on Xoah's staff on top of the Temple of the Springs. Xoah takes Tua and shows her the statue for the first time. Now Tua's flood of tears are happy ones. They disappear hand in hand into a dense garden.

Xaah, the psychologist, who is monitoring the Temple Processor, immediately receives a message from Xoth, via the Alpha Processor: Enjoying Xylanthia. Population exuberant. I will return in six Xylanthian sunrises. Scientist studies here have processed critical extensive Blue Planet data for us to calculate when I return.

Xoth suddenly appears in the courtyard near Tua's and Xoah's Temple. Xoth transmits a neuro-bio message to Xaah, Xoah and Xona, to meet together and calculate extensive data which Xylanthian scientists have compiled, with the intricate assistance of the Alpha Processor. The psychological data from Xaah, the psychologist, and the biological data from Xona, the biologist, was the basis for a sophisticated study on Xylanthia, regarding the mixture of dominant and recessive genes of Blue Planet beings.

Xoth initiates the crux of the meeting with Xoah, Xona and Xaah, as they enjoy the magic of the lush garden near a misty warm water pool. Xoth speaks: In the composition of all things that exist, there is a polarity within each whole. This is true, regarding any entity, whether it be made by beings or by natural evolution. Understand this universal statute.

Xoth continues to speak: The Universal statute of polarity within a whole can be confounding and seemingly paradoxical. We search for the end of endlessness. We attempt to set boundaries surrounding the boundless. We try to comprehend the incomprehensible. We resist change of inevitable evolution. We desire to normalize natural differentials. We strive to separate and isolate differentials in a inseparable monistic universal standard. We influence each other to be something other than that what we naturally are. We distinguish and classify one entities importance over another, not considering, that which we classify as lesser is the foundation for that which we distinguish as greater. The female constituent is lesser because she gave birth to a greater male. All of this reasoning nearly destroyed the entire Xylanthian Empire, one hundred thousand years ago. We can never tame the untameable beast within ourselves, we can only learn to peacefully coexist with it.

Xoth speaks further: Now we are confronted again with this dragon who will raise it's head in fury, for being awakened from its rest. We knew when we first came to this paradise planet, out mission would take fifty thousand years to evolve into a peaceful coexistive society. We also are aware of the chance that our mission can cause the complete destruction of this planet. Our duty now is to influence this new species, how to cope with the sleeping dragon as it awakens, not only in this new species, but also in the future Xylanthians who dwell on Blue Planet.

Xoth continues: We must realize, the dominant genes in this new species, prevent linkage to the Alpha Processor. Only one in many thousands will have the neuro-bio capability of Alpha Processor contact. In the distant future these few will become the prophets, masters and teachers on Blue Planet. As thousands of years expire, more and more beings will evolve into the full Xylanthian technological culture, with the possibility of constructing a super master processing chain which can regulate a peaceful coexistive cultural superstructure encompassing the entire Blue Planet. We are the roots of a tree that can flourish and grow or wither and die for the neglect of future caretakers of this magic paradise which we call Blue Planet.

Xoth: Our contemporary curriculum must be designed to address the inevitable fluctuation of the balance of polarity, beginning with the present embryonic stage, to the building of a Mighty Empire, which is beginning to expand beyond our expectations.

Xoth: The primitive beings genetics are programmed to a leader dependency. The Xylanthian genetics are programmed to the Alpha Processor dependency. The primitive beings are wandering nomads. The Xylanthians are Universal adventurers. These two genetic traits must be reckoned with , in organizing the cultural foundation of this new species. The leader dependency stimulates the adventure syndrome. This formulates a rebellious controversy between controlled conformistic equality and the desire to break away from leadership and become a leader, thereby exercising the simple statute of the strong surviving. Those who leave will create imaginary deities and animosity toward this empire. The raging dragon will eventually attempt to destroy us. It is necessary to prepare means of defense, which is contrary to Xylanthian culture.

I have just returned from a seventy two quadrillion mile journey. I would like a warm bath. Would you join me in the Temple of the Springs and continue our meeting tomorrow?

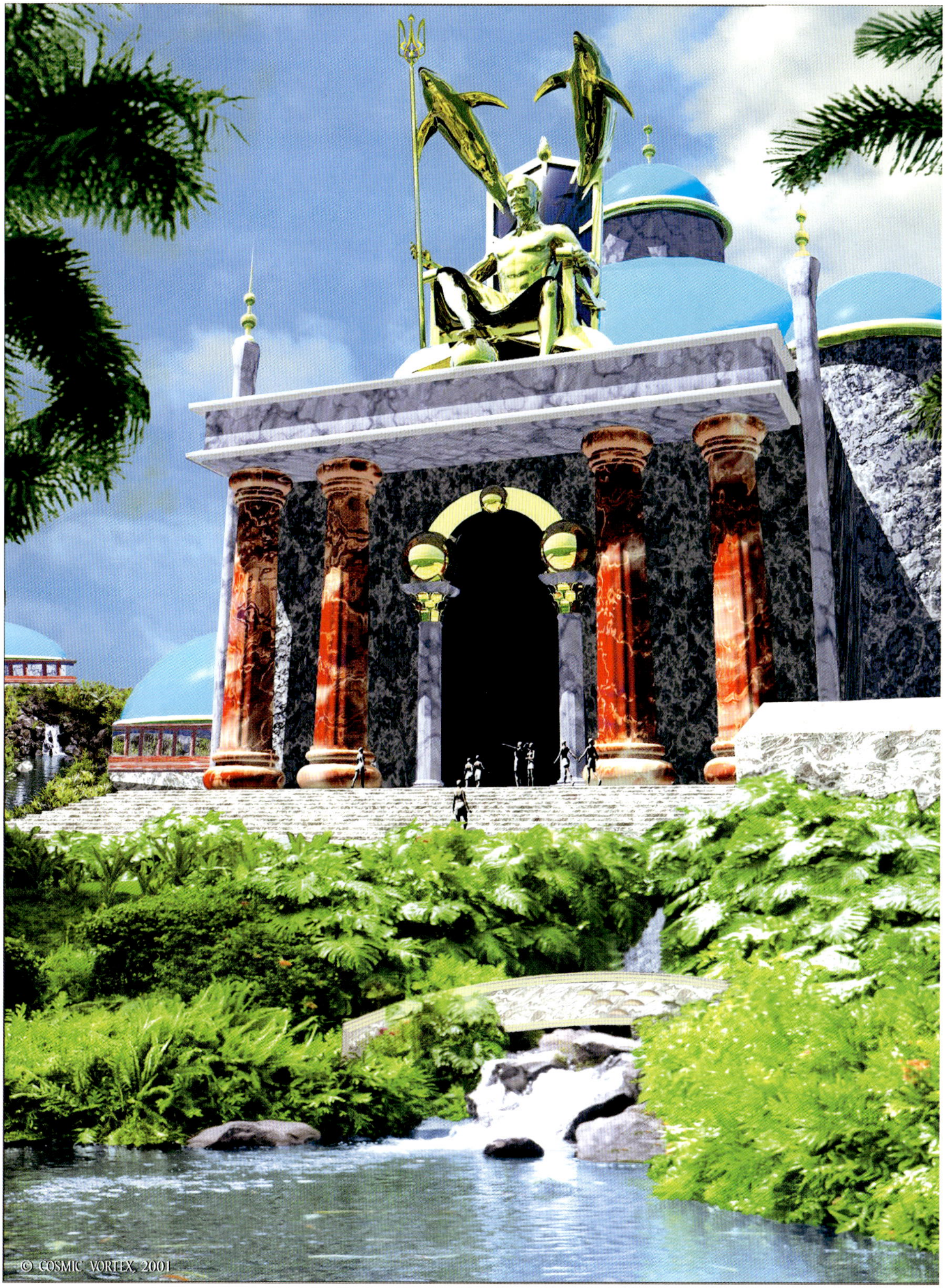
© COSMIC VORTEX, 2001

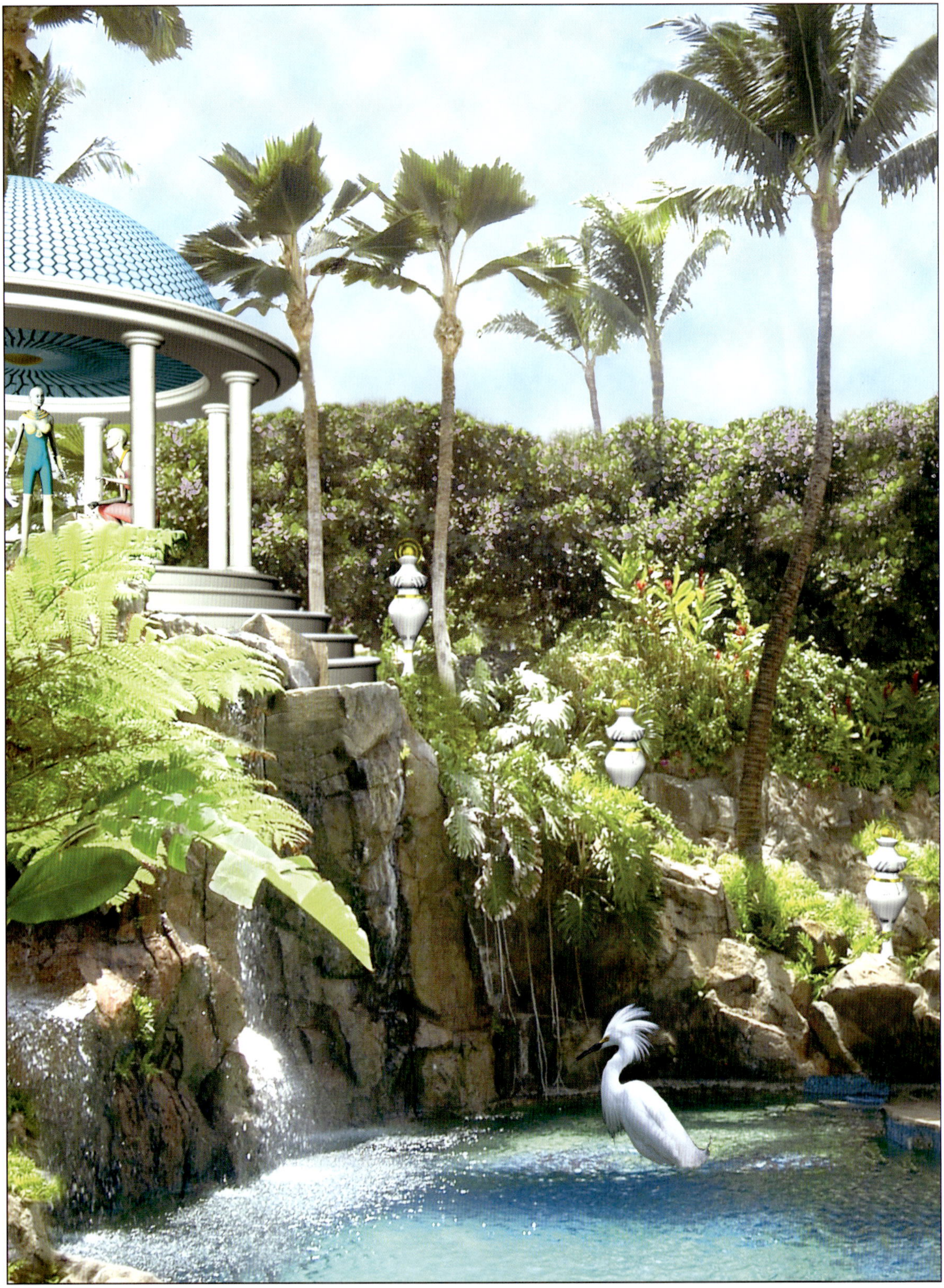

Xoah, Xoth, Xona and Xaah, simultaneously arrive in the Garden of Meditation. After an early morning greeting ceremony, Xoth begins to speak: This small waterfall is symbolic of our purpose on Blue Planet. These few drops of water gather in the pool which overflows and journeys on, to become a part of a mighty sea. A sea that gives birth to clouds that return the water to nourish the Garden again. We are the waterfall. This metropolis is the pool. The overflow is the ones who will leave. The sea is multitudes of beings. The clouds are the evolution of knowledge. This peaceful garden is Blue Planet.

Xoth: Today, I will present to you the continuation of the knowledge we covered yesterday. Twenty-one scientists on Xylanthia, with the aid of the Alpha Processor, have thoroughly calculated all the information the six of us have transmitted to them during the past seventy-five years. The analogy of our evolution on Xylanthia was a database to the projection of the evolution of this new species. With the exception of our androgyny and our advanced technology, there are striking similarities to the projected evolution of this new Blue Planet species.

Xoth: True equality is the basic existence of universal monism. Any entity in existence is dependant on everything else that exists. When eating the fruit of the tree, be thankful and aware of the water and the minerals in the soil that nourishes the roots to grow the trunk with limbs and leaves which gather the light from the far away heavens which also gives life to the bees to fertilize the flowers that makes the fruit which is your life sustenance. None of these is any less important than the other, although each function is different. We must emphasize the values of differentials.

Xoth: We must prepare for the inevitable. This new species will have a desire to look outside themselves for something greater than they are. Therefore rulers and leaders are necessary to fulfill this desire. The break-away can be minimized by contentment and reward for effort. Give praise for accomplishment and excuse errors, this increases self-esteem.

The four Xylanthians continue their conference in the Garden of Meditation. They agree to the necessity of organizing a military force. Xoth informs them of data from the Alpha Processor which outlines vessels of transportation, that float and maneuver upon the water bodies. There are no ships on Xylanthia. The data was gathered from probes on other advanced planets that use boats as a means of travel.

The vast plain surrounding Tua's hill has an abundance of waterways formed by several rivers that empty into the plain from surrounding mountain ranges. The waterways all empty into the nearby sea. The entire plain is laced with streams. This creates swamp areas and marshes. The scientists call Xeti, the geologist to join their meeting.

The five scientists agree to excavate a very deep ditch circumventing the entire plain. Xeti, with E-Gu and many helpers have extensively explored the entire plain. The ditch would be 1,150 miles in length, with a width of 600 feet and a depth of 100 feet. This depth would lower the water level of the plain and expose 60,000 square miles of rich fertile farmland.

The ditch will empty into the sea where the rivers converge and break through the coastal mountains. 100 feet wide canals will divide the entire plain into 11.5 mile sections. Each section will contain 10 lots, 1.15 miles square, to form a total of 60,000 lots which are encompassed by smaller irrigation canals. These lots will provide a bountiful supply of food for the future need of this exploding population. This engineering will create a navigation system wherein boats and rafts can transport produce from the farmlands and forest products from the distant mountains. It will also grant access to the open sea.

Xoth volunteers to select a large group of young males, females and pure Xylanthians, to teach them shipbuilding and navigation principles.

Xeti agrees to perform the tremendous task of building the outer ditch and canals. E-Gu who is now over 100 years old, has taught hundreds of beings the various facets of farming and supplying food to the thousands of workers and artisans who are building the metropolis. The five scientists discuss building a monument to honor E-Gu. They tease Xona about E-Gu's extended attraction to Xona. Xona retaliates by reminding the scientists of the motivating factor for longevity.

Xiza is invited to attend the Meeting in the Garden of Meditation. The scientists plan a comprehensive method of dividing the entire region into 10 areas. Each area will be governed by one of Xoah's sons whose successors would be the firstborn of each generation. Xoah's first born son is named Atlas who is selected to become the king of the metropolis and the surrounding walled city. The city is to be named Atlantis and the nearby ocean will be called Atlantic, in honor of Atlas.

The City of Atlantis

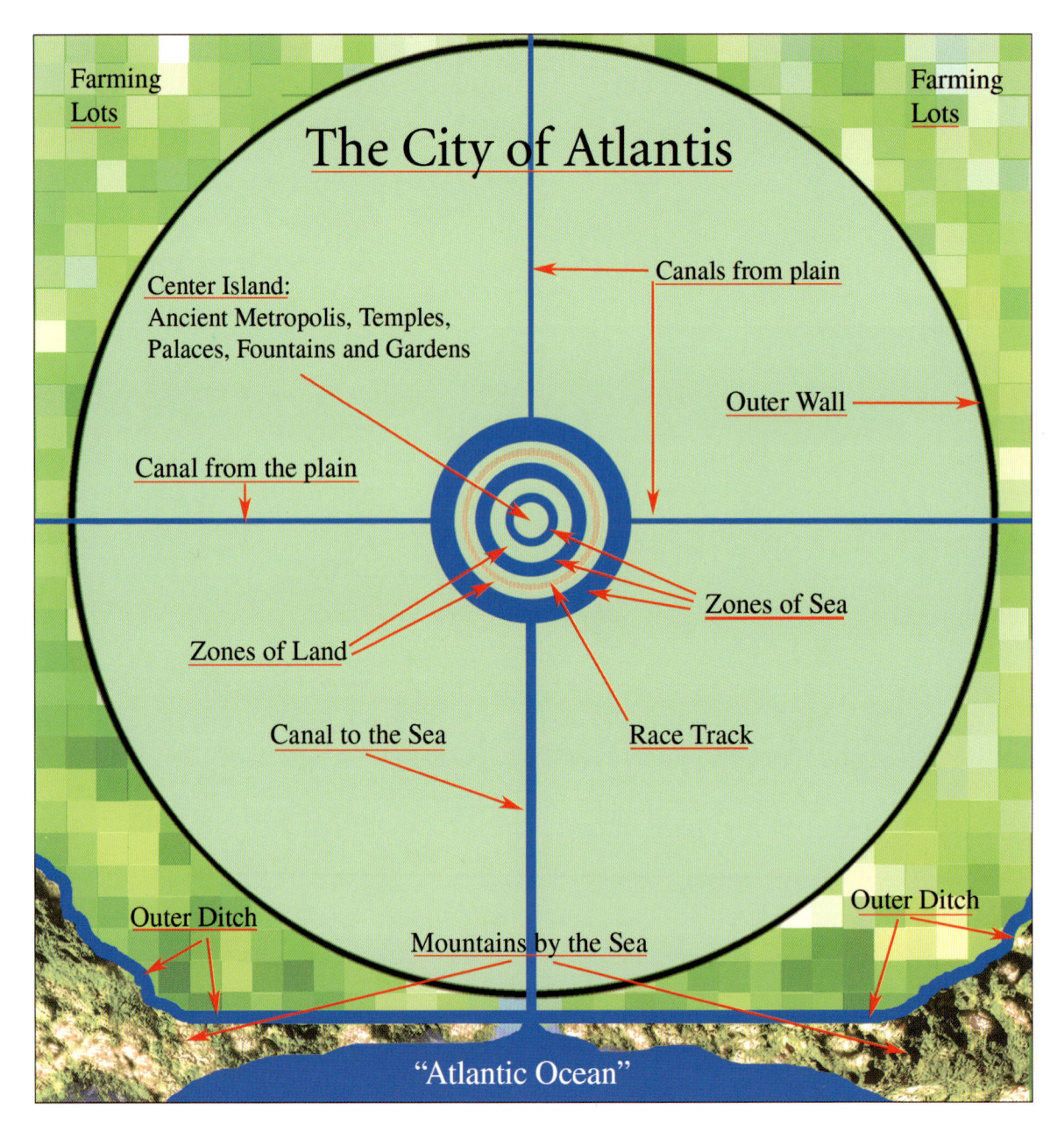

- Farming Lots
- Farming Lots
- Canals from plain
- Center Island: Ancient Metropolis, Temples, Palaces, Fountains and Gardens
- Outer Wall
- Canal from the plain
- Zones of Sea
- Zones of Land
- Race Track
- Canal to the Sea
- Outer Ditch
- Outer Ditch
- Mountains by the Sea
- "Atlantic Ocean"

Atlas mated with a female who was the daughter of Xoth and a primitive female. All ten sons of Xoah and Tua mated with females who were Xylanthian and primitive female mix. They all have many children who are extremely talented. They are leaders and teachers in different categories. Xoah calls the ten sons, to a meeting in the King's garden. Xoah reveals the comprehensive plan for this fast growing Empire. Xoah speaks: Atlas you are the first born. You are now the King of this Empire. You and your family will reside in your Mother's and my temple. You will govern all that is inside the wall of this metropolis. Your nine Brothers will each rule over their allotted portion of this kingdom.

64

5.75 Miles to Outer Wall

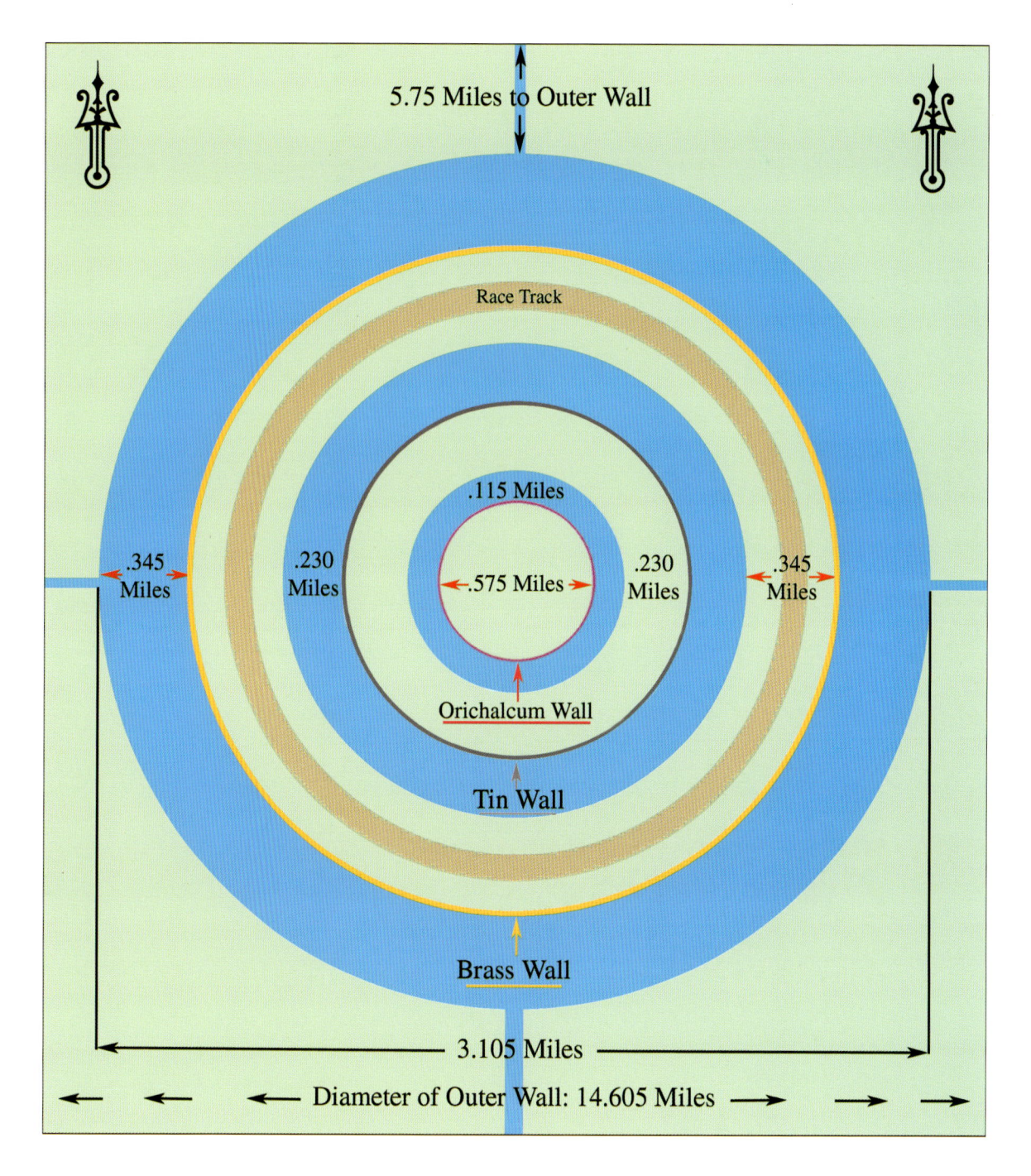

Race Track

.115 Miles

.345 Miles   .230 Miles   ←.575 Miles→   .230 Miles   .345 Miles

Orichalcum Wall

Tin Wall

Brass Wall

3.105 Miles

Diameter of Outer Wall: 14.605 Miles

   Xoah continues to speak to the ten sons: Do not forsake the friendship and respect you have for each other. The rules for harmonious co-existence are inscribed on these pillars. Abide by them and you will all prosper. Atlas will be ruler of all within the boundaries of the outer ditch. Honor him as your king. Govern the subjects of your kingdoms with equality. Your lands are far apart. All of you meet here, every five and six years alternately.

65

Xoah continues speaking: You have tamed the wild horse, to ride upon it's back and carry heavy loads. You have built ships to sail upon the water. Communicate with each other. Plan means to trade products that fulfill all your needs, thereby forming a powerful and beautiful Empire. Your Mother and I are proud of each of you. You have taught your family and many others all the skills that are necessary to build your kingdoms. You have helped build this remarkable metropolis. If some of your children wish to stay here, they are welcome to have your temples. The visitors temple is always available for any of you or your emissaries. Have pleasure without prejudice and your kingdoms will survive in excellency.

    The power of this great empire is our ability to work together, with respect for the unique talents and interests of each individual. We have built a great complex of waterways to sustain agriculture upon this vast fertile plain. The Channel to Sea, which Xeti with a vast crew of helpers has now completed, is an opening to many lands. Go forth and explore. Build your kingdoms with the foundation stones of respect and love for each other. Protect the land and create gardens for the sustenance of your people. Always remember that the king is no greater than any of the people. Everyone has different talents and desires. Understand this difference and provide a diverse culture and environment so that all of your people will find comfort and joy in their work and leisure time. Make your laws fair and just. Honor all of your people for they are the true wealth and power of your future kingdoms.

A person's home is their castle.   A Castle is a state of mind.

Visitor's Temple Complex

Main Entrance to the Race Track, located on the outer Zone of Land.
The Race Track is a popular attraction for social gatherings and recreation.

Royal Boat Dock, located beneath the center island, stairs lead to palaces above.

A ten year frenzy of boat building produces a fleet of ships that establish a communication system between the nine kingdoms and the city. Each vessel is a piece of art, some are small for personal use and others are large enough to carry various products and animals. The outer zone of water surrounding the metropolis is filled with docks. Narrow passages permit smaller boats to enter the 2 inner zones of water, where docks are carved into the zones of land. The outer ditch is navigable. Forest products from the northern mountains and farm produce from the sixty-thousand farm lots are brought to the city on ships and barges.

The visitors quarters are continually full, with merchants and dignitaries from the nine provinces, eight of which are outside the outer ditch. The visitors complex is where trading and bartering take place. The merchants trade gold, silver, ivory, wood products, art, grains, nuts, fruits, oils, spices, fragrances, tame animals, fine cloth, boats, weapons, pottery, salt, jewelry. animal skins and many other things.

Horses are a main commodity. Horse trading becomes addictive. Every full moon, a three day racing festival is held at the race track. Chariot racing and single horse racing are equally enjoyed. A code of honor develops between the traders. If a person promises to deliver a product on a future date, in trade for something that is readily available, the promise is honored without question.

69

Cold Water Fountain

Hot Water Fountain

Xoth is in continual contact with the Alpha Processor. Xoth learns that Big Bird has been replaced by an upgraded model and Big Bird will be de-materialized. Xoth requests the return of Big Bird to Atlantis to be used as a monument in the park surrounding Tua's cave which has been preserved, in the middle zone of land. Everyone on Xylanthia is extremely pleased. The Alpha Processor transmits a simple message; Come and get it.

Atlas has summoned his nine Brothers to come to the metropolis, on the third full moon, to celebrate the one hundred year anniversary of the landing of Big Bird. Xoth and Xoah agree, for Xoth to land Big Bird, as a surprise during the celebration.

Tua is now 115 years of age and E-Gu is 120 years of age. Xylanthian technology has extended their life spans to the maximum, due to the dominant gene pattern. The normal life span, for primitive beings, is 35 years.

E-Gu has been honored many times for his extraordinary accomplishments and loyalty to Xoah. A monument with the symbol of E-Gu's encoder, was erected outside the Temple of Records where E-Gu's life history is tabulated. Of all the fabulous buildings, E-Gu helped build, he prefers to live in his primitive hut which he had given to Dai and Tai to live in, until they expired, many years ago. E-Gu's invaluable ability to co-ordinate the innumerable facets of building this great Empire pleases the Xylanthians scientists. E-Gu's deep love for Xona never ceases.

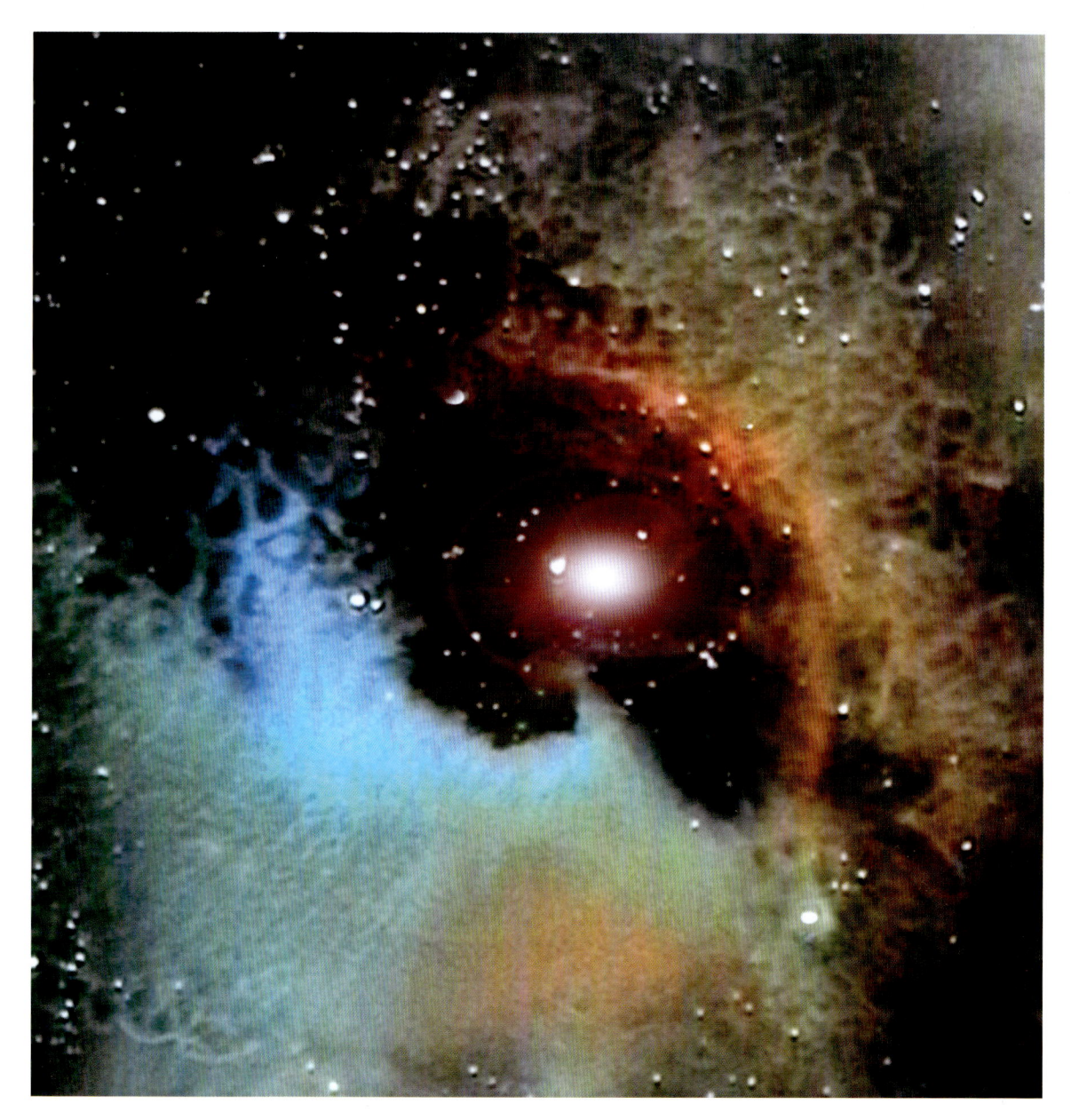

It is two moons before the centennial celebration. E-Gu asks Xona to spend the night in his hut. They know it is time for E-Gu to die. They spend the night, laughing, weeping and caressing each other.

A radiant sunrise lights the glorious city which they can see through the open doorway of E-Gu's hut. E-Gu places his jeweled encoder in Xona's trembling hands. He lays his head on Xona's lap, gives Xona a meaningful smile, closes his eyes and his life spirit leaves his body. Xona strokes his long white hair and kisses him on the forehead. Amid a flood of tears, Xona contacts the Alpha Processor. E-Gu vanishes into the cosmos. Xona transmits a message to the five Xylanthian scientists; E-GU IS GONE. They will always remember their Dear Primitive Friend, Mighty E-Gu.

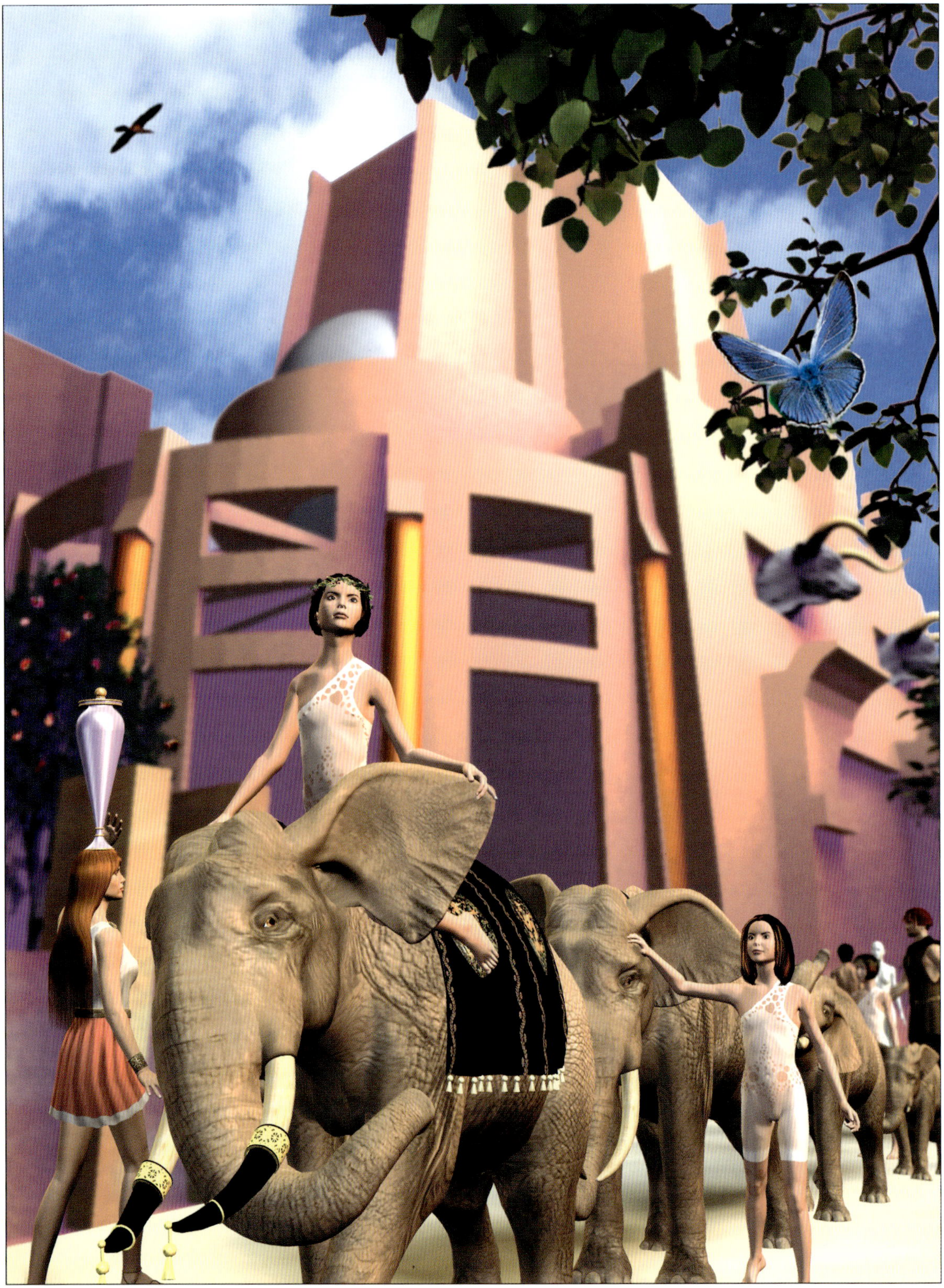

A pristine sunrise heralds the awakening of this centennial day of celebration. The golden spires and orichalcum pillars in the city glisten in the morning sunlight. A powerful energy force envelopes the entire region as the populace of the ten provinces begin this special day. Each kingdom and selected areas of the farmlands surrounding city are enjoying their separate festivals. The ten sons, portions of their families and their favorite race horses, have arrived at the city which is crowded to maximum. The main gathering in the City is in the large park where Tua's cave is located. Xoah created a regal white horse which Tua has treasured for many years. Xoah assists Tua to mount her horse. Xoah leads them across the bridge to the middle zone where the ten sons and hundreds of others are gathered in the park near Tua's cave. An extremely loud greeting with the sound of horns and drums, welcomes their Queen Mother as she arrives.

Suddenly, the tumultuous roar of the crowd changes to an awesome breathless silence. All eyes are looking skyward as Big Bird slowly descends, nose down, into the center of the park. Tua is so excited, she jumps off her horse into Xoah's arms and weeps with joy, while shrieking; E-Tua, E-Tua, E-Tua! As Xoth emerges from the craft, Xoah carries Tua into Big Bird and places her in a special seat. Xoah speaks: My Queen would you like to go for a ride and see your Empire. Tua claps her hands like a happy child and nods approval through her normal flood of happy tears.

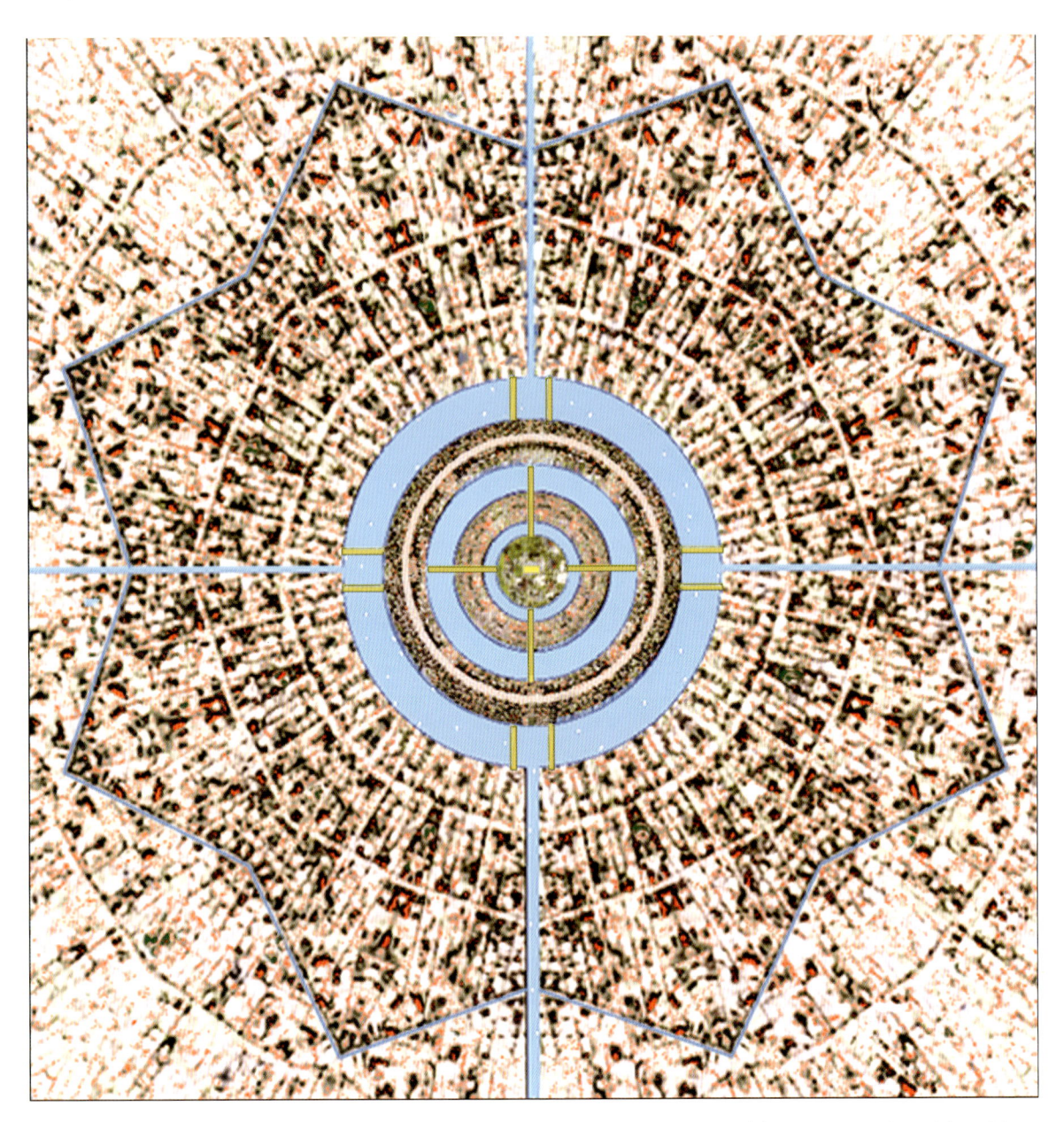

The ground trembles with the exuberant noise of the people as Big Bird silently raises to a low altitude and circles several times over the city. Xoah flies Big Bird low over the vast farmland as a greeting to the many festivals in various places. Xoah flies low over the nine kingdoms being built along the edge of the Great Ocean and on different islands in the Sea. Xoah speaks: My Precious Queen, you are the Mother of this vast Empire. Your Empire is the Motherland of billions of people who will populate this entire planet. I will show you your planet. Xoah accelerates Big Bird which climbs to a very high altitude. When Tua sees Beautiful Blue Planet, she is speechless. Her countenance changes as if a brilliant light is shining on her. Two crystal rivers of tears are flowing down her cheeks.

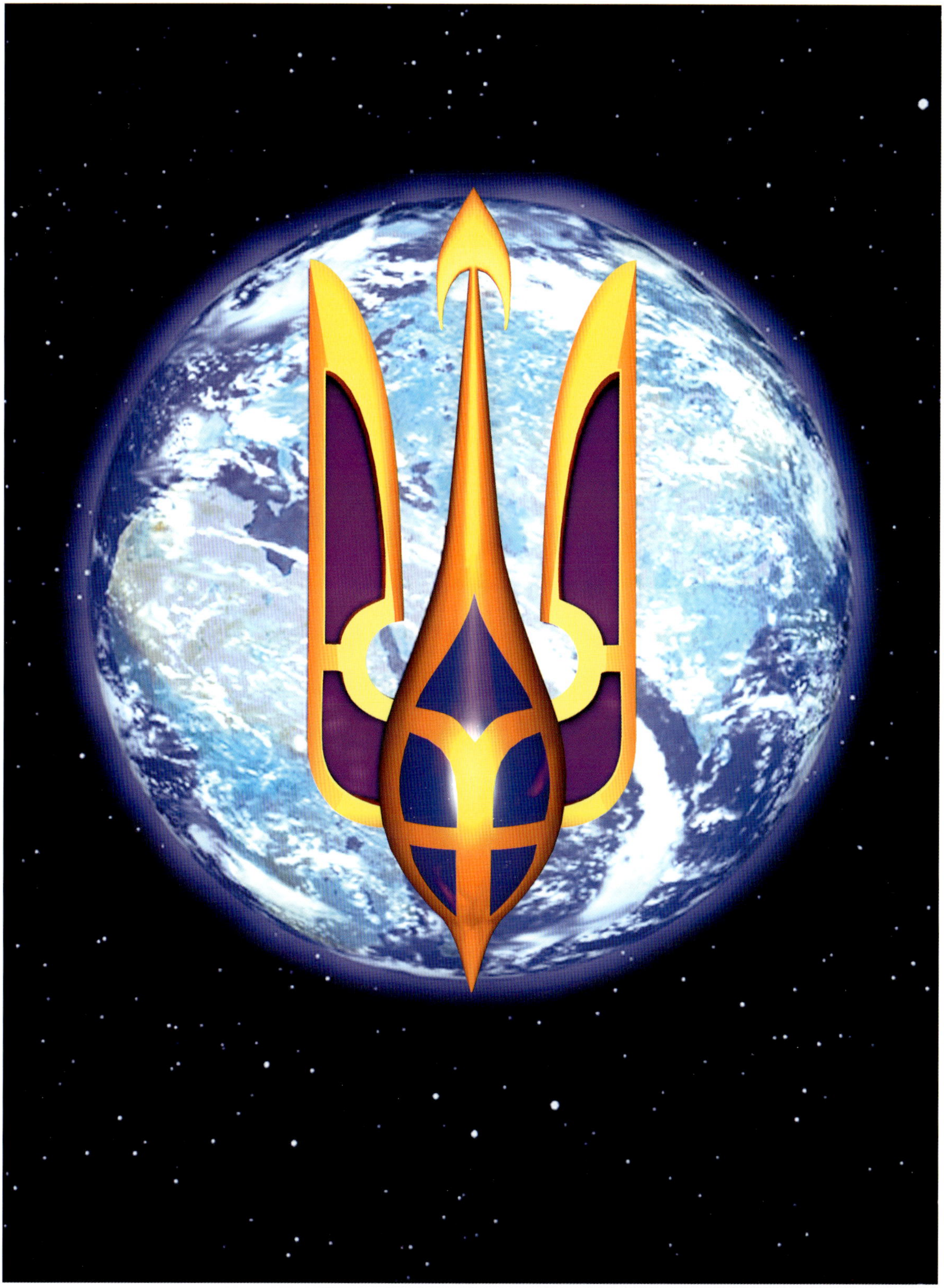

The three hour journey ended as Xoah settles Big Bird down in a favorite place near Tua's Cave. Everyone, except the ten sons and the five scientists, are at the race track on the outer zone. Xoah permanently disables the manual controls and the anti gravity power bank. As they exit from Big Bird, Xoah seals the opening. This majestic symbol will be a monument commemorating the amalgamation, of two different species, into one peaceful coexistence.

The ten sons and five scientists greet Tua and Xoah as they descend from Big Bird. Xoah asks them why they are not at the races. Atlas speaks: My Father, you ask a question which you already know the answer to. We know it is time for our beloved Mother to leave us and surely you will go with her as you two are never apart. As you know, my Father, we would not let you leave without honoring your departure. Mother Tua, there are no words a son can find that can fully express our love for you. You gave us life, the precious gift of existence. You gave us the individual freedoms to be what we truly are. You taught us equality without prejudice, not by your words but by your behavior. You selected our Father for a mate, that gave us the genetics of a knowledge that prevented our primitive ancestors from extinction. Dear, Dear Mother and Father, your love for each other has been our greatest teacher, the gift of true love is a rare eternal force which balances all emotions. Our sorrow, for your farewell today, will be balanced by the joy of our children and their generations of children when they see this monument and know that without you two very special beings, they could not enjoy the gift of life. Dearest King and Queen, we love you, there is no reason for a farewell. You will always be with us in our hearts and memories.

After a lengthy exchange of hugs, kisses and tears the scientists and the ten sons are off to the races. Tua and Xoah are caressing Big Bird. Tua feels something touching her back. She turns around. Her white horse is nuzzling her. Tua sees tears falling from her horse's eyes. Tua throws her arms around his neck and bursts into tears. Her horse moves his head up and down as if to nod an affirmative approval. Then with a very majestic prance he bounces away and disappears into the dense foliage.

During the late afternoon, Tua and Xoah are strolling around the park near Tua's cave. They are like two children, holding hands and laughing about the pleasant events of their many years together. The sun is setting as a full moon rises over the opposite horizon. They are at the entrance to Tua's cave as the moonlight night begins. Xoah lifts Tua and sets her on the rock where she sat so many nights, communicating with Xoah on Xylanthia. Tua, begins humming her musical chant, then squeals excitedly and points to the brightest star in the sky. Tua slips off the rock into Xoah's arms. They embrace amid crystal fountains of joyful tears. As their lips are pressed together in a lengthy meaningful kiss, the Alpha Processor blends Tua and Xoah into the eternal life essence of the infinite monistic universe.

79

The races ended at sunset. News of Tua's and Xoah's departure has spread throughout the multitude. An abundance of lamps are lighted everywhere in the metropolis. Everyone dampens their sorrow by joining a furor of festivities which continue all night. New relationships are formed between members of different provinces. This increases the solidarity of the Atlantian Empire. Future trading principles are arranged. Knowledge, of boat building, mining, farming, animal breeding, leather and cloth production, preservation of food, arts and many other crafts, are shared equally. Many male and female friendships are established, which will eventually progress into mating couples. Artistic principles and architectural grandeur is freely shared. Philosophical views are debated and unified.

The five Xylanthian scientists are an extremely rare commodity. They will only travel together, to the different provinces. A special ship was designed for the Xylanthians and their equipment. These nine kingdoms are in their early stages of development. The knowledge and teaching of the scientists are in great demand as each province has different topographical, geological and meteorological constituencies to contend with. On this memorable night, a comprehensive schedule is created to cope with the needs of each province. Priority is given to the comfort and care of the five Xylanthian scientists. The energy force of true friendship is prevalent everywhere in the closing hours of this Grand Centennial.

Xoah, who was a scientist in animal husbandry, created bulls that had a gentle nature and a very powerful physical body. These bulls had the freedom of the King's Garden. Tua gave each bull a name, the bull she called, would come to be caressed. Xoah perceived the bull to be a symbol for the inhabitants of the Empire, Strength with Justice.

As a glorious sunrise appears, the ten sons and their families meet together in the King's Garden. They swear an oath to abide by the laws of their Father, which are inscribed on the pillar; to love and honor each other and rule their kingdoms with justice and equality. After a brief ceremony, they all cross the bridge to the center island and gather in the Garden of Tua's Cave.

No words were spoken. After many tearful embraces, the nine families go to their separate boats which are tied in the outer harbor. Atlas and his mate, stand on the temple balcony and watch the beautiful boats of the nine Kings sail down the Channel to the Sea. As the boats reach the ocean, each one sails off in a different direction. Atlas and his mate watch until all the boats disappear from view.

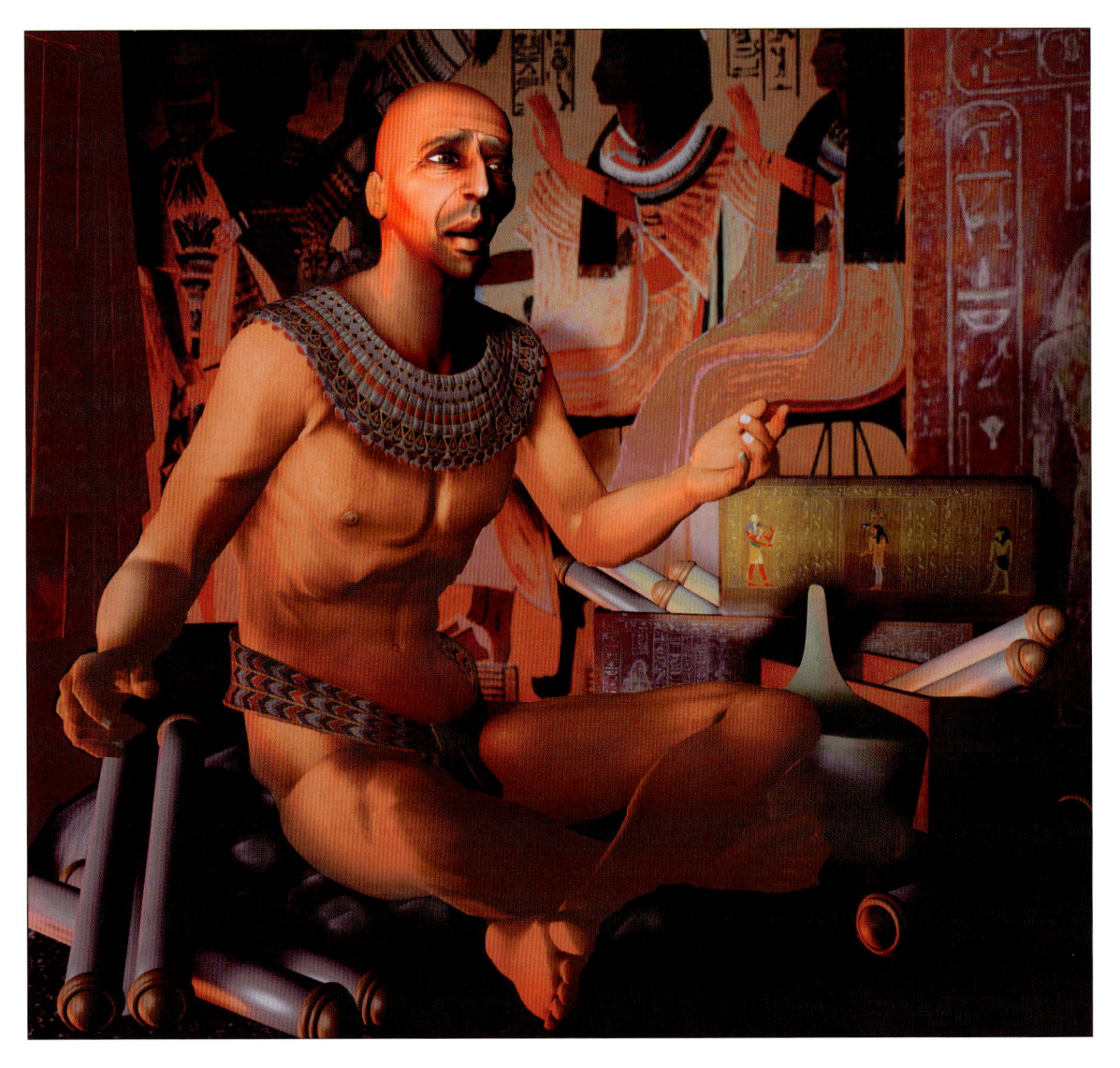

Hidden in the dark corners of ancient history, are many great and noble persons who were never acknowledged for their invaluable gifts to human evolution. One of the greatest of these forgotten masters, was an Egyptian Priest, Philosopher, Teacher and Historian, named SONCHIS.

Sonchis was noted throughout the known world, for his knowledge and wisdom. He was visited by Roman Emperors, Greek Statesmen and scientists. The Egyptian Priests preserved valuable ancient historical records that would have been lost forever. Sonchis's student Priests were scribes dedicated to preserving these records. Their Deity was Seshat, the Goddess of records, who was believed to have a male counter part named, Thoth. Historical records were treasured more than gold. Through the ages of time, Rulers, Emperors and Kings possess an ego-maniacal desire to present themselves as God, or an emissary of God. Destroying records, prevented their subjects from worshipping former Deities. The Egyptian Goddess Seshat was a threat to them.

590 BC

In 590 BC, Solon, a prominent Greek statesman, visits the City of Sais in the Nile Delta region of Egypt. News of Solon's visit has preceded his arrival and spread throughout Sais. As his ship docks in the harbor, a great multitude gathers to welcome this noted person who's wisdom has abolished the tyrannical Aristocracy of Greece.

Solon is a charismatic exhibitionist, he uses his songs and poems to maintain his popularity and sway others to reasonable wise decisions. After entertaining the multitude, Solon escapes and gives a young man a gold coin to guide him to the temple of Seshat.

Solon is bored with the political instability in Greece and changes his life to an adventurous quest for more knowledge. He is aware of the knowledge and wisdom of Sonchis. As Solon enters the temple of Seshat, he recounts the many times in his life, when he had a desire to meet Sonchis.

A young student priest greets Solon at the entrance to the temple. When Solon introduces himself, the student priest is exuberant to be face to face with the great Sage. The young priest is so excited, he grabs Solon's hand and hurriedly pulls him to a chamber where some forty student priests are busy with records of stone, parchment, wood and papyrus. As the priest introduces Solon to the other young priests, they all gather near Solon. They beg him to tell them about Greece.

As the young priests sit down in a semicircle on the stone floor, Solon takes a stance in his familiar theatrical pose. As he begins his poetic oratory about the history of ancient Greece, Solon notices a very old Priest sitting quietly in a corner of the room. Solon's heart pounds, he knows, after many years of longing to meet Sonchis, he is now in the same room with him.

Solon is a politician, he knows all the tricks. He now considers that if he stands here and makes a jackass out of himself long enough, he can get a retort from the Old Priest. This would give Solon the prestige of being recorded in history as outsmarting the wise Sonchis. The young priests are captivated for one hour by Solon's antics.

Sonchis is one hundred and five years of age. His voice is like the sound of distant thunder. As he begins to speak an eerie hollow echo fills the room; Solon! Solon! Solon! You have done a great service for your country. You are wise in your search for knowledge. Your rudeness in this Holy Temple today is excusable because you, like all the Greeks are little children living in a world of fantasy. You take reality and truth and distort them into myth and unreality. You come to this temple to seek wisdom. How do you expect to find wisdom from one whom you perceive to have less wisdom than you? This creates a paradox. You taught your country equality as a better form of government. Today you deviate from your own teaching, by presuming you are wiser than me and can maneuver me into retorting. The truth is you place yourself lesser than me by assuming there is a need to outsmart me, thereby causing me to be the lesser one. This is not equality. The wisdom that we learn together today is, Teacher, hear your own teaching.

As Sonchis speaks to Solon, the student priests are busy transcribing every word. Solon, many catastrophes in your country are the reason you have no ancient records. You spoke to the priests today about a deluge, there have been many deluges which destroyed your records. You talk about myths instead of scientific reality, that Phaethon drove a flaming chariot and burnt up all that was upon the Earth. In reality a fiery heavenly body fell to the earth and scorched the high places in your country. Your country's loss of the ancient records of your heritage is the primary reason why the Greeks create myths and fantasies, like little children.

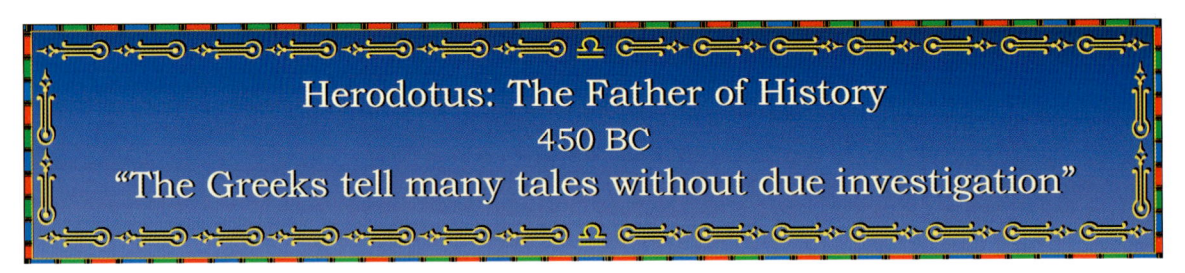

Herodotus: The Father of History
450 BC
"The Greeks tell many tales without due investigation"

Sonchis deep voice resonates in the stone temple, like living knowledge awakening from thousands of years of the ancient past. Solon, your search for the heritage of your country persons, is the greatest gift you can obtain for them. One's heritage is a part of the person. If one does not know their heritage, one does not know a part of their self. If a part of a person is missing, all the days of their life is spent searching for their own being. This is why you are here, Solon. You are a lonely wanderer searching for the true Solon. The tears on your cheeks, tells me this is so.

These young priests are finding their true beings. They have dedicated their lives to preserve over 30,000 years of knowledge of human heritage, from stone, wood and ivory to parchment and papyrus. From hieroglyph, petroglyph and symbols, to languages. This is our contented lives. Ancient records reveal that this Earth is a sphere. Humans will eventually migrate around this sphere. If they do not know their true identity, they will always be discontented and full of trouble. Solon, we are exhausted. Please, dine and retire with the student priests, they will enjoy your songs and fairy tales. You will appreciate a hot mineral bath and exercise with them, in the refreshing water of the sacred pool of Seshat.

I will return here tomorrow at sunrise. Meet me here and we will search the ancient registers. You will find what you are searching for. That is the Motherland where the ancestors of your country and mine, originated.

Good Morning, Solon. Last evening you bathed in the sacred water of Seshat, the Goddess of ancient Records. The minerals in the water, awakens the sleeping ancient knowledge stored in the memory realms of your brain system. We have a duality in our genetic composition, the nature of the primitive Earth person and the nature of our cosmic ancestry. As the mixture of these two natures vary from generation to generation, also varies the ability of persons to find balance within their constituent behavior. Solon, knowledge is an infinite universal force. All entities in existence have varying degrees of access to this force. Our primitive nature limits this access. We must learn to maintain a balance of our two natures. The genetic ability of our cosmic nature, permits us to contact this universal knowledge and communicate with each other without words. I knew you were coming to meet me when your ship was crossing the sea. Even now as we speak of balance, there is a great teacher in Asia, called Lao Tzu, who is, at this very moment, explaining the universal law of polarity, wherein every force that exists, has an inseparable opposite force which regulates the function of the two, in an attempt to attain the illusive force of balance. I will now implant this image in your memory for your future contemplation.

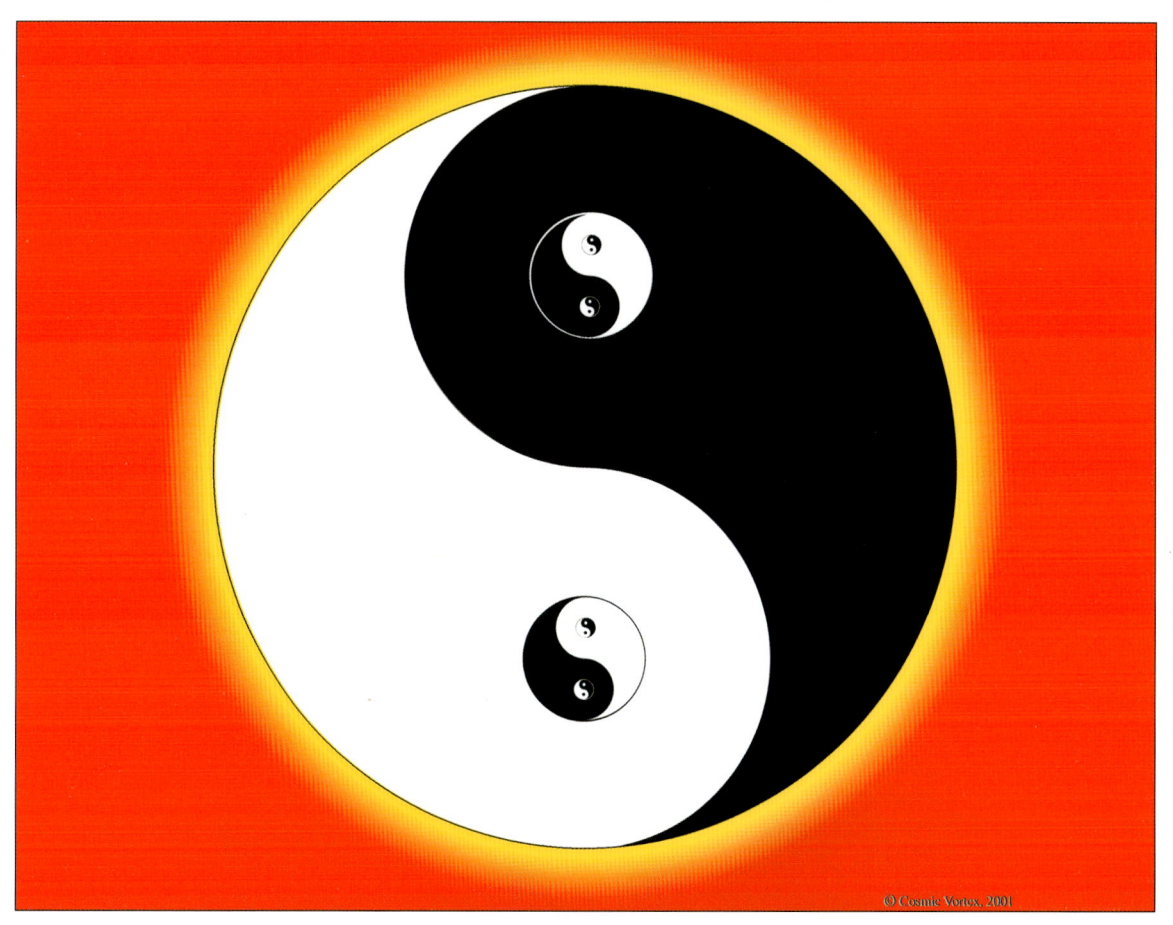

© Cosmic Vortex, 2001

85

Solon, the reward for living is self respect. The greatest self respect one can attain, is to fully understand basic reality. You are 40 years on this Earth. I have seen 105 years. Life is our teacher. I am no wiser than you, I have had more schooling. The maximum of learning is realizing, the more you learn the more there is to learn. The fool's self respect is contentment with ignorance.

O-Solon, your desire to find the foundation stones of your heritage, reaches to the depths of your soul. These foundation stones sank into the depths of the sea, from a terrible earthquake and flood, 9,000 years ago. At the same time all of the mighty valorous warriors of the Hellenes, from your great country, were buried in the Earth. Our history tells of a majestic wonderful vast empire which was founded 36,400 years ago, by beings from the cosmos, who the Greeks call Gods, and primitive Earth Beings. This lost civilization of Atlantis, was the Motherland of all humans on Earth. This magnificent Empire flourished with peaceful balanced equality for a thousand years, until Aristocracy and military oppression forced your ancestors and mine to migrate to distant areas on this Earth. This migration preserved the most valuable gift we all possess, the foundation of our two fold genetics. The excellent intelligence of the cosmic beings and the survival qualities of the Earth beings is our true heritage. Awareness of these two natures, is the key to open the doorway to that endless pathway within each of us. This awareness guides us along the infinite journey into our true being. Open the door, Solon, you are a great man. Your desire is your motivating power. Go visit the land of our Ancestors. The ancient knowledge still resides on the mountain tops, in the depths of the sea, in the legends of the remaining inhabitants of that land and in the fertile lands which still exist there.

Your ship can sail to the location of this lost empire. In those days, a stone barrier prevented travel from hence to there. A great flood 5,000 years past, removed this barrier. If you sail due east from the northern part of your country, you will enter what you call the straights of Heracles. This body of water is only a harbor, leading to a narrow passage which forms the pillars of Heracles. Past the pillars of Heracles is a real sea. 36,400 years ago this ocean was named Atlantic, and the Empire was called Atlantis, in honor of Atlas the first born of the original founders. The other nine sons of these founders and their descendants established kingdoms surrounding this ocean. My Ancestors came from the east side of this sea. Your ancestors came from the western region. Many islands, which are now inundated, existed in the western part of the ocean. The main Island of Atlantis was to the north. These nine kingdoms and this large island were the components of this Empire which is the common heritage of humankind.

Solon, many great and wonderful deeds of your state are recorded in our records. One of those deeds exceeds all others in greatness and valor. Our histories tell of the mighty military power of the Island of Atlantis, subjecting the entire population of the surrounding Empire to slavery. This vast military gathered into one and came forth out of the Atlantic Ocean for a fatal blow to your country and the whole of the region within the straits of Heracles. Solon, in the excellency and strength above all nations, your country, with the power of Athene and the Hellenes, defeated and triumphed over the invaders and liberated those of us who were subjected to slavery. True facts, not fantasies is the heritage of your country. I perceive you are anxious to go to your ship and I must council Amasis, who is waiting. He will be the next ruler of Egypt. The scribes have prepared duplicate transcripts, of the history of the roots of humankind, for you. Be proud of what you are. Please visit me again on your next journey to Sais.

Dear Sonchis, your wisdom is priceless. Before we leave, my crew will deliver ten luxors of gold for the temple. Your greatness knows my gratitude. You are truly the full power and essence of Seshat and Thoth.

1975 AD

In 1975 AD the authors of this book came together in a passionate love affair. They immediately discovered that each of them had a life long ambition to find the LOST CIVILIZATION OF ATLANTIS, each had a psychogenetic memory of its existence. Both had actual dreams and had searched legend, history, myths and records for factual evidence of its reality and location.

Whispering Wind was 20 years of age and Flying Eagle was 54 years of age. OH! How they loved each other. They compared their dreams and memories and were astounded at the identical versions of their visions. They decided to dedicate their lives, to locate this LOST ISLAND OF ATLANTIS,

Whispering Wind and Flying Eagle compiled their previous knowledge and spent years searching for records and locations throughout the entire Earth. This search caused them to realize that solving the mystery of ATLANTIS required the amalgamated contemplation of many sciences: geography, topography, oceanography, geology, archeology, bathymetry, tectonics, seismology, botany, history, cartography, hydronymy, onomastics, genealogy, mythology, anthropology, zoology, meteorology, geothermalogy, astronomy, biology, psychology, sociology and especially chronology.

Chronology is the crux of discovery. For 2,000 years the legend of ATLANTIS has been attributed to Plato. There is no record of Plato ever writing anything about ATLANTIS, nor is there any record of Plato being a playwright or dramatist. Plato was born 133 years after Solon died. He lost his father when very young and idolized Socrates. Plato was a dear friend and probable lover of the famous and disheveled philosopher, Socrates. Plato was 17 years of age when he transcribed conversations between Socrates, Critias, Timaeus and Hermocrates. These transcribed dialogues, of Timaeus and Critias, contain the transcript which Sonchis gave to Solon, 180 years previously. Plato was heartbroken over the death of Socrates. He traveled for many years before he opened the Academy which was an institute of philosophy, science and research. Plato taught many renowned scientists.

Scientists and scholars, in various categories of science, are incapable of combining their separate discoveries into one comprehensive solution. THIS INABILITY CREATES A WARP IN TRUE KNOWLEDGE AND DISTORTS REALITY. One distortion is the location of the Pillars of Heracles and the location of the ancient Atlantic Ocean. The present Atlantic Ocean was named by the Romans, 100 years after Solon died. At this same time they named the Rock of Gibralter; the Pillars of Hercules, in honor of the Greek hero, Heracles. There were at least two Heracles. The Greeks worshiped their hero, Heracles who's name the Romans changed to Hercules and they also worshiped the God, Heracles.

Sonchis; *"the sea in those parts is impassible and impenetrable, because there is a shoal of mud in the way."* **THE STRAIT OF GIBRALTAR HAS BEEN OPEN TO THE ATLANTIC FOR 5 MILLION YEARS.**

Myths and history are intertwined into a genetic umbilical cord which connects present day humans to their ancestors. All myths contain history and all history contains myths. A thin thread of reality is woven into this interlacing, as this cord winds it's pathway through the ages of time. Follow this cord back to it's point of origin and true knowledge can be unveiled.

The myth that ATLANTIS was an island in the present Atlantic Ocean, outside Gibraltar, is completely absent of sound reasoning. Or, if ATLANTIS was on the Mediterranean side of Gibraltar, this is also unreasonable. Both of these myths have no scientific foundation whatsoever. Atlantis *"disappeared into the depths of the sea"*, 11,600 years ago. Atlantis had existed for 27,400 years when it *"disappeared"*. There is no scientific evidence of any human, except the Neanderthal, living near the Gibraltar region at that time.

One key to this thin thread of reality, is the word PILLARS. In the science of geology, pillars and columns are synonymous terms. Pillars are generally formed, in a massive group, by the cooling and crystallization of heated volcanic igneous basalt. THERE IS ONLY ONE ROCK OF GIBRALTAR, it is not a volcanic geological formation. It is a sedimentary limestone rock formed 55 million years ago, by the African tectonic plate pushing into the European plate, creating an 8 mile wide strait between the present Atlantic and Mediterranean Sea. The Bosporus opening to the Black Sea is less than one half mile wide. *"The sea which is within the straits of Heracles is only a harbor having a narrow entrance."* This quotation refers to the Sea of Marmara, the Dardanelles and the Bosporus. THE GEOLOGY OF THE BOSPORUS CONTAINS VOLCANIC CRYSTALLIZED BASALT PILLARS.

The Bosporus was called Symplegades or Clashing Rocks. Basalt columns in geological formation, are pillars formed in a series of stacked segments. There are many tales recorded in history, of rocks falling on ships.

The top of the spectacular Rock of Gibraltar is over one thousand, two hundred feet above the sea. The ancient geological formation of the sedimentary limestone layers, is indicative of the uplift of the tectonic plate.

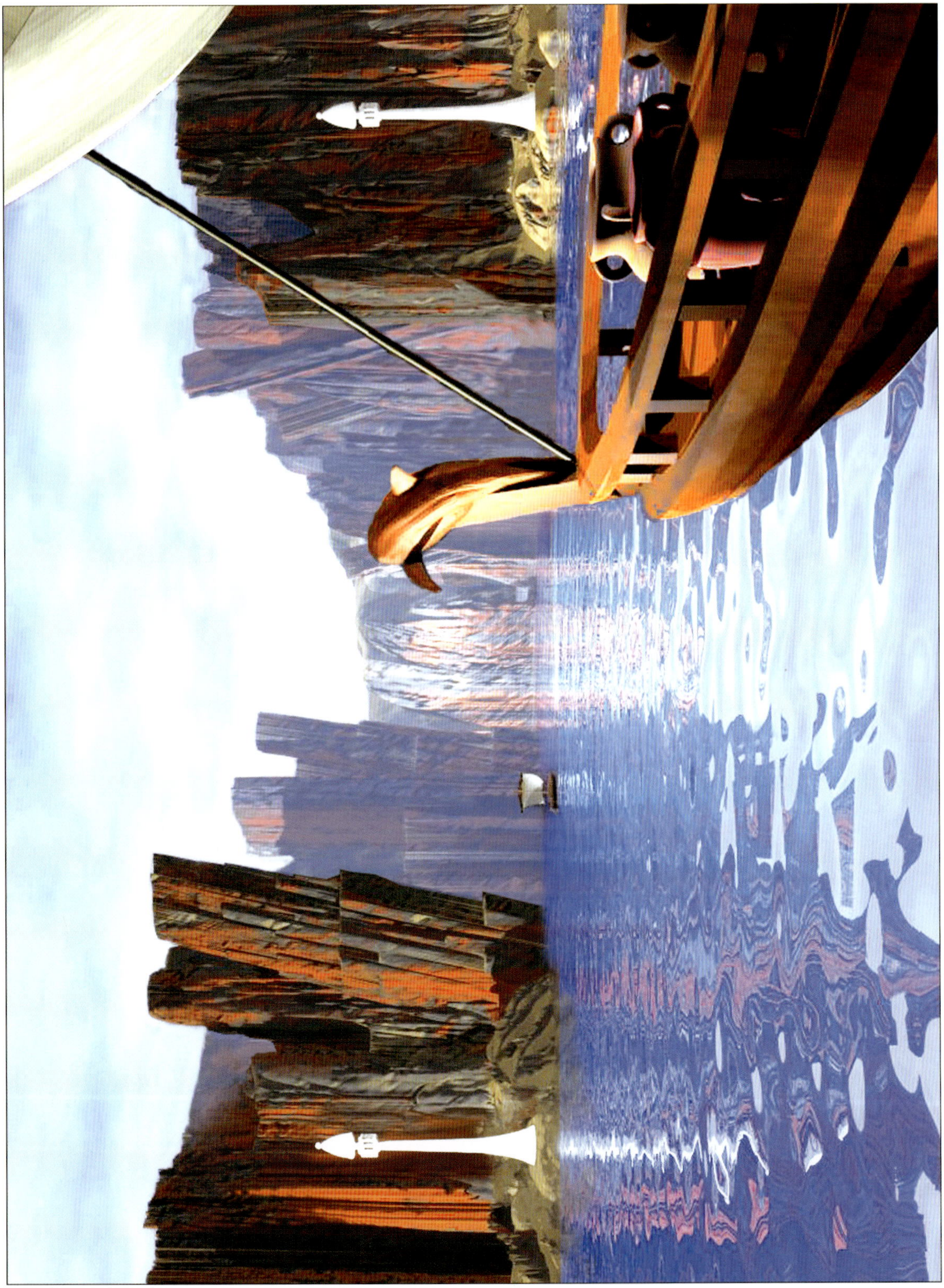

THE PILLARS OF HERACLES AND THE PILLARS OF DARIUS THE GREAT

Sonchis speaking to the Greek Sage, Solon: *"there was an island situated in front of the straits which are by <u>you</u> called the Pillars of Heracles."* In the 6th century BC, the Greeks begin to colonize various regions of the Black Sea Region, as far north as the southern tip of Crimea. They earnestly worshiped the God, Heracles. They named several cities, in this area, after their God Heracles.

In the 4th and 5th century BC, King Darius of Persia made an onslaught against the Greek Black Sea colonization. Those who would join his mighty army would be rewarded, others were destroyed. King Darius wanted to conquer Greece. His strategy was to disrupt extensive trade, from the plush colonies, to Greece. He built a bridge across the narrow Bosporus, for his armies to intercept this trade from the fertile northern Black Sea region.

King Darius was power-mad. The Greek God, Heracles was a threat to his ego-mania. He constructed two giant white marble pillars, in front of the Pillars of Heracles, at the narrow opening, of the Bosporus, which leads through the Dardanelles and the Sea of Marmara, to Greece. The geological formation of this opening is what the Greeks called the Pillars of Heracles. On these white marble Pillars of Darius where inscriptions of the military might of Persia. The purpose of these pillars was twofold, to deter merchant shipping to Greece and especially to belittle the Greek God, Heracles. The God Heracles won this strategic battle. The Byzantine, a short time later, removed the white marble Pillars of Darius the Great. The Pillars of Heracles have withstood many wars and may withstand many more wars of egotistical, power-mad humans.

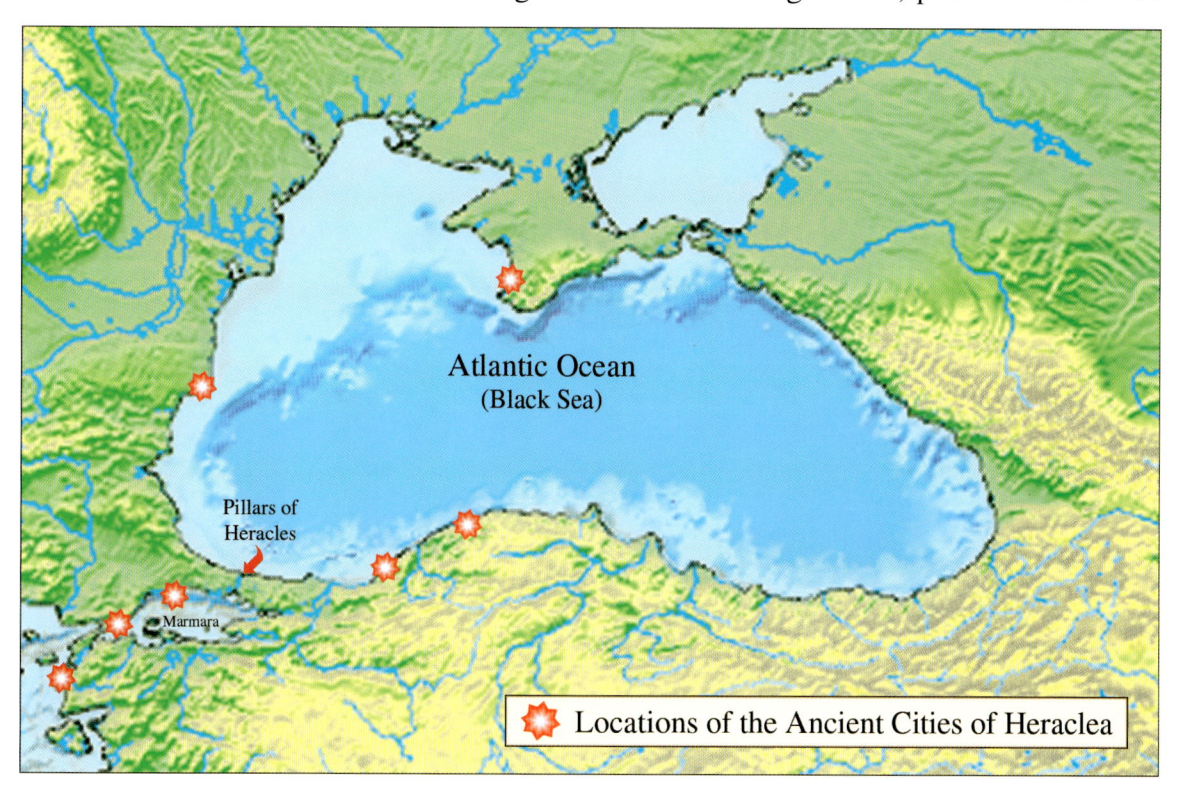

Locations of the Ancient Cities of Heraclea

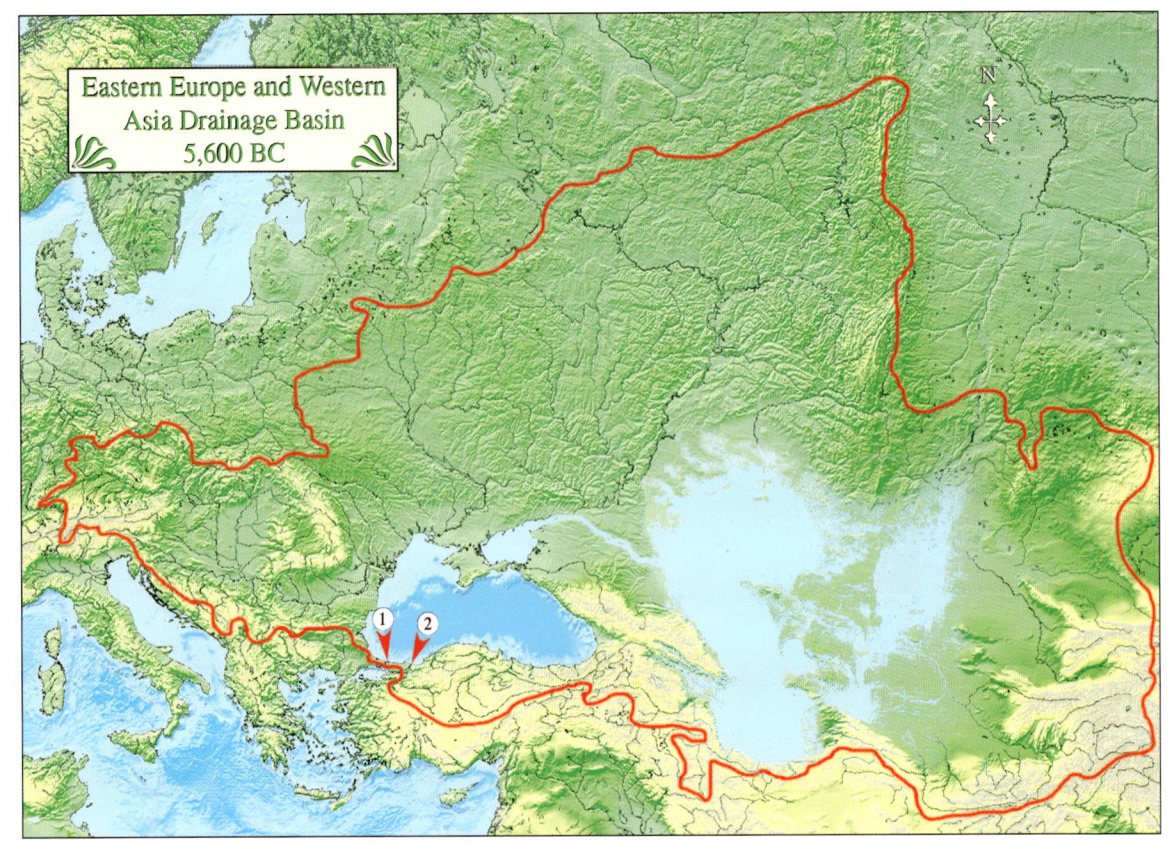

Eastern Europe and Western Asia Drainage Basin 5,600 BC

The Bosporus was a land bridge before 5,600 BC. For millions of years, the vast drainage area, of Eastern Europe and Western Asia, emptied into the Black Sea. This ancient Black Sea discharged through a subterranean tunnel under the Bosporus (arrow #1 on map) and through the Sakarya River delta (arrow #2 on map) into the Sea of Marmara and thence through the Dardanelles, to the Mediterranean Sea. When the great flood from the last ice age occurred in 5,600 BC, the Black Sea level rose 300 feet. This massive sur-charge created a phenomenal hydraulic pressure which undermined the tunnel overhead and opened the Bosporus, from the bottom upward, with the possible assistance of seismic activity. This tremendous thunderous hydraulic discharge displaced rock segments from the tunnel overhead and deposited them as far away as 175 miles, in the alluvium surrounding the Dardanelles. Spectrographic analysis proves these alluvial samples are different from the Dardanelles base rock, but are identical to the Bosporus geological formation. Spectrographic analysis also proves alluvia, from Lake Sapanca and the Gulf of Izmit, are identical to geological base rock samples from the nearby Sakarya River delta region.

The Mediterranean Sea could not have spilled over the Bosporus into the Black Sea. The Bosporus rises 300 feet above the present Mediterranean Sea. The Mediterranean has never raised 300 feet above its present level.

The depth of the bottom of the Bosporus and an adjoining deep channel in the Black Sea, substantiates the existence of an underground discharge through the Bosporus, from the Black Sea to the Mediterranean Sea.

Black Sea

Bosporus

Sakarya River Delta

Marmara Sea

Gulf of Izmit

Lake Sapanca

The present Bosporus has a maximum depth of 400 feet. There are two opposite currents thru the Bosporus, an upper current from the Black Sea to the Mediterranean Sea and a lower current from the Mediterranean to the Black Sea. This lower current is responsible for identical life forms in the bottom of the Black Sea and the Mediterranean Sea. There is a fresher water layer on the surface of the Black Sea, from extensive input of the fresh water drainage area. The upper current thru the Bosporus carries the fresher water to the Mediterranean Sea.

Thru million of years and many ice ages, the Black Sea level raises and lowers. When the Sea level raised, overflows thru the Sakarya River basin, created Lake Sapanca and the Gulf of Izmit. During these overflows, the channel underneath the Bosporus was not large enough to handle the entire volume increases of the Black Sea. However, the tremendous continual hydraulic power, from the tunnel, deepened the Sea of Marmara to a depth of 1,600 feet. The overflows, thru the Sakarya River basin, have a lesser hydraulic effect, due to a minimal sur-charge. The Gulf of Izmit and Lake Sapanca are shallow. There is no evidence of any massive overflows in the Sakarya River basin and the surrounding overflow area. Red arrows on the map, show the path of the overflows. There is no evidence of any overflows since the Bosporus opened in 5,600 BC.

"Boundless Continent"

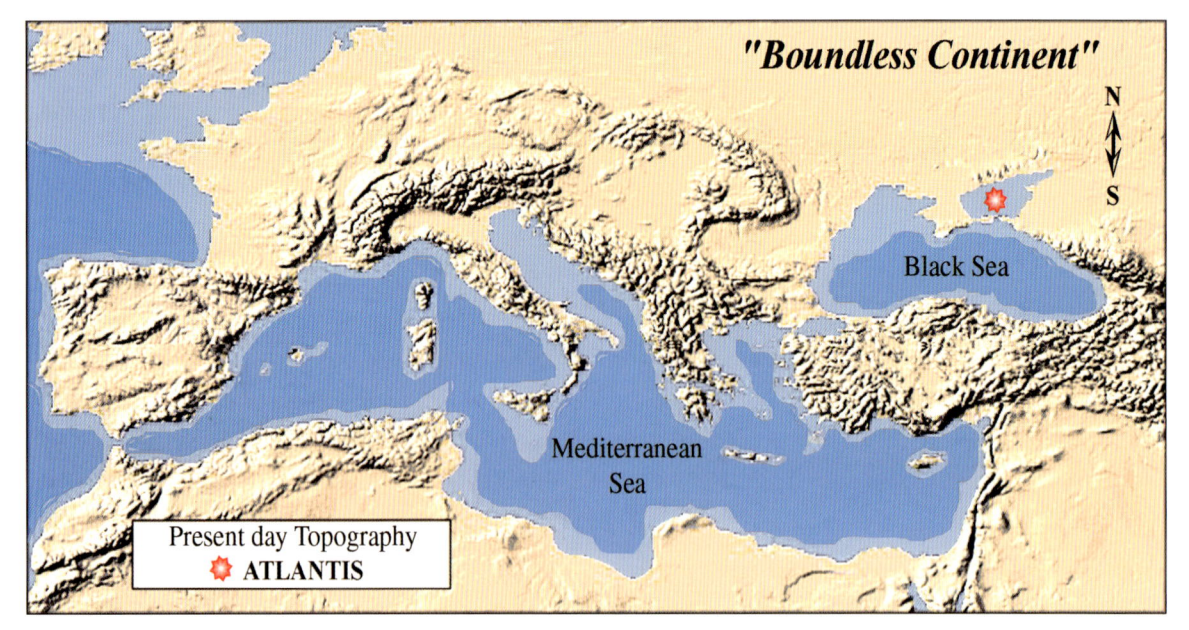

Present day Topography
✷ ATLANTIS

During the past 2,400 years, ATLANTIS has been "FOUND" in 51 different places on Earth. Thousands of books, articles, songs and poems, about ATLANTIS have been published. No authentic physical or scientific evidence has ever been presented, to prove any of this publicity. ATLANTIS IS ONE OF THE WORLD'S GREATEST MYSTERIES. As neuro-psychology evolves, it will disclose the existence of a psychogenetic memory of ATLANTIS, in one form or other, in over 90% of all humans living today. Millions of dollars have been spent on research and explorations of this illusive mystery.

A great philosopher one said, "simplicity confounds the wise." Twenty five years of research by the Authors, thru-out the entire Earth, and a 2 million dollar expenditure, revealed the simple discovery of only one place on Earth which coincides with ALL recorded legend, myth and history, pertaining to the LOST CIVILIZATION OF ATLANTIS. THIS ONE PLACE IS THE SEA OF AZOV BASIN, ADJOINING THE NORTHERN BLACK SEA SHORE.

Present day Geography
✷ ATLANTIS

One simple basic fact must be contemplated to establish a firm foundation for the discovery of Atlantis: ATLANTIS was an ISLAND. An island is a body of land surrounded by water. The ISLAND OF ATLANTIS was surrounded by an *"incredible"* ditch of water. This island contained a vast grid-work of canals which formed over 600 smaller islands within the main island. Each smaller island was divided into 100 separate lots. Simple reasoning determines this island had to be located on a very large body of land, and not in an open body of water.

SONCHIS: *"He begat and brought up five pairs of twin male children. The island and the ocean were named after the first born, Atlas, other sons inhabited diverse islands in the open sea. The whole country was very lofty and precipitous on the side of the sea, but the country surrounding the city was a level plain; it was smooth and even, and of an oblong shape. It extended in one direction 343 miles. Across the center it was 230 miles. This part of the island faced THE SOUTH and was sheltered from the north by mountains. An incredible ditch surrounded the entire island. It was excavated to the depth of a hundred feet, and its breadth was 607 feet. The length of the ditch was 1,150 miles, it carried abundant water, from many rivers to the fertile plain, thence to the city and into the sea. Navigable canals, 100 feet wide, were connected to the ditch at intervals of 11.5 miles, creating a massive transportation system."*

NOTE: In recent times, the construction of the 300 mile long Krim'Kii Kanal revealed strong evidence that the ancient ditch followed the same route. SHOWN IN RED, ON MAP.

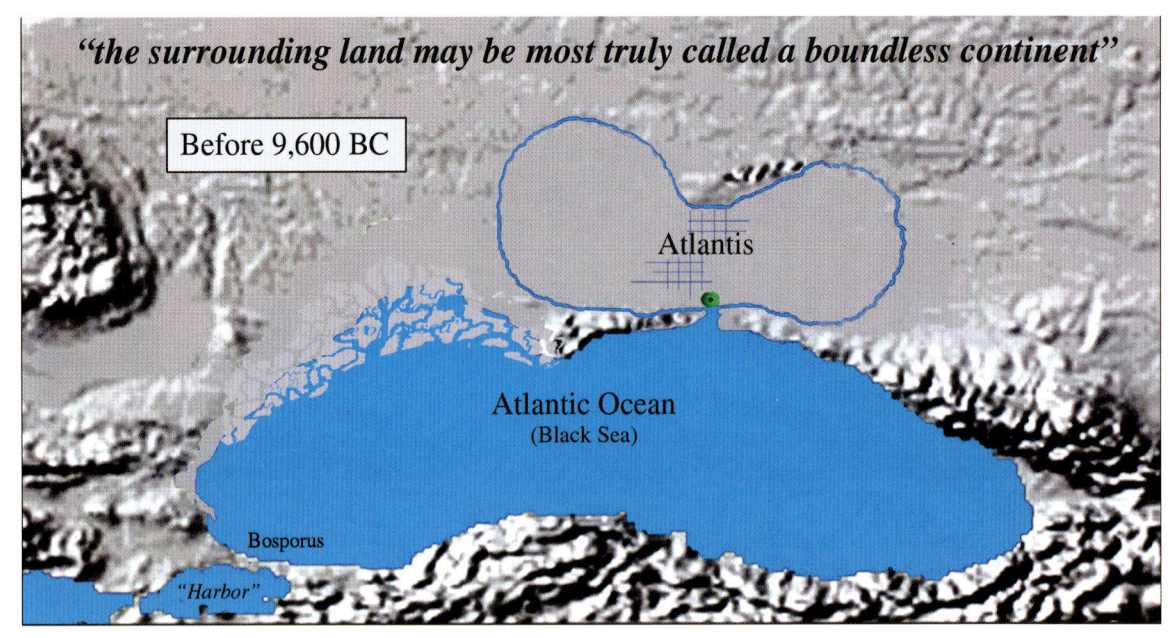

"the surrounding land may be most truly called a boundless continent"

[Before 9,600 BC]

Atlantis

Atlantic Ocean
(Black Sea)

Bosporus

"Harbor"

    Atlantis "disappeared" in 9,600 BC. The SEA OF AZOV did not exist until 5,600 BC, when the last ice age melted and raised the ocean levels. The *"diverse islands in the open sea"* and many ancient coastal provinces, located in various places surrounding the Black Sea, were also submerged during the ocean level rise. The present depth, of the Sea of Azov, varies from 1 foot to a maximum depth of only 40 feet. The bottom of this very shallow sea consists of a thick layer of sedimentary silt, which the many surrounding rivers have deposited during the last 5,600 years. Beneath this silt, lie hidden secrets of our lost Motherland. The Sea of Azov covers only one third of the original Island of Atlantis.

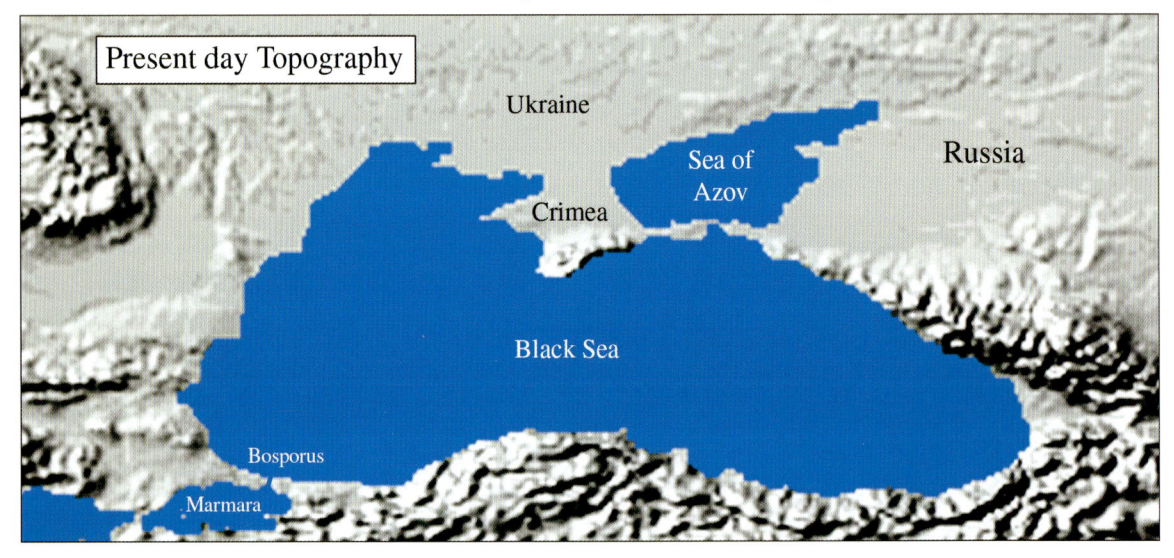

[Present day Topography]

Ukraine

Sea of Azov

Russia

Crimea

Black Sea

Bosporus

Marmara

> Herodotus, the father of history, when visiting this area, in 450 BC:
> "The VASTNESS OF THE PLAIN is worthy of noting; It is level, well watered and abundant with pastures. The rivers are larger and more numerous than any other land."

The portion of the great plain of Atlantis, to the west of the Sea of Azov, in the Ukraine, possesses the world's greatest resources of fertile black soil called chornozem. Known for centuries as the "Breadbasket of Europe" with cereal crops, wheat, rye barley, oats, hops, corn, flax, vegetables, sugar beets, potatoes, orchards, vineyards, tobacco, hemp and cotton.

Krasnodar Kray, the portion of the island of Atlantis, adjoining the east shore of the Sea of Azov, is the main rice producer in Russia and is ranked first in Russia in total agriculture production. This area is Russia's largest producer of canned fruits and vegetables, producing 2 million cans per year. This food industry produces meat, especially canned meat products and dairy products, especially canned milk products and dried milk.

The ancient Atlantis pattern of individual farm lots, separated by canals, is presently prevalent, in the immense areas to the east and west of the Sea of Azov. This expansive canal system is one of the worlds most remarkable irrigation systems.

Recent satellite photography shows this canal system, covering vast areas of farmlands. This area is located within the boundaries of the great plain of the ancient Island of Atlantis.

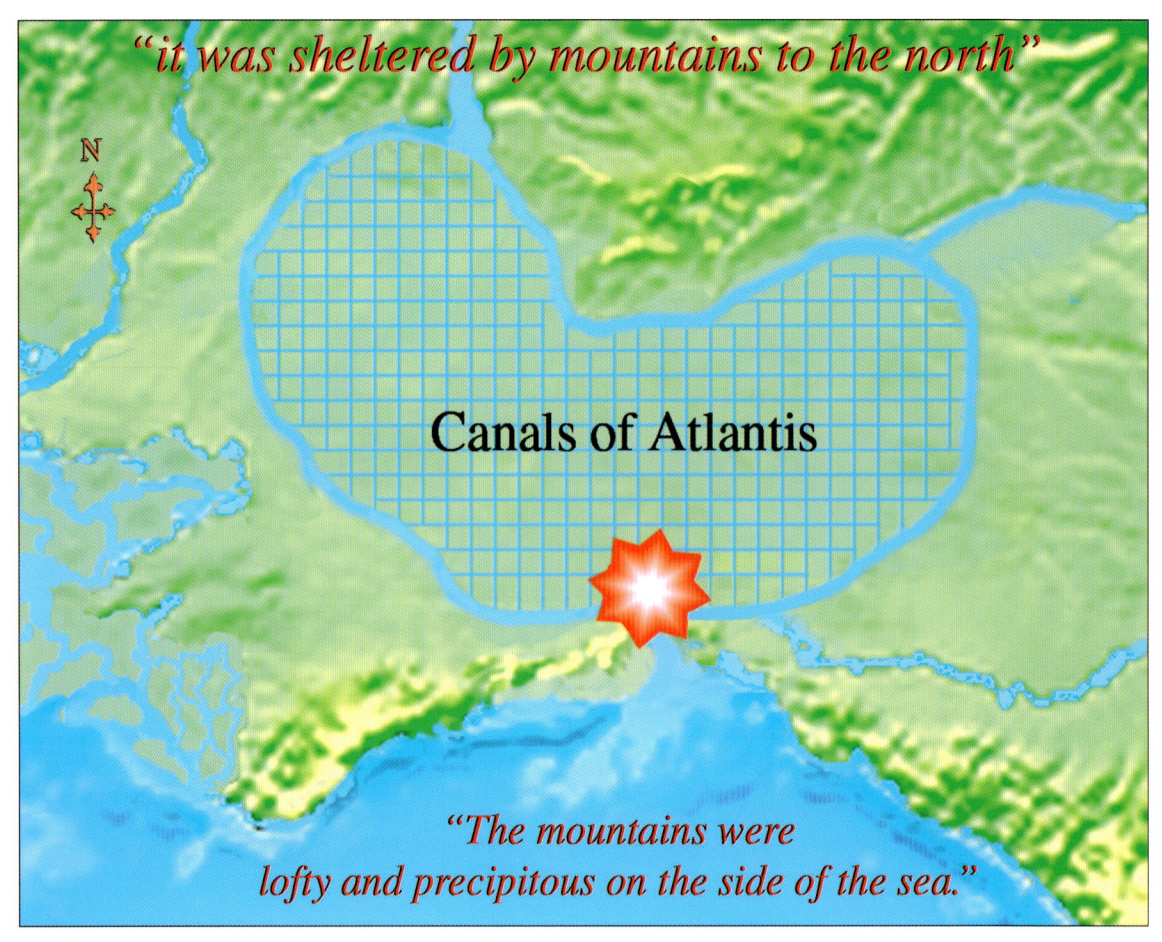

"it was sheltered by mountains to the north"

Canals of Atlantis

"The mountains were lofty and precipitous on the side of the sea."

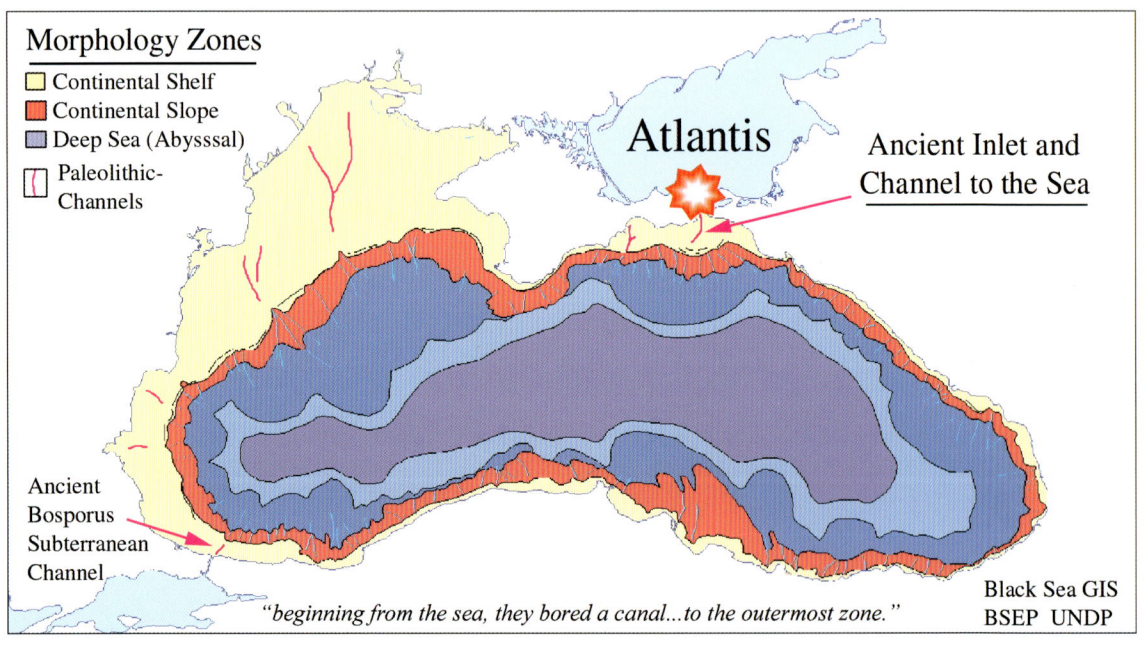

Morphology Zones
- Continental Shelf
- Continental Slope
- Deep Sea (Abysssal)
- Paleolithic-Channels

Atlantis

Ancient Inlet and Channel to the Sea

Ancient Bosporus Subterranean Channel

"beginning from the sea, they bored a canal...to the outermost zone."

Black Sea GIS
BSEP UNDP

Crimea South Coast

Crimea South Coast

The photographs of this cave, in the Crimea Mountains, and the foregoing Southern Crimea cliffs, are courtesy of Aleksei Korsakov, in St. Petersburg, Russia. She has many photographs of the beauty of Crimea. Her web site is http://www.korsakov.ru.

The Crimea mountains and the surrounding lands contain many Neanderthal caves and archeological sites which at the present are under extensive exploration. SONCHIS transcript notes, a great plain which is said to be the fairest and most fertile of all plains. In the center of the plain was a hill, not very high on any side, the hill faced south and was five miles from the sea. On this hill lived a ***primitive earth man***," his mate and an only daughter. The "God," who founded Atlantis, fell in love with the daughter and the present race of humans began.

SONCHIS TRANSCRIPT: *"The stones they used in the work was quarried from underneath the center island, one was white, another black, and a third red.---some of their buildings were simple, but in others they put together different stones, varying in color to please the eye, and to be a natural source of delight."*

The most prominent stone in the area where Atlantis is located, is white limestone. Black basalt is found in some places, from ancient volcanic eruptions, which also formed layers of red igneous iron oxide stone.

Millions of years of geological history is written in layers of stone. A layer of sedimentary stone can be indicative of an ancient ocean floor which was raised thousands of feet above sea level, by tectonic movement. Layers of igneous stone on top of sedimentary layers, indicates volcanic eruptions after the ocean floor was raised. Seismic action creates perpendicular fissures thru multiple layers of stone. Heated aqueous ejections thru these fissures, deposit valuable metals and crystalline treasures of the Earth. Depressions in tectonic plates can cause multi-layered formations to shift from original horizontal positions to as much as a 90 degree perpendicular formation, or fold completely over with the top side down.

There is at the present a large complex of underground tunnels, called Adjimushkay quarries, at Kerch, on the Yenikale Peninsula. This is the exact location of the metropolis of Atlantis. These quarries support Sonchis statement; *"The stones they used in the work was quarried from underneath the center island."*

EARTHQUAKES DISRUPT ORIGINAL SEDIMENTARY LAYERS

Map labels: Azov Sea; Atlantis City Outer Wall; Russia; Mithridat Hill; Kerch City; Atlantis Metropolis; Crimea; Kerch Strait; Black Sea

The historical hill of Mithridat is located in the center of the Crimean city of Kerch. In the 6th century BC, the Greeks colonized this location. In 100 BC this hill was named after Mithradates, King of Pontus. A stone castle was built in his honor on top of the hill, ruins of this castle remain to the present time. Many dynasties have occupied this strategic region since it was founded by the Greeks.

This Motherland of all Humankind, has suffered the worst damnable rape of heritage, that has ever happened on Earth. To this day, greedy, psychotic grave robbers are molesting the essence of their own Mother. The yellow dots on the above map are the most treasured archeological spots on Earth, all of them are being pilfered, not for knowledge, but for the price of the treasures.

Beneath the Hill of Mithridat and many other burial sites within the outer wall of Atlantis, are numerous underground quarries, catacombs and rooms, which have been consistently robbed of gold jewelry, statues and other artifacts, for 2,500 years. Stones of Atlantis temples have been excavated to build beautiful castles, only for marauding, warring hordes to completely destroy at a later age. One fabulous gold statue weighing over 2,400 ounces was melted down and divided between three men to settle their dispute of ownership.

In the Heritage Museum at St. Petersburg, Russia, is a "Special Golden Treasury" of art, robbed from the catacombs beneath Mithridat Hill. The English plundered this area of priceless gold and art treasures, during the Crimean War. The Russian Mafia, in Odessa, Ukraine, purchases treasures from grave robbers. The United States, the French, the Nazis, the Romans and many others grabbed their portions of these valuable treasures.

Atlantis accumulated more gold than has ever existed in one place on Earth. Gold has a personality. No two gold deposits are identical. A close spectrographic analysis can pinpoint the origin of raw gold. There is no such metal as pure gold. Raw gold contains varying amounts of other minerals, any raw metal has this same characteristic. The majority of ancient gold in Atlantis came from the Caucus Mountains, in Georgia. After Atlantis "disappeared" the Scythian raw gold came from the Carpathian mountains in Ukraine. The Greek raw gold was primarily from Macedonia.

Art forms vary in different ages of time. Genealogy can be traced by the evolution of art forms. The Heritage Museum in St. Petersburg and the Kerch museums, list the art as mostly Greek and Scythian. A detailed analysis determines some of the treasures are ten thousand years older than Greek and Scythian art form and gold content.

Masonry is an art. The stonework in the ruins of Mithridat hill and other archeological sites within the outer wall area of Atlantis, is a graphic history of the ages of time and culture. A detailed study of existing masonry segments of Mithradates Castle ruins, clearly indicates the mixture of 3 types of stones: ancient Atlantis building stones, stones from structures erected after Atlantis *"disappeared"* and stones that were quarried when the Castle was built. Stones talk to those who listen.

If you like scuba diving, try 50 feet offshore in Kerch Strait (near yellow dot next to the Atlantis Metropolis on the map). You can walk upon the ruins of an ancient Atlantis tower 20 feet in diameter and a stone wall 7 feet thick. Many more hidden treasures await.

The mammoth ivory carvings in the museums, portray symbols of Atlantis and the ancient culture. These carvings definitely suggest ages of time from 25,000 BC to 300 AD. Place your ear to an elaborate vase and listen to the beat of mammoth skull drums accompanied by bone flutes. The intricate golden jewelry, mirrors artisans and their techniques, from the early years of Atlantis to the many cultures that occupied this peninsula after Atlantis *"disappeared"* 11,600 years ago.

SONCHIS TRANSCRIPT: *"They had fountains, one of cold and another of hot water, in gracious plentiful flowing; they were wonderfully adopted for use by reason of the pleasantness and excellence of their water."*

Kerch is world famous for medicinal mud baths and mineral spring waters. There is a natural mud bath in the city of Kerch and another, 9 miles north, at Lake Cokrac. Mineral springs are plentiful in the area. The Kerch peninsula possesses a tremendous geothermal energy supply, several industries, in Kerch, use this power source.

A hot water geyser on top of the Atlantis Hill, serviced the entire metropolis. The seismic action that destroyed Atlantis, fractured the fumarole that produced the geyser. This fracture decreased the geothermal pressure, causing mud to be emitted instead of water. This seismic action split the original fumarole into tributaries, which accounts for the multiple therapeutic mineral springs and mud emissions clustered within the original Atlantis City wall area.

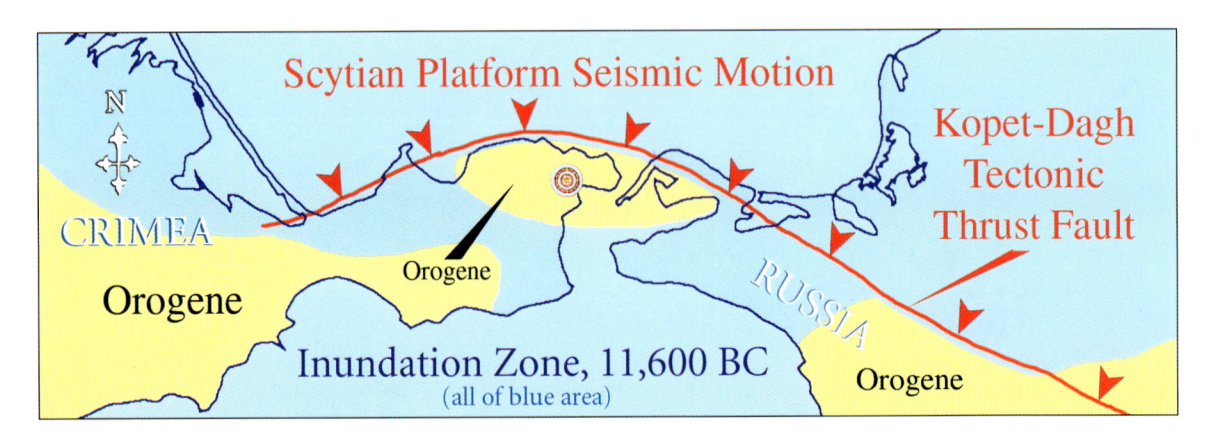

SONCHIS TRANSCRIPT: *"...there occurred violent earthquakes and floods; and in a single day and night of misfortune all your warlike men in a body sank into the earth, and the ISLAND OF ATLANTIS in like manner disappeared in the depths of the sea."*

Kopet-Dagh tectonic thrust fault is one of the most vicious faults on Earth. It winds it's way for over 2,000 miles, like a deadly desert serpent; from the Kerch peninsula, thru the Caucasus Mountains, thru Georgia and Azerbaijan, across the Caspian Sea, into Turkmenistan where if coils southward thru Iran to Armenia. This viper's victims include; 20,000 in Iran 2003, 50,000 in Iran 1990, 25,000 in Armenia 1988 and over 1 million in Atlantis 9,600 BC.

Atlantis City was built on an oval orogene formation. The surrounding area was alluvial deposits covering ancient tectonic depressions. An extremely violent earthquake and 24 hours of after shocks, lowered the tectonic depressions and turned the alluvium into "jelly". The initial shock, of the earthquake, leveled the city and caused the surrounding farmlands to sink. This seismic movement, created a 24 hour series of massive tidal waves in the Black Sea. With a devastating hydraulic force, these tidal waves rushed inland and flooded the entire Island of Atlantis. A gigantic wall of water reached the mountains to the north, generating a churning backlash of mud and silt, forming mud shoals in the present Kerch Strait region. *"the sea in those parts is impassable and impenetrable, because there is a shoal of mud in the way."*

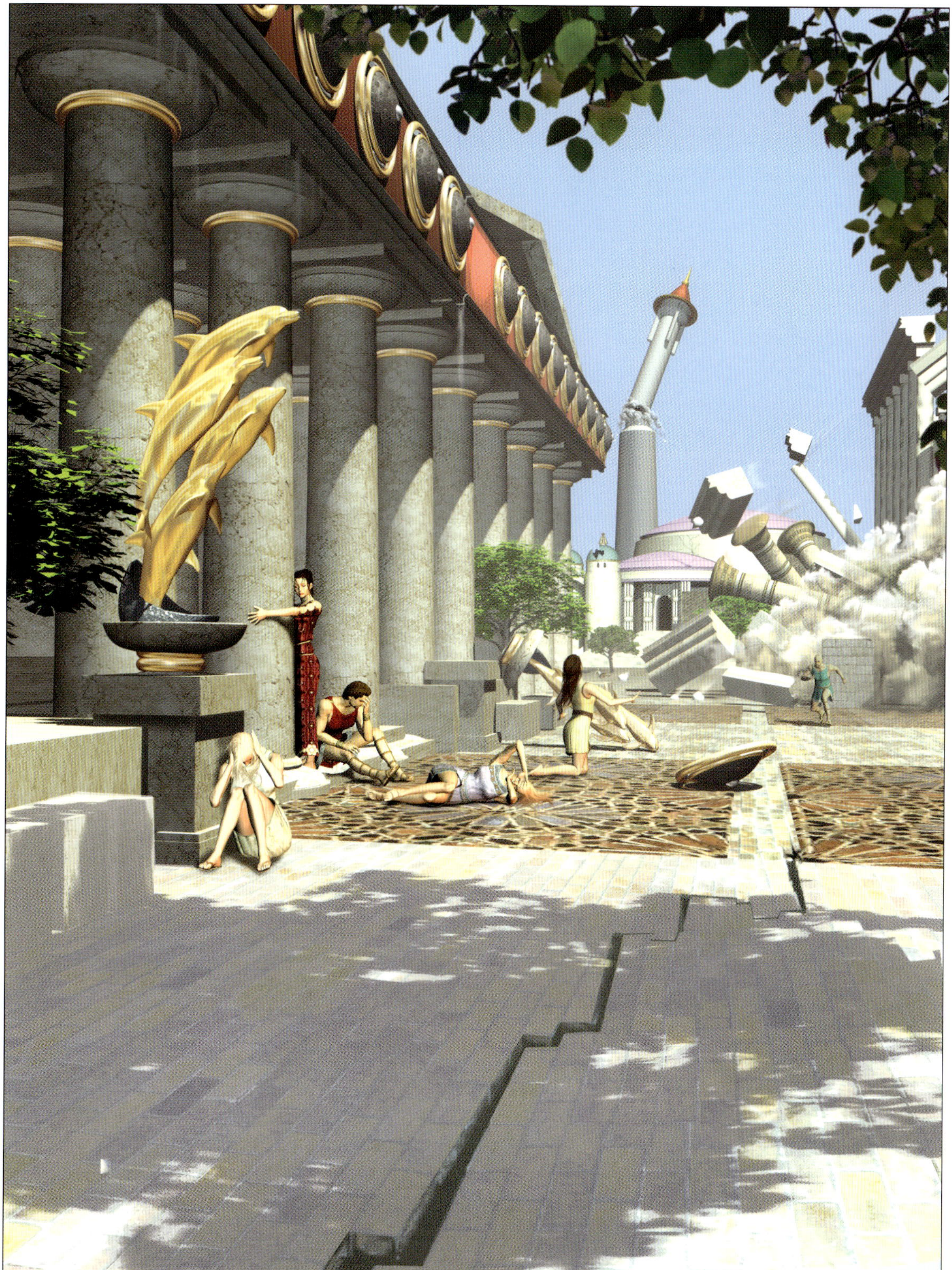

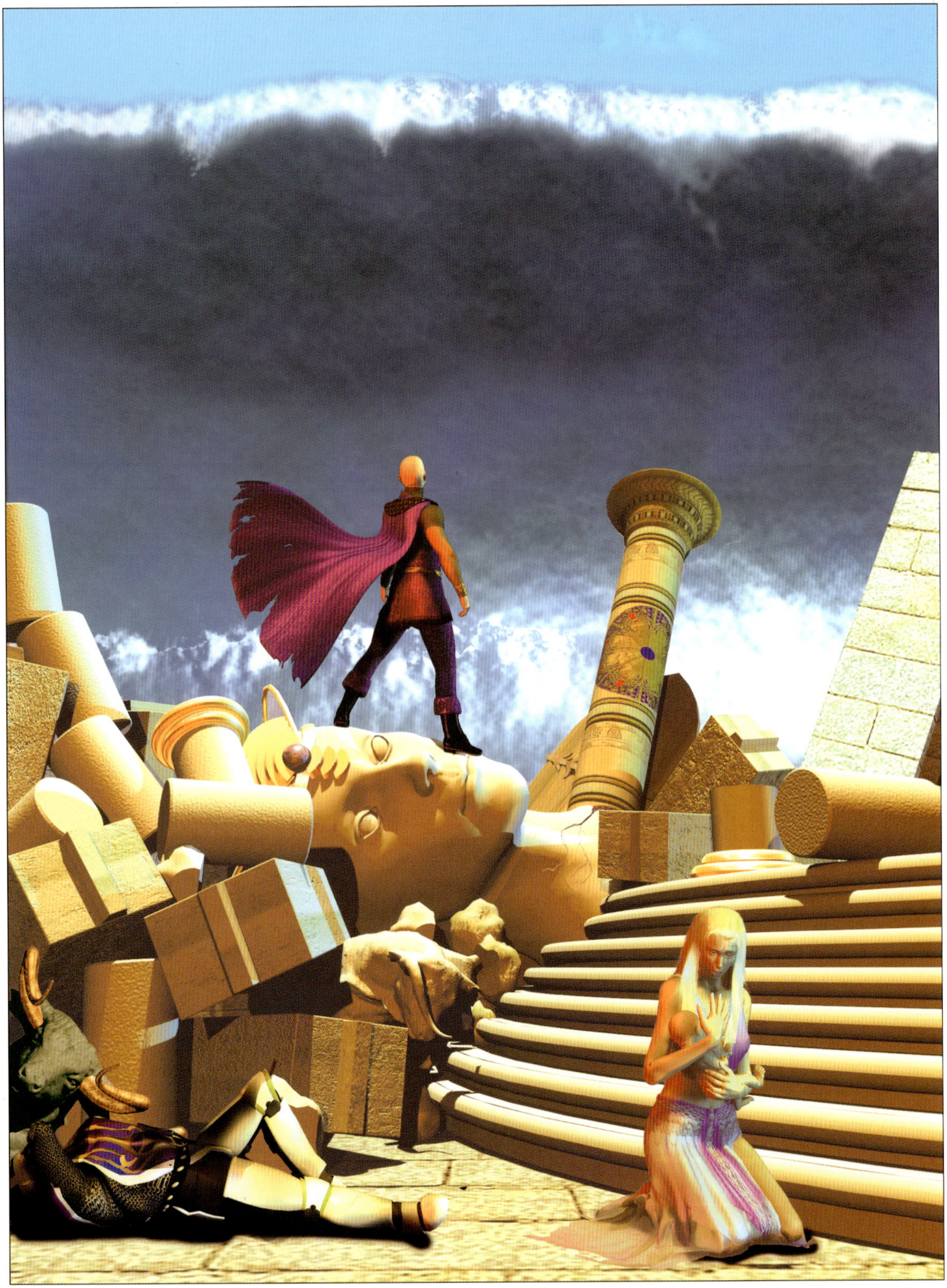

This wall of water does not obey my command

I am a Great Ruler Now I am so small

A time to die

I should have told her I loved her

My Military 1 Million Strong is powerless

My Golden Treasures are valueless

My bodyguard is dead

My Prince will never be a King

The Gods have no mercy

Is this my punishment for Greed

I am no greater than my slaves

I know she loves me

My Scepter and sword are lost

WHY

My Temples are gone

There is no place to run

The Hellenes are advancing on my City

My Sailors are buried in the Sea

My favorite wine is spilled

I am powerless

Our First Born

I have oppressed my Subjects

She loves her baby Prince

I must comfort her

Catastrophe instigates migration. A migration of Atlantians began long before the earthquake and flood. Aristocratic oppression, which, to the oppressed, was a catastrophe, combined with the primal adventure syndrome of humans, motivated a migration from the Atlantian Empire to every direction. There were survivors from the destruction of Atlantis, they were the second major migration.

The successive descendants of Atlas created a powerful military force which enforced the Aristocracy of Atlantis and dominated the nine provinces of the descendants of the other nine sons of Xoah and Tua. The size of the military force is calculated in the transcript of Sonchis: There were 1,200 ships and 4,800 sailors, 10,000 chariots and 10,000 charioteers, 120,000 chariot-horses, 120,000 horses and 120,000 riders, 10,000 men-at-arms, 120,000 heavily armed soldiers, 120,000 archers, 120,000 slingers, 180,000 stone-shooters and 180,000 javelin-men; A total of 864,800 men and 240,000 horses.

As the Xylanthians observed this military force, they recounted the database memory of their planet's military control, which nearly destroyed all life on Xylanthia. Their deep sorrow prompted them to prepare to leave Atlantis before the inevitable happened. Military power invites war. One day of battle, can destroy one thousand years of cumulative culture and architectural grandeur. The peaceful Xylanthians were a minority, they were aware of the increasing prejudice against them.

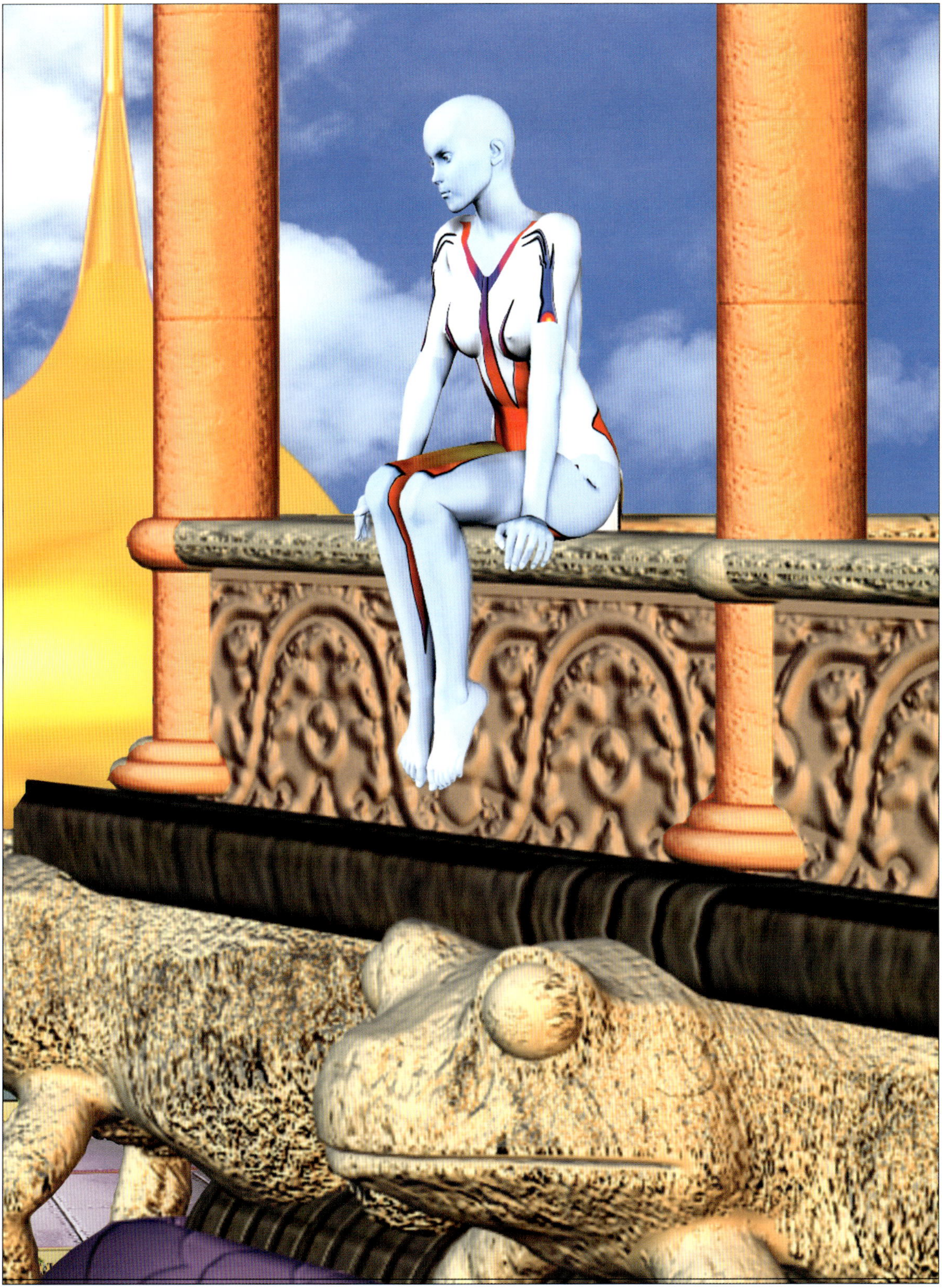

The superior intelligence of the Xylanthians, placed them in a cultural class wherein they were distinguished as Gods or Goddesses. Androgyny of these divinities, influenced an opposite sex counterpart syndrome of divinities, which has prevailed for millennia, to the present. The Catholic Regime, in recent history, declared the Virgin Mary to be the Mother of God.

There was a primitive genetic element, of tribal leader dominance, in the psychological constituency of the successive Kings of the ten provinces of Atlantis. The genetic need for dominance was responsible for their ambiguous mental conflict. The rulers wanted complete authoritative control, however they needed the expertise of the Xylanthians wisdom and technology. This conflict between Xylanthian total equality and Atlantian aristocracy, was the beginning of prejudicial energy forces, which was uncomfortable to Xylanthian peaceful nature. This discomfort, social inequality, dominant control, injustice, rebellions and oppressive tariffs, prompted a mass migration of all Xylanthians and their closely associated freedom-seekers and adventurers. The first migration began thousands of years before Atlantis *"disappeared."* The second migration began with the survivors of the earthquake and flood. These migrations spread in multi-directions and can be traced by the characteristics of recessive genetics. During these adventuresome journeys, several primitive tribes were contacted and interbreeding was inevitable. There is abundant anthropological evidence of Xylanthians co-existing with primitive beings, beginning in 35,000 BC, two thousand years after Atlantis was founded. Pure primitive beings vanished from this part of the world in 30,000 BC.

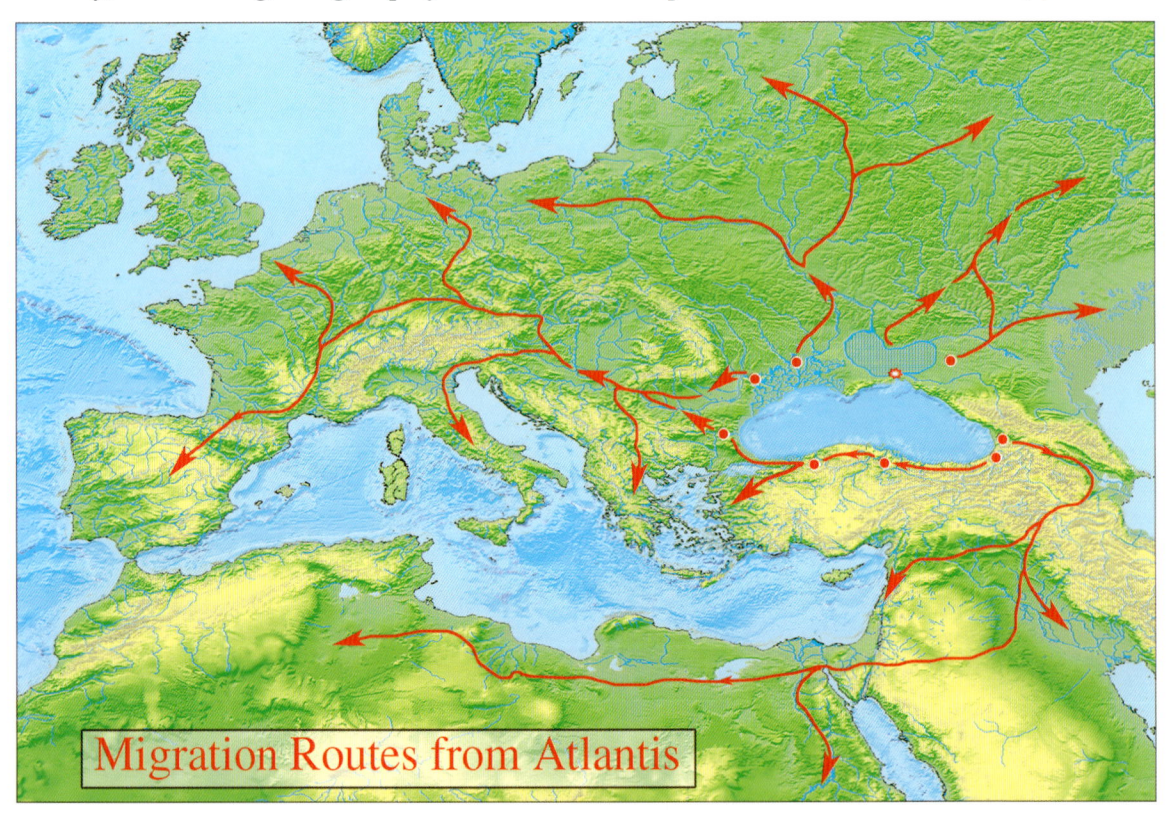

Migration Routes from Atlantis

Locations of the Origin of Language

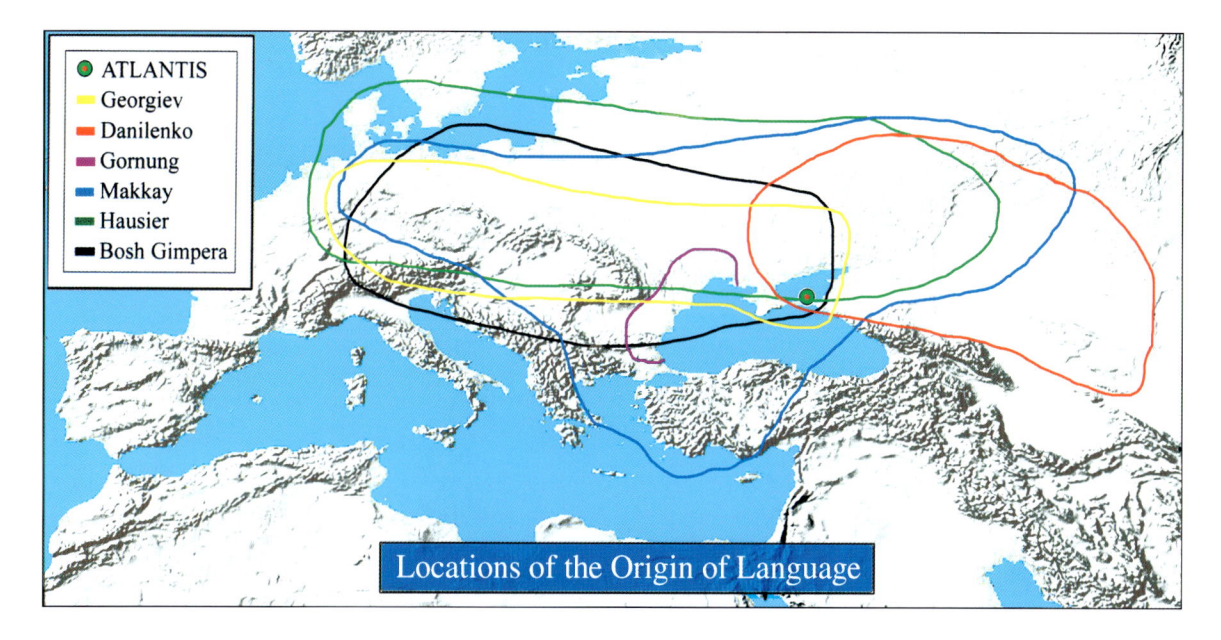

Legend:
- ATLANTIS
- Georgiev
- Danilenko
- Gornung
- Makkay
- Hausier
- Bosh Gimpera

Ancient history has been recorded in many languages, symbols, art forms and hearsay. As dynasties changed, records were destroyed and hearsay was distorted. Migration transplants names of geographical locations, from homelands to colonies. Genetic mixtures influence language evolution. These facts have retarded the ability of scientists to decipher the illusive mystery of Atlantis.

The above map clearly indicates the spread of ancient languages. These seven onomastic scientists spent their lifetimes tracking the origin of languages; Each of these scientists placed the origin north of the Black Sea, where Atlantis existed.

Primitive Beings had a limited vocabulary, which differed among the various tribes. The Xylanthians had an extensive vocabulary, which was common to all Xylanthians, however their audible language was minimal, as they used mental telepathy to communicate with each other. Xylanthian interbreeding with various tribes, was responsible for the development of different languages based on the vocabularies of the different Primitive tribes.

Atlantis was not only the Motherland of all languages, the origins of blood types can also be traced to this region. Oxford University studies have determined the existence of seven genetic Mothers of Europeans. As the science of DNA research advances, the existence of extra-terrestrial inter-breeding with primitive beings will be proven.

The migrations, from the Empire of Atlantis, were multi-directional. The Western and Southern movements have been emphasized, with slight contemplation given to the Northern and Eastern migrations. The languages of Asia are vastly different from the Mediterranean and European languages. The origin, of the Oriental Human, is very controversial. It is not reasonable to believe the Oriental races evolved from the original South African migration to the Mediterranean. There is evidence that an aquatic creature, evolved in the South Pacific region, about the same time as the South African evolution. These South Pacific beings migrated westward and northward and eventually interbred with the eastward and the northern migrations from Atlantis.

Empire of Atlantis
Xylanthian Migrations

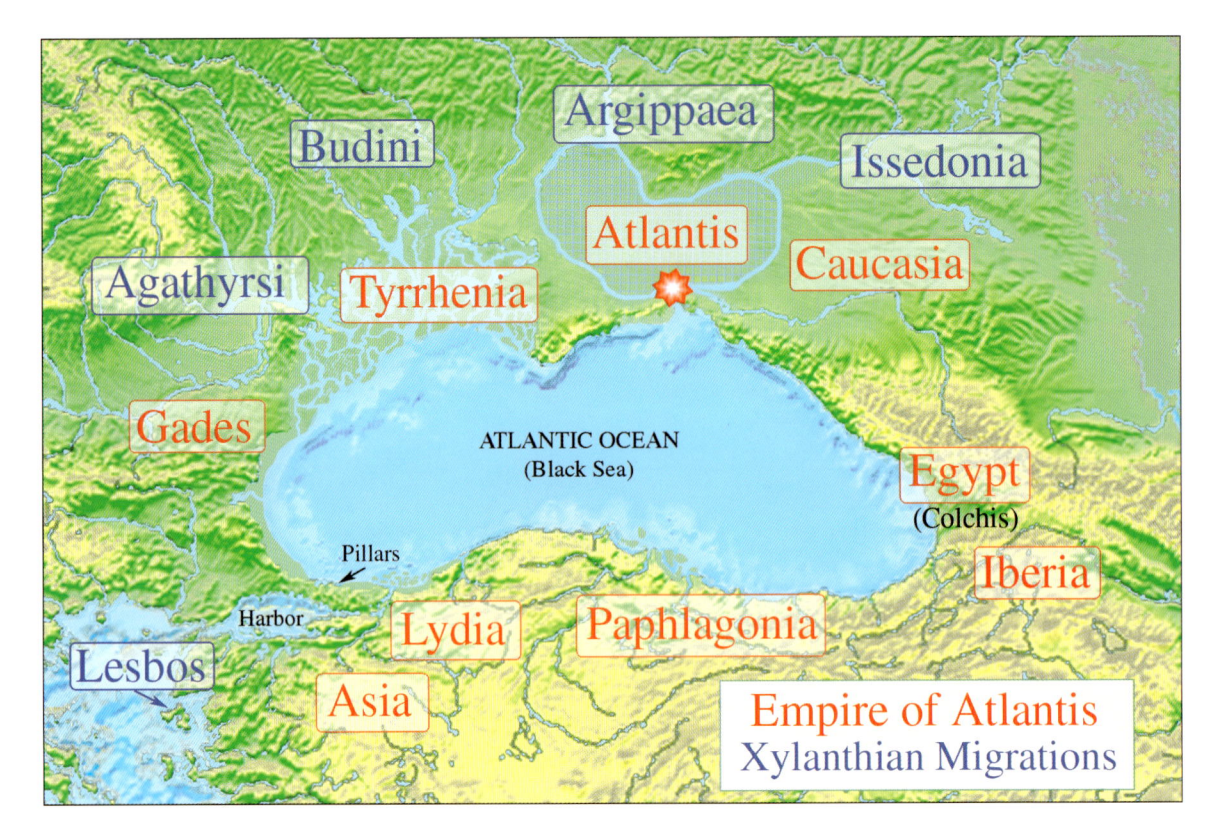

The ten sons of Tua and Xoah and the descendants of theirs sons, founded kingdoms along the shores of the Black Sea and on the many islands of the Danube Delta region. Sonchis transcript: *"Their descendents for many generations were the inhabitants and rulers of diverse islands in the open sea."* The ancient islands of the Danube River Delta, disappeared when the sea level of the Black Sea raised in 5,600 BC. Future scientists will find these lost civilizations, in their quest of knowledge. Sonchis transcript refers to these kingdoms as *"within the pillars."* Sonchis specified; *"those of us within the pillars."* Sonchis was Egyptian, the word *us*, places Ancient Egypt on the shores of the Black Sea.

The Island of Atlantis contained the territory surrounded by the *"outer ditch."* The Empire of Atlantis included the Island of Atlantis and the provinces on the shores of the Black Sea. Sonchis notes *"the Island of Atlantis was larger than Libya and Asia put together."* This notation confounded scientists into believing Atlantis was a vast continent, due to the massive size of the present continent of Asia. Asia and Libya (Lydia) in ancient times were two small provinces where Turkey is today. The Island of Atlantis was larger than these two provinces.

The Ancient kingdom of Egypt (Colchis) produced the major supply of gold and golden treasures for the Metropolis of Atlantis. Recent finds of unearthed ornate and elaborate golden artifacts, in the Colchis area, carbon date to as early as 25,000 BC. Xylanthian technology unveiled the science of mining and smelting metals, thousands of years before this knowledge was mastered in Europe and Asia. It is sorrowful to contemplate the existing political strife and poverty in Georgia (Colchis).

Herodotus, the father of history, when visiting Colchis, in 450 BC:

"There can be no doubt that the Colchians are an Egyptian race. Before I heard any mention of the fact from others, I had remarked it myself. After the thought had struck me, I made inquiries on the subject both in Colchis and in Egypt, and I found that the Colchians had a more distinct recollection of the Egyptians, than the Egyptians had of them. Still the Egyptians said that they believed the Colchians to be descended from the army of Sesostris. My own conjectures were founded, first, on the fact that they are black-skinned and have woolly hair, which certainly amounts to but little, since several other nations are so too; but further and more especially, on the circumstance that the Colchians, the Egyptians, and the Ethiopians, are the only nations who have practised circumcision from the earliest times. I will add a further proof to the identity of the Egyptians and the Colchians. These two nations weave their linen in exactly the same way, and this is a way entirely unknown to the rest of the world; they also in their whole mode of life and in their language resemble one another. The Colchian linen is called by the Greeks Sardinian, while that which comes from Egypt is known as Egyptian."

In this land of the "Golden Fleece" (Colchis), many hidden art treasures will reveal the glorious past history of Atlantis

Sonchis Transcript refers to kingdoms founded by Xylanthians migrations, as *"outside the pillars"*, (blue captions on map). The records of Herodotus lends a bountiful proof, relating to the origin of the modern human race and the birthplace of recessive genes which spread *"outside the pillars"* by the migration of Xylanthians and freedom seekers as they escaped the avarice of Atlantian dominance.

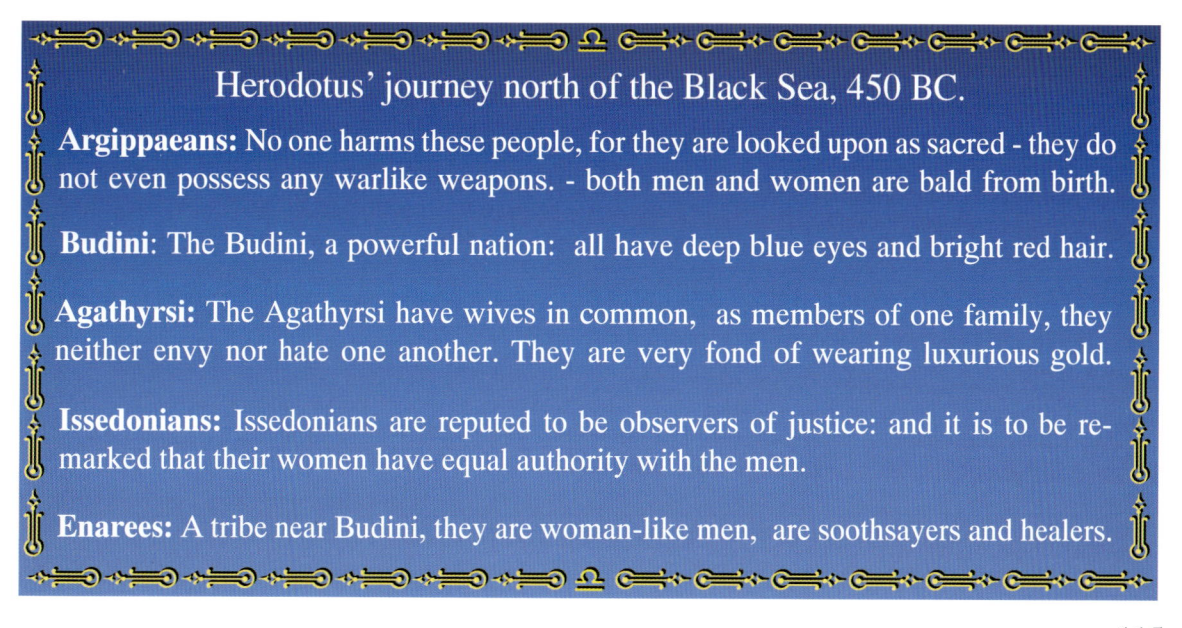

Herodotus' journey north of the Black Sea, 450 BC.

Argippaeans: No one harms these people, for they are looked upon as sacred - they do not even possess any warlike weapons. - both men and women are bald from birth.

Budini: The Budini, a powerful nation: all have deep blue eyes and bright red hair.

Agathyrsi: The Agathyrsi have wives in common, as members of one family, they neither envy nor hate one another. They are very fond of wearing luxurious gold.

Issedonians: Issedonians are reputed to be observers of justice: and it is to be remarked that their women have equal authority with the men.

Enarees: A tribe near Budini, they are woman-like men, are soothsayers and healers.

Scythes, First King of Scythia, Son of Heracles

Xoth (Zeus) was sexually prolific, producing many offspring, some by breeding with primitive females, some by androgynous Xylanthian breeding and Athene (the Greek God/Goddess) by asexual reproduction. Heracles was the son of Xoth and a primitive female. History relates to Heracles as half God and half man, however he was worshipped as a popular God. Many temples were erected, throughout the Mediterranean Region, in his honor. Heracles bred with a primitive female. They bore 3 sons, the youngest was named Scythes, who became the powerful, notorious leader of the Scythians.

SONCHIS TRANSCRIPT, referring to Atlantis, 36,800 BC: *"Zeus, the god of gods, who rules according to law, and is able to see into such things, perceived that an honourable race was in a woeful plight, and wanting to inflict punishment on them, that they might be chastened and improve, collected all the gods into their most holy habitation, which, being placed in the centre of the world, beholds all created things. And when he had called them together, he spake as follows-* The fragment "Critias" thus breaks off in the middle of a sentence. Critias the tyrant, was a cunning politician. In the works of Plato it is noted that "Critias" breaks of in the middle of a sentence, where Zeus begins to speak. The Greeks deleted his oratory to eliminate any offense to their Divinities, Athene and Heracles who were chastised. Sonchis' original transcript contained the words of Zeus. Solon gave the original transcript to Critias' Great Grandfather, Dropides, who gave it to Critias' Grandfather, then to Critias.

ZEUS spoke as follows: *Your countenances portrays your shame, and reveals that you have a foreknowledge of the purpose of this gathering. You have abandoned the laws which are inscribed on the pillar. The laws of wisdom, friendship, equality, virtue, dialogue, respect for all life, moderation and justice. Do not think that I am the God of Gods. The God of Gods is Life in its infinite boundlessness. I called you here not to pass judgement upon you or punish you. You have done that to yourselves already.*

You have enslaved the subjects of your kingdoms. You have placed yourselves above them instead of equal. You drink the life blood of beasts to strengthen your weakness. In this strength you take the lives of beings for violating the law, while you excuse yourselves for the same violations. You have glutted yourselves with wealth and luxury that you rob from your subjects. You have massed a military, causing great fear to all your subjects. You have brought judgement upon yourselves. Your subjects will leave your kingdoms. They will travel far and establish Kingdoms of their own. They will form armies and create weapons, they will come against your Kingdoms with the violence you have taught them. Your mighty empire will disintegrate. Your seed will spread throughout the earth, creating violence, hatred and greed which you have bred into them. This is your punishment that you have brought upon yourselves and all your offspring. Your ancestors left their world to come to this beautiful garden. Their culture had no greed, no hatred, no inequality, no injustice, no male or female, no King or ruler, no greater or lesser. You have violated your laws of peaceful co-existence. You have brought a curse upon the land whereon your temples and palaces are used for revelry, instead of judgement and thankfulness. The land will become a stagnant quagmire, its putrid stench will be a reminder of your avarice, forever. I have spoken.

Sonchis: *"The progress of history will unfold the various nations of barbarians and families of Hellenes which then existed, as they successively appear on the scene."*

Athene and a band of freedom seekers left Atlantis early in it's existence. They migrated up the Danube River Basin, breeding with far away primitive tribes, becoming the Acheans, the Ionians and the Aeolians. They all invaded Greece and formulated the Mighty Hellenes. Athene was their God/Goddess and military leader. Successive generations had an inbred memory of their ancestors' oppression in Atlantis. This generated hatred and vengeance.

Sonchis Transcript: *"Now in this island of Atlantis there was a great and wonderful empire which had rule over the whole island and several others, and over parts of the continent, and, furthermore, the men of Atlantis had subjected the parts of Libya within the columns of Heracles as far as Egypt, and of Europe as far as Tyrrhenia. This vast power, gathered into one, endeavoured to subdue at a blow our country and yours and the whole of the region within the straits; and then, Solon, your country shone forth, in the excellence of her virtue and strength, among all mankind. She was pre-eminent in courage and military skill, and was the leader of the Hellenes. And when the rest fell off from her, being compelled to stand alone, after having undergone the very extremity of danger, she defeated and triumphed over the invaders, and preserved from slavery those who were not yet subjugated, and generously liberated all the rest of us who dwell within the pillars. But afterwards there occurred violent earthquakes and floods; and in a single day and night of misfortune all your warlike men in a body sank into the earth, and the island of Atlantis, in like manner, disappeared in the depths of the sea.*

Hellenes and Atlantian War Zone (red area)

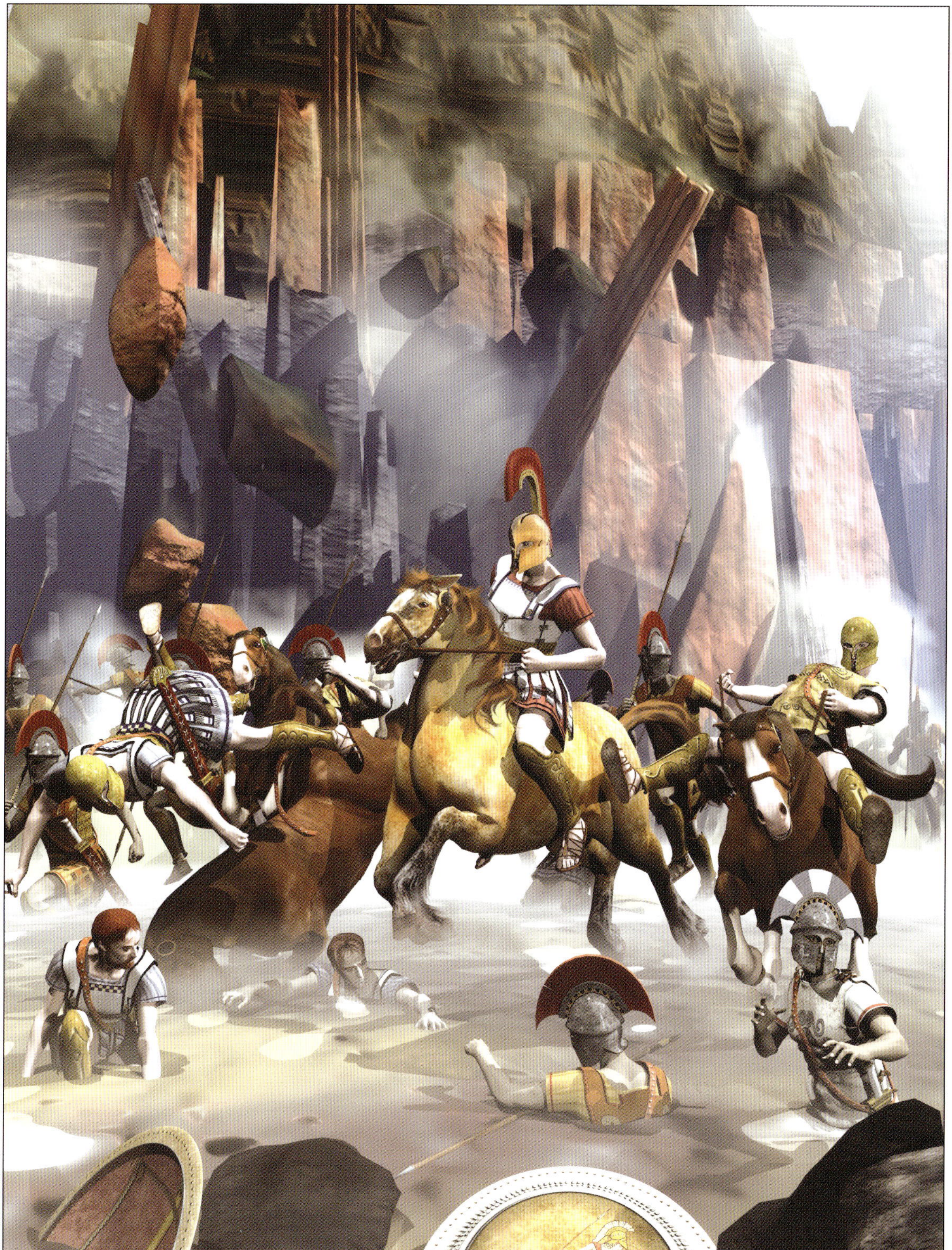

Scythes' Brothers: Agathrysus and Gelonus

After the inundation of Atlantis, the land was slowly re-populated over the passing millennia. Civilizations and nations rose to power and then fell. Scythes founded Scythia. One of his older brothers, Agathrysus, founded the Kingdom of Agathyri and his other brother Gelonus, joined the Province of Budini. They all possessed Xylanthian genes thru Heracles.

Atlantis was the Motherland of Artistry. The Xylanthians taught smelting and casting of metals, thousands of years before the bronze age. Genetics transferred this knowledge and artistic ability to the Scythians. The Scythians gold jewelry and artifacts surpassed imagination with its excellence and intricacy. The Scythians and their neighboring kingdoms were fond of gold jewelry. They placed gold jewelry on their infants. This trait was adopted by the Iberians who migrated to Spain. The Basque Gypsies of Spain's highlands, place gold jewelry on their infants.

Xylanthian artistic genetics prevailed in Ancient Iberia and Egypt, in the Atlantian Empire. Art forms are a road map of migrations. The fabulous golden art techniques of Atlantis Motherland can be traced to Ancient Troy and thence to Santorini. The mass migrations, thru the Danube River Basin, thence to Greece, Italy, Spain, spread Xylanthian genetics westward from the Atlantian Empire. The Southern Mediterranean migration of Xylanthians, spread to the island of Lesbos, Phoenesia, Persia, Egypt, and thence to Libya. Archeological discoveries, in these regions, reveal artifacts and jewelry identical to ancient Atlantian Empire artistry.

The Etruscans had a BISEXUAL GOD (Xylanthian), named Voltumna, they were noted for their exquisite gold jewelry design which was identical to Scythian forms. The Etruscans who evolved from the Danube River Basin migration, taught the Greeks and the Romans their art techniques. The Iberians taught the same style to Spain. Archeological discoveries in these various locations verify the chronological migration of art forms.

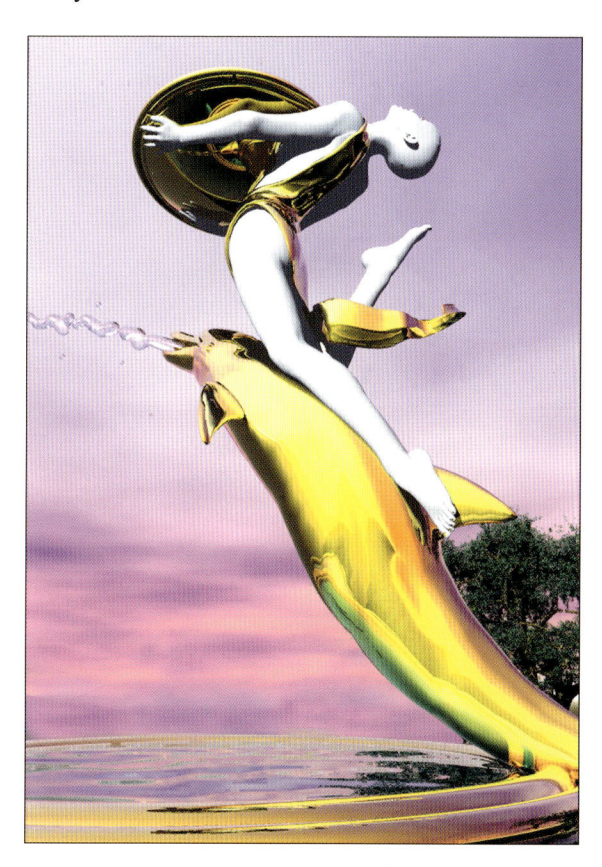

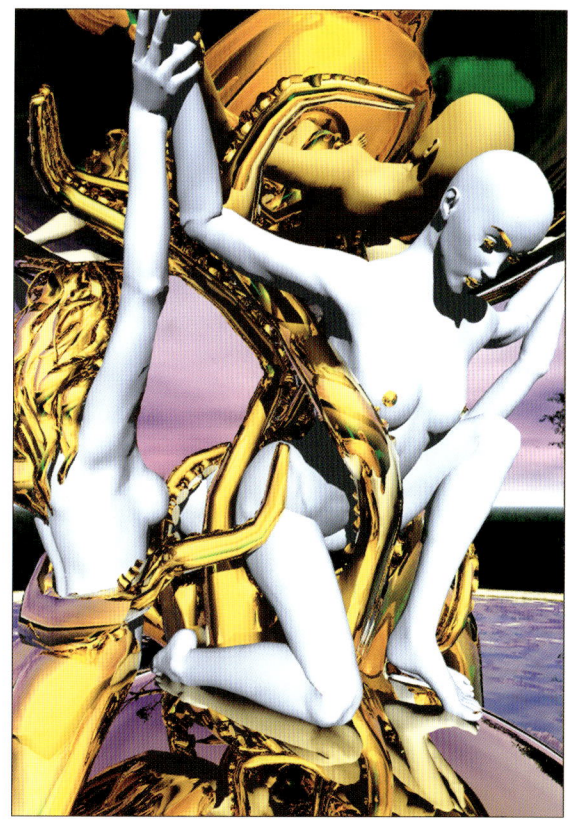

ATLANTIS was the MOTHERLAND of Horses on Earth. In Greek mythology, XOAH (Poseidon) "created the horse from an ocean wave." Herodotus: *"The Greeks tell many tales without due investigation."* Xoah did create the horse, However "from an ocean wave?" Xoah was an animal husbandry scientist. Xylanthian technology was a million years more advanced than Earth sciences today. The only prehistoric horses on Earth, prior to Atlantis, were small animals, only 3 feet tall. Sound reason indicates that there were small horses in the Atlantis area, which Xoah genetically cloned and altered to create large horses of various anatomy.

In Atlantis the horse was used in transportation and military service but was also an important part of their recreational and spiritual culture. The horse was honored in their temples and depicted as a mythological winged creature harnessed to the chariot of the Great God, Poseidon. SONCHIS: *"Here was Poseidon's own temple ... In the temple they placed statues of gold: there was the god himself standing in a chariot - the charioteer of six, winged-horses - and of such a size that he touched the roof of the building with his head."* There was an extremely large amount of horses in Atlantis. There were 240,000 horses procured for war effort against the invading Hellenes. This number consisted of 120,000 horses to be used as mounts for cavalry, also another 120,000 horses which supplied additional war-chariot horses.

To protect these valuable horses, 10,000 men were procured to guard the horses in battle. These men (horsemen), carrying small shields, were ready to fight on foot in defense of the chariot horses. SONCHIS: *The leader (of each lot, the total number of lots was 60,000) was required to furnish for the war the sixth portion of a war-chariot, so as to make up a total to ten thousand chariots; also two horses and riders for them, and a pair of chariot-horses without a seat, accompanied by a horseman who could fight on foot carrying a small shield, and having a charioteer who stood behind the man-at-arms to guide the two horses;"*

Within the center islands of the Metropolis, the Atlantians built special accommodations for horses. Bathing facilities were created for horses showing the great care that was taken of these revered animals. The very most prized of the Atlantian horses were kept within the center islands (zones) of the Metropolis for the protection and amusement of the Royalty, honored citizens and visiting potentates. SONCHIS: *" they had fountains, one of cold and another of hot water, ... They constructed buildings about them and ... they make cisterns ... there were the king's baths, and the baths of private persons ... and there were separate baths for women, and for*

HORSES." The Outer Zone of Land in the Metropolis consisted of a race track that was exclusively used to race horses and chariots. This race track was 607.2 feet wide with a distance of 6.5 miles and was situated in the center of the Outer Zone. Surrounded by a crowd of excited onlookers, the races were a main activity where participants practiced military maneuvers and competed in contests of speed and endurance. SONCHIS: *"there were many temples built and dedicated to many gods; also gardens and places of exercise, some for men, and others for horses in both of the two islands formed by the zones; ... in the centre of the larger of the two (zones) there was a circular racecourse (607.2 ft.) in width, and in length (6.5 miles)... for horses to race in."*

The land within these zones was the most highly valued and protected in all of Atlantis. The use of such a large portion of the Outer Zone shows that these races were a very important part of their culture. The fastest and most beautiful horses would certainly have been of great value and highly prized. The Metropolis was protected by guard towers on the bridges leading into the Zones. Access to these areas was restricted and only the most prominent persons were allowed entrance. A special relationship between the Atlantians and the horse developed over many ages of time, as the Kingdom of Atlantis itself developed. This relationship between humans and horses has continued from generation to generation, from thousands of years past to the present.

The horse was first domesticated in Atlantis, 39,000 years ago. The first material evidence of domestication of the horse comes from France where horse teeth were found showing evidence of crib-biting (chisel or wedge-shaped wear of the teeth). This only occurs in horses that are held in captivity. They press their teeth against any hard object and breath heavily. This behavior is common and probably caused by boredom. Crib-biting has NEVER been known to occur in wild horses. These prehistoric teeth are, at least, 30,000 years old. This discovery is strong evidence that domestication of the horse occurred before 28,000 BC. The Atlantians took horses with them on their migration to France.

The Vogelherd Horse is a carving made from Mammoth Tusk Ivory. Found in a cave in Germany, it also dates from 28,000 BC. The reason why this prehistoric artist created this piece of art is lost in antiquity. Perhaps it was a "Good Luck" charm for hunting horses, perhaps a reminder of a beloved horse, or maybe it had a special utilitarian purpose. Whatever the purpose, we know this artist had an important relationship with the horse. Many similar carvings have been found in Spain, France and other places in Europe.

Paleolithic carvings clearly show "horses with bridles". Discoveries from the Pyrenees has caused great controversy. The Creation Theory that the Earth is 6,000 old has caused many archeological discoveries to be called "the work of Satan". Many theories have been rejected and suppressed and important archeological evidence has been discredited or destroyed. Close examination of ancient artworks show that horses were used for domestic purposes tens of thousands of years ago.

There were a number of different breeds of Horses created in ATLANTIS; The most common was probably the **Tarpan**, which is very strong and easy to domesticate. The Tarpan, though small, is very sturdy with strong legs and can easily carry a large adult. Their hoofs are so strong they never need shoes. Tarpans are extremely intelligent and agile with amazing endurance. Their disposition is calm and affectionate. They enjoy being ridden, pulling carts and are especially good jumpers. Treated with kindness, they respond well, but balk if they are treated with cruelty. It's soft and wooly dun coat resembles that of a deer, and turns white in the winter.

The ATLANTIANS had a greater purpose for the horse, beyond meat and milk. The Xylanthians taught the primitive beings that these small but powerful horses could be used for hauling, pulling and riding.

According to Legend, Xoah's (Poseidon) greatest gift to mankind was the horse. The ancient legend of the Centaur (a mythological creature which was half-man and half-Horse) arose from sightings of Atlantians migrating on horseback. Centaurs were honored in these legends for their great intelligence. Chiron was a famous Centaur, the teacher of many great Heroes, including Heracles.

The importance of the horse throughout the history of Humankind is well documented. Yet this wonderful animal almost became extinct. After the destruction of Atlantis, the knowledge of horsemanship was almost lost. Fortunately a band of horsemen remained on the steppes north of the Black Sea. If not for these remnants of the Atlantian culture all horses would be nothing but a vague memory. Horses became extinct everywhere else in the world, by being eaten by Humans. The only remnant was in the Ukrainian Steppes.

There is abundant evidence that all horses living today are directly descended from this remnant of horses from Atlantis. The first documented evidence of men riding horses comes from the Ukrainian steppes. Excavations from Dereivka, Ukraine have unearthed horse-teeth which show distinct signs of bit wear. These teeth are dated at 4,000 BC. This is 2,000 years before any other known evidence of horseback riding. Some of the world's oldest Chariots have been found buried in tombs in this steppe grassland. It is known that horses for war-chariots were brought from the *"barbarian north"* (this refers to the area north of the Black Sea- Atlantis) to the *"civilized"* Near East, about 2,500 BC.

The Tarpan was immortalized in many ancient artworks, this art has been found from Ukraine to the caves of France and Spain. This shows the importance of this little horse in prehistoric culture. Today Ukraine is leading the way in saving the Tarpan, by creating breeding programs and sanctuaries for this mighty little horse that helped build Atlantis.

A Good Home

The Bureau of Land Management of the United States Government, manages wild horse herds, in the western U.S. Hundreds of horses are routinely rounded up with helicopters and placed in confinement. Many are adopted out to have a good home. If you ask the horses, they will tell you that they already had a good home, before they were captured. Most wild horses live on federal land, leased to cattle ranchers. A balance between the populations of cattle and horses is maintained.

Both the horse and humankind must find a balance between two cultures. One life is living free and in harmony with nature and the other is an artificial cultural confinement of rules and programming. Finding a good balance and a "good home" takes intelligence and adaptability in this highly complex social culture.

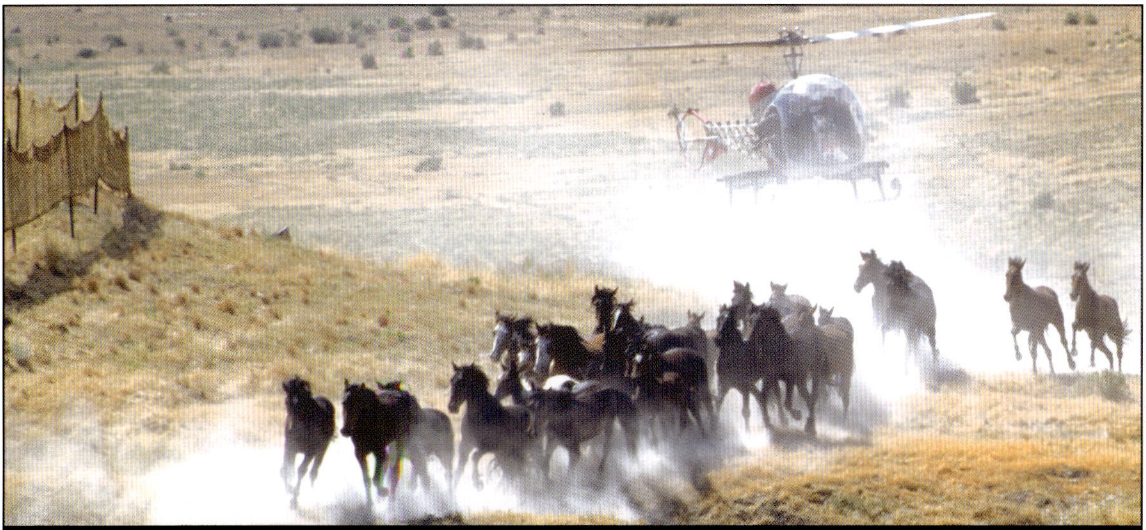

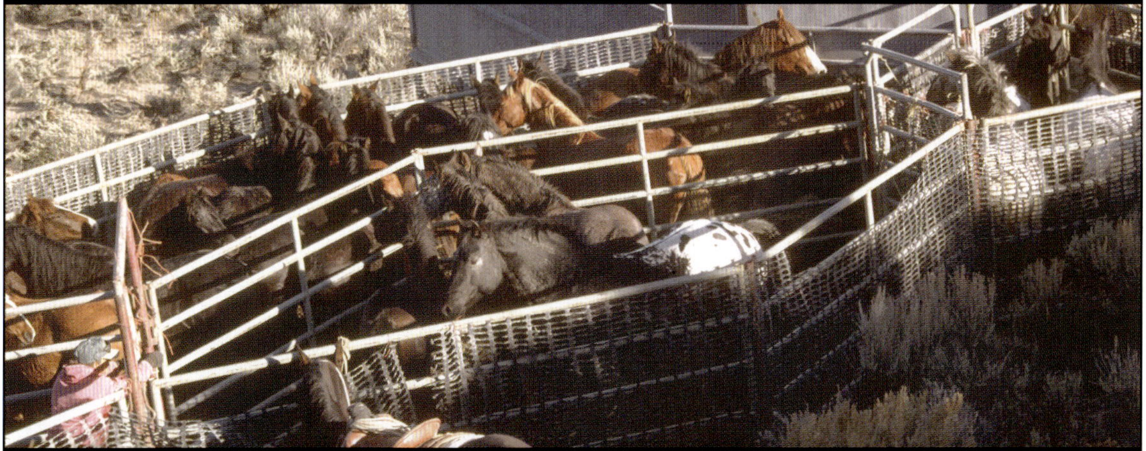

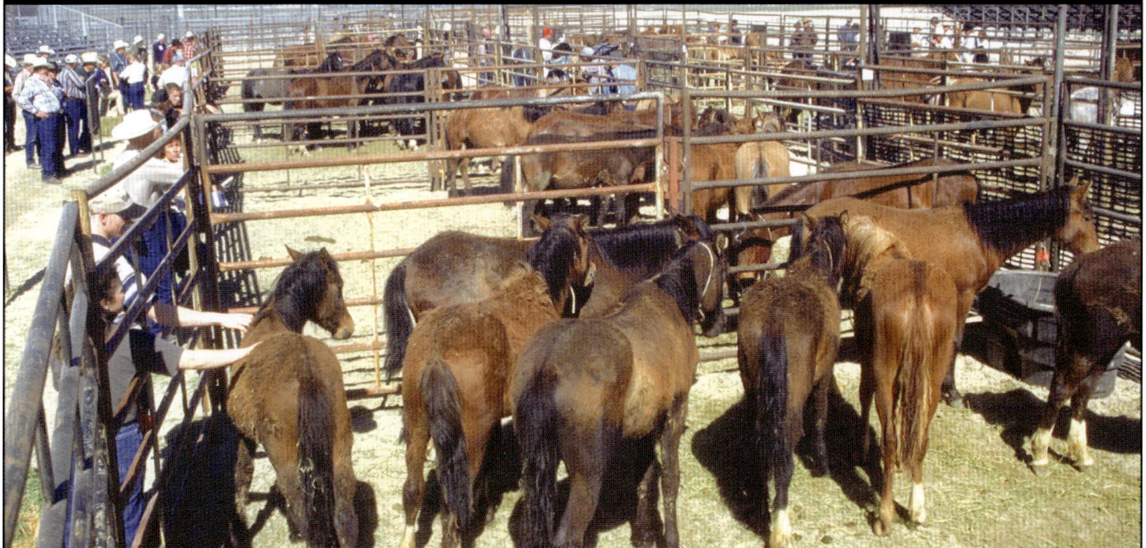

Bulls originated in Atlantis Motherland. Xoah (Poseidon) DNA altered a small prehistoric wild bovine of the Bos species and created a larger animal. The Bull and his torture, has evolved, from 39,000 BC to the present.

SONCHIS TRANSCRIPT: *"There were bulls who had the range of the temple of Poseidon; and the ten kings, being left alone in the temple, after they had offered prayers to the god that they might capture the victim which was acceptable to him, hunted the bulls, without weapons but with staves and nooses; and the bull which they caught they led up to the pillar and cut its throat over the top of it so that the blood fell upon the sacred inscription. Now on the pillar, besides the laws, there was inscribed an oath invoking mighty curses on the disobedient. - after slaying the bull in the accustomed manner, they burnt its limbs, they filled a bowl of wine and cast in a clot of blood for each of them."*

Bulls are still tortured for the pleasure of massive spectators, to satisfy the primitive "hunting for food" dominant genetics of primitive origin. This psychosis resides within each of us. It existed in the Coliseum in Rome, where large audiences cheered as lions ate Christians and Gladiators waited for the "thumbs down" sign to murder their victim. The "thumbs down" evolved to Spain and Mexico where Bull Fighting is enjoyed by spectators, to this present day. The Picadores torture a Bull in an arena. They pierce the front shoulder muscles many times to weaken the Bull. Then the Great Matador exhibits his skill, he teases the Bull with a cape, causing him to tire from running, with blood streaming from his shoulder. The roar of the audience reaches a thunderous maximum. The spectators are standing and yelling "Muerto - Muerto" (Murder - Murder), then the sword of the Matador pierces the heart of the weakened Bull.

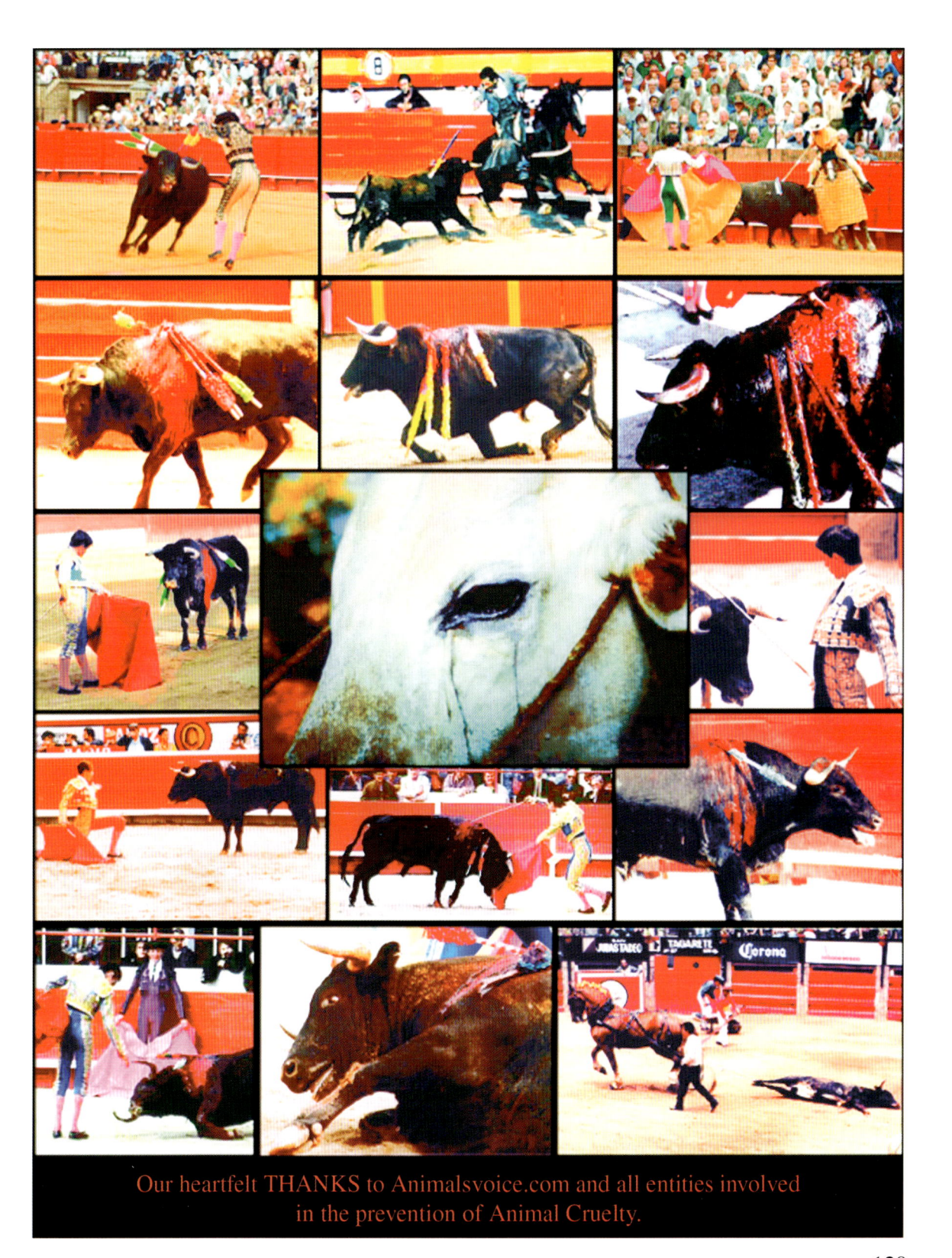

Our heartfelt THANKS to Animalsvoice.com and all entities involved
in the prevention of Animal Cruelty.

The United States condemned Spain and Mexico for Bullfighting and made it illegal to fight bulls in the U.S. However, this animal torture syndrome spread to the United States. On July 4th there are dozens of Rodeos, celebrating independence from the oppression of the British. To celebrate Freedom, we imprison horses, bulls and baby calves. We put them in an arena and torture them. Young calves are frightened when they are released from confinement and start running out into an arena where thousands of spectators are cheering. Not for the calf, but for a cowboy riding on a giant horse, chasing the calf. The cowboy throws a rope around the calf's neck. The cowboy has taught his horse to stop suddenly when the calf is lassoed, almost breaking the neck of the calf. As the crowd begin to cheer louder, the mighty cowboy jumps from his horse, pounces onto the calf, grabs it by the head, twists it's neck and picks the calf up and slams it to the ground. The cowboy then ties the feet of the calf causing it to squall for fear, because it is immobile. The roar of the crowd of spectators reaches a maximum. This famous champion cowboy has just tortured a young calf, faster than any other cowboy. These frightened little calves are only a very few months old.

At Rodeos, horses and bulls are, severely physically and mentally tortured. A horse and a bull possess a genetic defensive instinct. When something is on its back, it could be a giant cat trying to reach around the neck and grab the jugular vein to choke the animal to death. Wild horses and bulls share the same rangeland, peacefully. When a horse or a bull has been tortured, it is in a state of shock and life survival fear. In this state of mind, their natural instinct is to attack anything they think is endangering their life. The survival instinct of these beautiful wild creatures, causes them to buck off whatever is on their back. They have a few seconds of a terrible fear of death. The spurs on a cowboy's boots, viciously goad the horse's rear flanks with razor sharp rowels (wheels) on their spurs. This pain amplifies the fear of being killed and devoured by another wild beast. The tortured bull becomes so frightened, he will attack anything in the arena, including horses. A horse or bull will buck, twist and turn to get this terrible thing off their back. The excited spectators cheer loudly, as the great rodeo champion cowboy has created a vicious mental and physical torture to one more beautiful wild animal, for a longer period of time than any other cowboy.

FREEDOM

The ritual of the Bull Sacrifice in Atlantis took many forms, which historically records the dual nature of humans. As these ceremonies evolved, the Bull became a symbol of both good and evil. The legends and rituals originated when the Ten Kings of Atlantis sacrificed the Bull, to consecrate the empire and join the people into a united kingdom, just as the Bull protects and holds the cattle together in a united herd. Many myths, legends and religions evolved, surrounding the slaying of the Bull. A form of this ritual is represented in Greek mythology as the legend of Poseidon creating a beautiful white Bull, from the sea, for King Minos of Crete. The "Bull of Marathon" was killed by Theseus. Gilgamesh, king of Uruk, killed the "Bull Of Heaven", which had been sent by Anu, the sky-god. Garlanded white Bulls were sacrificed to the deities, in Crete and Mycenae. Zeus, in the form of a Bull, abducted Europa and swam away with her. Zeus then seduced her and they bore three children. This myth is symbolic of the Atlantians coming forth from the Black Sea and by their power and persuasion, populated the three continents of Europe, Asia and Africa (their three children).

Tua's love for the Bull also migrated with the Atlantians. During the first exodus, these ancient adventurers returned to a life in harmony with nature and the wild animal kingdom. They created the cave art of western Europe, 14,000 to 35,000 years ago, honoring the Bull by often depicting him disproportionately larger than the animals around him.

After the inundation of Atlantis some of the survivors began new cities, located the highlands of Turkey, They created temples honoring the bull and painted a giant wall mural with a great Red Bull surrounded by Humans. There are many more sites in this area waiting for excavation.

As these first civilizations spread, the legendary power of the Bull was emulated and altered from one empire to another. Sumerian Royalty wore crowns with bull-horns as a symbol of their power. The Minoan civilization had elaborate ceremonies with both men and women dancing and leaping over Bulls. Ancient Egypt had many gods which were associated with the Bull. Isis had bull-horns supporting a Solar Disc which she wore as a crown. The Pharaohs were called Bulls. The Cow Goddess, Hathor, gave birth to the Earth and the Sun. Apis, the Bull of Memphis, was believed to be the incarnation of the God, Ptah, the mightiest of the Egyptian Gods. The Apis Bull was contemplated as a powerful oracle. When the Apis Bull died, officials from every realm of Egypt brought lavish gifts for the burial ceremony. Greatly Honored in death as in life, the Bull of Memphis was buried in a vast subterranean complex, called the Serapeum. The Gallic Bull God was honored in France. Norse Gods worn bull-horn helmets. The God Shiva, in India, is depicted riding a White Bull and carrying a Trident. These myths and legends evolved creating creatures that were part Bull and part Human. The Bull has been consider both good and evil, the great Bull is both loved and hated.

The images above courtesy of freestockphotos.com and Visipix.com

The Worship of Mithras, the Bull Slayer, was widespread in Persia, India and Asia Minor. The Taurobolium was a Mithraic sculpture depicting Mithras, reluctantly slaying the primordial Bull. As the honorable Bull died, the world came into being and order was born. From the Bull's dead body came all the vegetation to nourish mankind. Most of the knowledge and the beliefs of the many followers of Mithras philosophy, regarding the bull, were destroyed when this ancient religion was supplanted by Christianity.

Mithras was the god of loyalty, justice and war. Mithradates, which translates, descended from Mithras, was the name of six different kings of Parthia. Their empire began in Iran and expanded through generations of empire building, reversing the migration from Atlantis. The teachings of Mithras were taught in cavern temples built underground. The Taurobolium of Mithras is thought to represent the astrological constellations of Taurus, Scorpius, Orion and Canines Major, where our home-star, Sirius, is located. The teachings of this ancient cult, may have contained the knowledge of our Xylanthian heritage. Mithradates VI established his capital in Kerch, then called Panticapaeum, perhaps he had the knowledge that Kerch was the location of mighty lost Metropolis of Atlantis.

135

The erratic behavior of the human race is an apparent enigma. Infinite DNA composition of genes, creates a self-perpetuating hereditary transmission. The complexity of this genetic transmission and it's catalytic effect on the chromosomes, can never be fully understood, due to the primordial reality of incomprehensible infinity. DNA has no boundary. As we have stated before, boundaries are only that which is comprehensible in an incomprehensible boundless infinite universe.

There is no number large enough to classify genes. In all genetic types there are dormant genes. These dormant genes can lurk in a minute tributary in the river of life, undetectable for billions of years. A cosmic energy force that has traveled for thousands of light years distant, can awaken this sleeping gene. The DNA composition of this catalytic traveler, mixed with dormant genes, can completely alter the behavioral pattern of any species. This change can be regressive or progressive, promulgating extinction or survival.

Xylanthian culture evolved from a primitive violent survival mode. Primitive Earth Beings survival behavior was violent. The mixture of these two genetics, created the present progressive and regressive behavior of humans. We are entering into a golden age of technology, however the awakening of the dormant primitive survival genes, can use this technology to destroy all life on Earth.

Einstein commented, when the United States declared war against Hitler, "I am sorry to admit that I belong to this species of obnoxious idiots." Nuclear scientists begged Einstein for his advanced research. He replied, "I have given you too much already. You will destroy yourselves soon enough."

We must understand that everything in existence has a purpose. Violence, hatred, greed and war are natural survival traits, prevalent in all universal functions. These traits are not psychotic within themselves. Psychosis is paradoxical reasoning without wisdom. Self-destruction is not survival, this is a paradox.

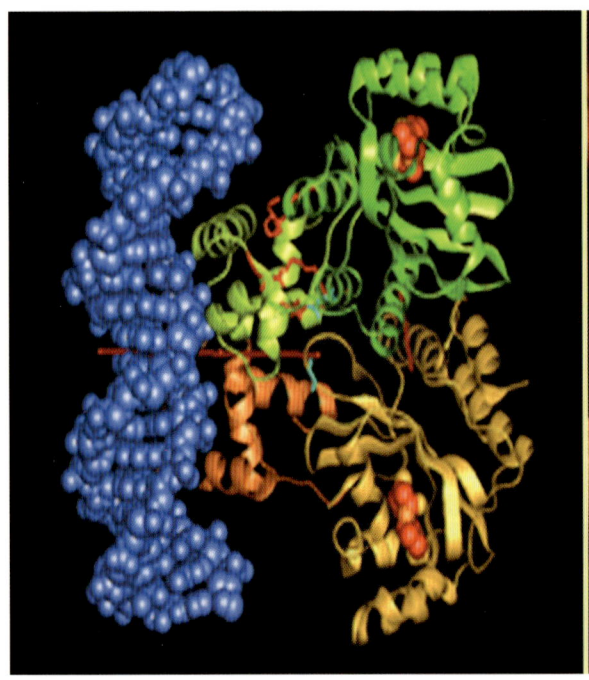

Eternal Universal Monistic Existence is inextricably intertwined with infinite inseparable purposeful differentials. All that exists is dependant on all that exists. If one differential attempts to eradicate another differential, this is suicidal. Suicide is not survival, it is paradoxical psychosis. Break the survival chain with wanton destruction for pleasure or greed and extinction is inevitable.

Thousands of sharks are captured, for the sole purpose of having their dorsal fins cut off. After this amputation, they are placed back into the sea. This altered condition questions their survival. Rhinos are slaughtered for their horns. The horns of the Rhinos and the fins of the shark are served in expensive, mens' only, restaurants, with the pretext of increasing male virility. If this psychosis accelerates, it may be possible, in the future, for wealthy women to eat Poodle Dog Pie, to make their hair curly.

Elephant tusk ivory has been a valuable commodity for 40,000 years. Ancient beings used the meat for food, the hide for shelter and the ivory for artifacts and tools. Present day humans slaughter this giant beast, for their ivory tusks and leather hides. A pair of fancy elephant hide cowboy boots sells for $1500. They are beautiful, however how beautiful was the giant elephant that sacrificed its life to make a hundred thousand dollars worth of cowboy boots for a wealthy Texas boot maker?

137

The foxhunter enjoys watching 20 vicious dogs rip a precious little fox to shreds.

The humans' brains were in the muzzles of their powerful buffalo rifles, as they slaughtered ten million beautiful animals, not for food, but for trophies. Bison were the major food supply for numerous American Indian tribes. The United States government murdered some Indian Chieftains, others were herded into railroad cattle containers and transported 2,000 miles away to prison. Their tribes were placed on reservations in desolate geographical locations, where they wept bitterly as they watched their beloved buffalo friends being senselessly murdered. Destroy a food supply, destroy a species. A Blue Jay has more common sense than a human. Give a Blue Jay 50 sunflower seeds, it will eat 40 and plant 10. Pollute the ocean, pollute the fish. Read the fine print on a cigarette pack while drinking alcohol. *Oh where, Oh where has the blue sky gone?* Which is it, Natural-Survival or psychotic Self-Destruction?

Great and wonderful knowledge has evolved from the Xylanthian recessive gene implant in Atlantis. Technology has abolished deadly diseases, longevity has increased, instant worldwide communication is possible, benevolent entities respond immediately to natural catastrophes. However, the yin/yang principle of balance prevails in all universal functions. As the benevolent force evolves, so does the destructive force. The present state of human behavior is completely out of balance. Paradoxical behavior is overwhelming the benevolent forces of the Cosmos. This imbalance originated in Atlantis, as did all existing human behavioral traits. Creating a military in Atlantis was the seed that grew the tree whose fruit is greed and hatred. Military force breeds war. Oppression destroys self-respect. The lack of self-respect gives birth to self-hatred and vengeance which spreads like wildfire thru the entire species. The survivors of Atlantis migrated thru-out Europe, Asia and Africa. Empires with power-mad rulers waged thousands of years of wars which continue globally to this present-day.

SONCHIS TRANSCRIPT: *"when the divine portion began to fade away, and became diluted too often and too much with the mortal admixture, and the human nature got the upper hand, they then, being unable to bear their fortune, behaved unseemly, and to him who had an eye to see grew visibly debased, for they were losing the fairest of their precious gifts; but to those who had no eye to see the true happiness, they appeared glorious and blessed at the very time when they were full of avarice and unrighteous power...they deliberated in common about war...The king was not to have the power of life and death...unless he had the assent of the majority of the ten* (Kings of Atlantis).*"*

Two precedents were based in Atlantis, rules for war and capital punishment; The Geneva Convention and the Justice Jury System. One person is guilty for taking another persons life, however 12 persons can take the guilty persons life. Killing is Killing; whether it be by burning at the stake, the executioner's beheading axe, the guillotine, the hangman's noose, the firing squad, lethal injection, the electric chair, the gas chamber or war.

7 million humans were starved and murdered in Ukraine. 6 million were baked in the Auschwitz ovens. 110,000 men, women and children were scorched to death by atoms bombs in Hiroshima and Nagasaki. 1000's of genuine American Indians scalps were sold for $1.50 each. African slaves were sold like animals at public auctions. America, "the land of the free," was stolen from the American Indians, the Alaskan Indians and Hawaiians. Cyril and a band of Christians killed a librarian in Alexandria. In the name of Jesus, they scraped all the flesh from her bones with abalone shells and burned her bones. They destroyed the library of Alexandria and the valuable records of our Atlantian heritage.

OH, GENEVA! Symbol of Peace on Earth. Many birds are nesting in the cornices of your beautiful buildings. The vultures make rules for humane methods to kill in war. These warlords have a desire to devour each other. However, they have copulated together and are impregnated with an egg that will hatch a nuclear monster that may devour them all. GENEVA! GENEVA! Listen to the gentle cooing of the Dove of Peace and the Joyous song of the Bluebird, echoing the heartbeat of millions of people who are laying the foundations stones of a cultural superstructure, wherein brotherly love and equality are the catalysts to generate peaceful coexistence.

GENEVA

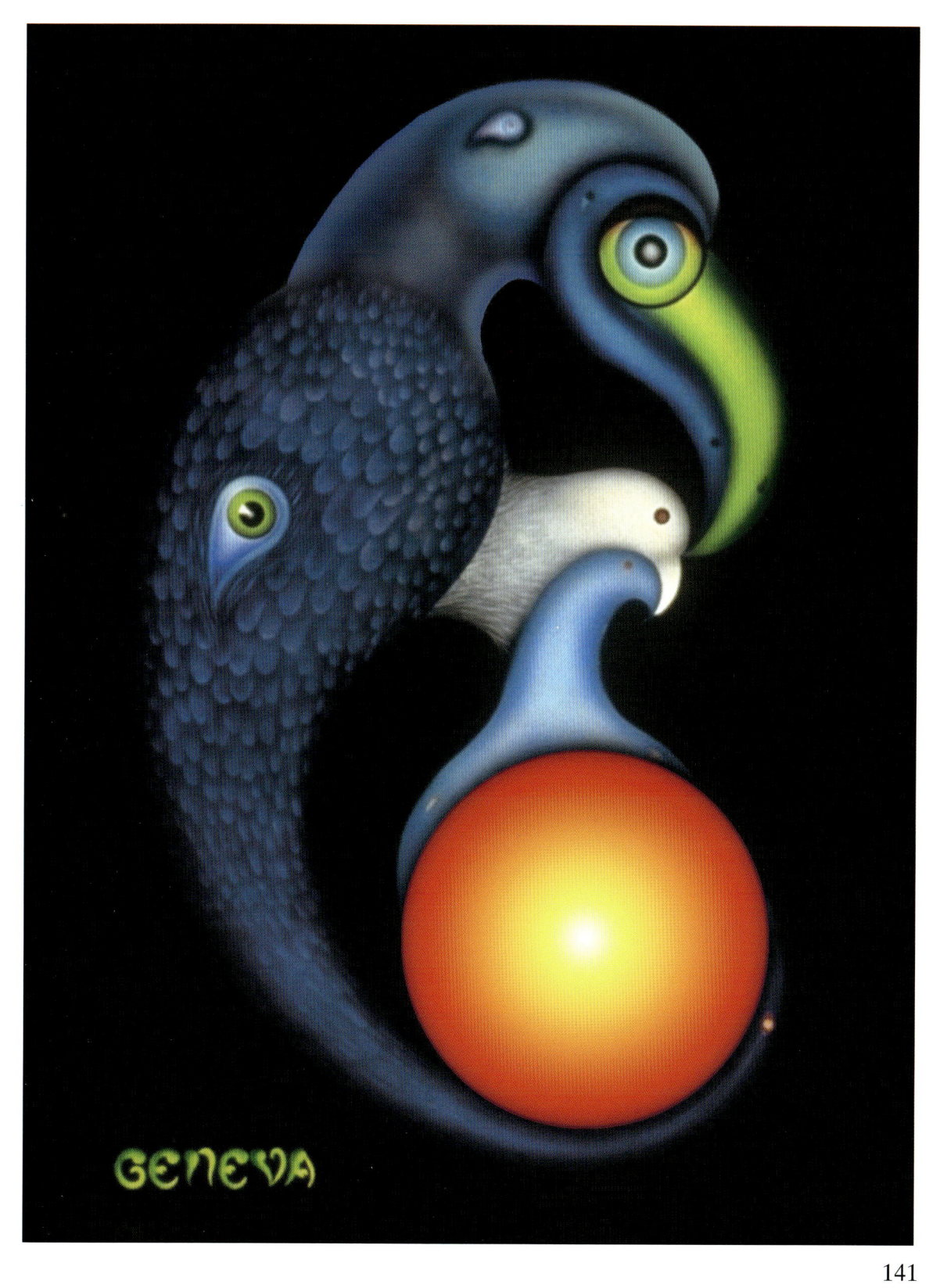

Some modern Humans' mental capacity is incapable of fully understanding basic reality. The simplicity of existence is confounding to the learned. The first stepping stone in the pathway of understanding, is to accept the universal statute that everything in existence is purposeful. Adversity motivates change. Change is evolution, either regressive or progressive. Every force in existence has an opposing inseparable counterpart, this is the universal law of polarity. Psychosis and paradox are a part of natural reality. Universal function is paradoxical and psychotic. A cosmic body is hurled out of a nuclear mass, to survive for a time, then falls back into the mass from which it originated. A wild comet or meteor can suddenly disrupt the apparent stability of any celestial process. All entities are born to die.

All humans are blessed with the greatest gift in existence; the free will to survive and progressively procreate or to become celibate and regress into extinction. Protesting or condemning, any human behavior trait, agitates and increases the velocity of that which is condemned. Protest is merely asserting that natural reality is unnatural. The only way to attain balance in the present self-destruct modes of human society, is to create a cultural superstructure based on peaceful co-existive survival. This energy force is now in a formative mode thru-out the Earth.

Within the genetic code of ALL humans is "Good and Evil." Humans are the most helpless animal on Earth. They have developed a need to seek for something outside themselves, which is greater than they are. They have created hundreds of Deities, to moan and groan to, about their unworthiness. They blaspheme their own Deities by deviating from the principles of their Deities. This deviation has initiated a fear complex which distorts sound reasoning. "An angry sadistic Deity will reincarnate a human to be tortured"???

Conformism destroys individualism. If one has no self-awareness, what is there to respect? Entire life spans drift by, controlled by dictatorial fascist concepts that all humans should think and behave identically. This eliminates individuality and is contrary to the Universal law of difference, wherein no two entities in existence are identical. The absence of identity, stalemates progress and prevents communication which is the media for peaceful co-existence.

There is a time for everything that exists; a time for war and a time for peace, a time to hate and a time to love, a time for joy and a time for sorrow, a time to build and a time to destroy, a time to be born and a time to die. Now is the time for the benevolent forces of the cosmos, the Xylanthian technological knowledge and the bountiful treasures of the Earth to be combined into a comprehensive energy force that will become the surrogation of the existing behavior of the Humans.

A novel surrogate force is now being formed by the unison of immaculate cumulative human mind power, focused on the revival of dormant Xylanthian genetics wherein equality and peaceful co-existence prevailed.

Procreation

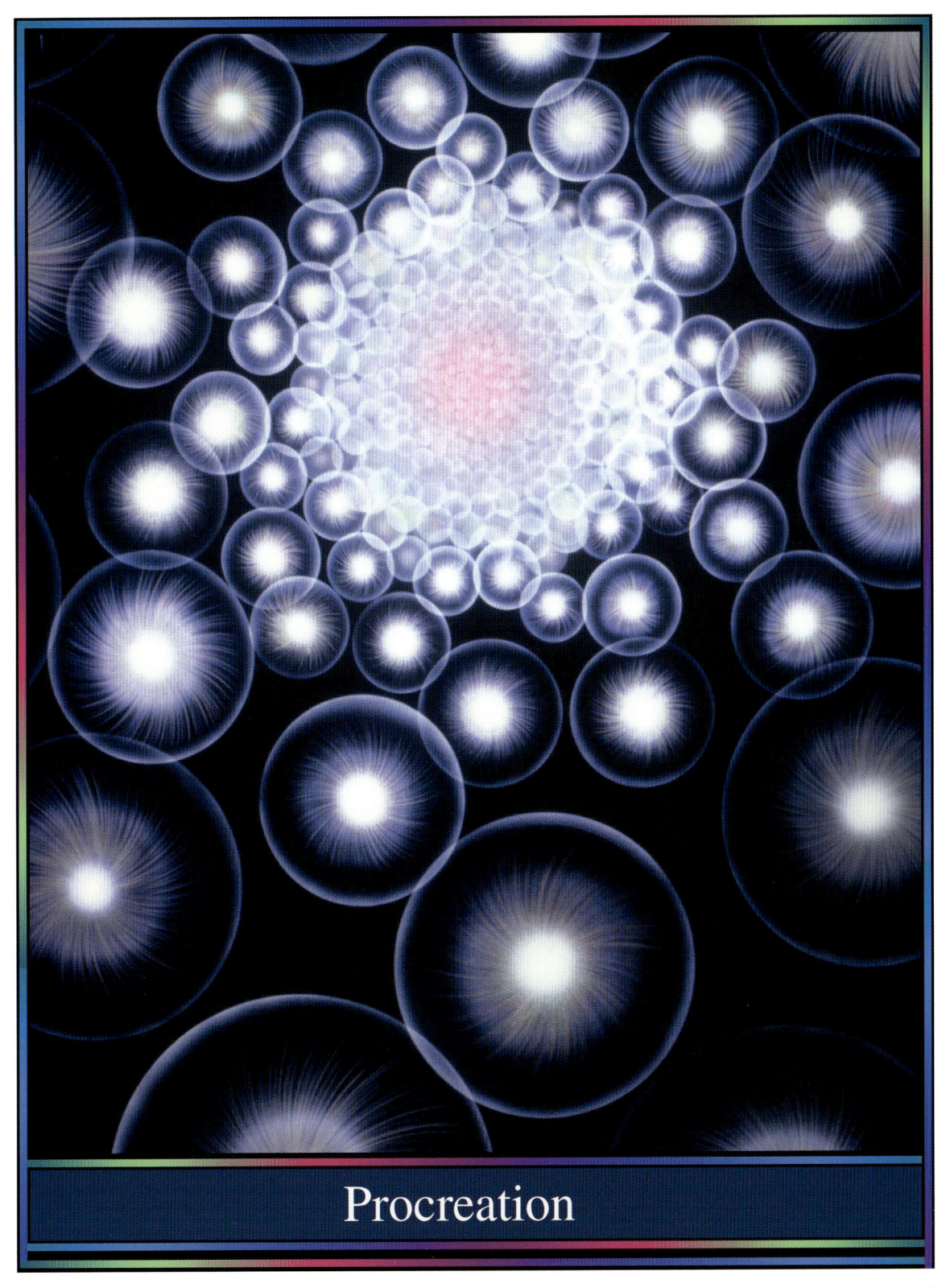

Trident

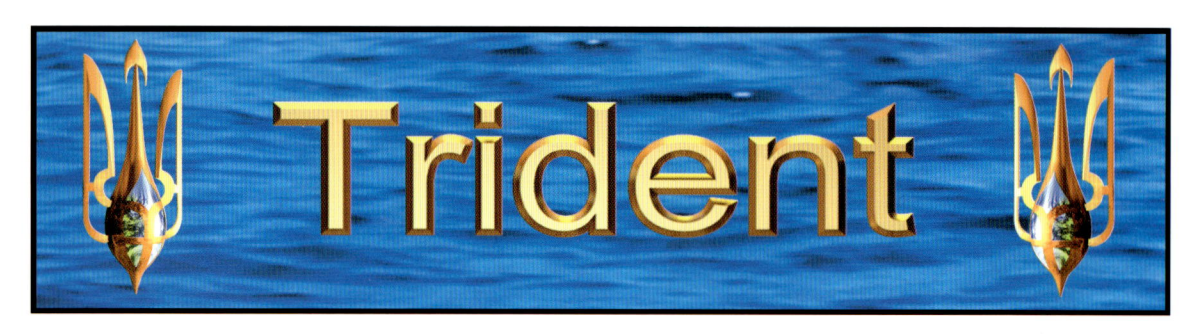

The Trident is one of the most powerful symbols on Earth. Xoah's spacecraft, Tua's beloved "Big Bird", became the symbol of Atlantis. Its three great prongs represented the Primitive Earth-Beings, the Xylanthians and the new species created by their interbreeding. The Trident represented the three species living in harmony together. Paradoxically, it also became the symbol of the military force of Atlantis. As the Atlantians spread in every direction the symbol of the Trident spread with them. Archeological discoveries in the countries surrounding ancient Atlantis have revealed over 200 various designs of the Trident. It's multiple meanings have migrated around the world. It is used by political governments and military forces as a symbol of their power and control. The Trident is a symbol of the power of various Deities. The Trident is also a deeply spiritual symbol representing love, harmony and peace.

Trident Missle

Trident Submarines patrol the world's oceans

145

SONCHIS Transcript: *"Orichalcum" was dug out of the earth in many parts of the Island, being more precious in those days than anything except gold... The third wall which encompassed the citadel, flashed with the red light of Orichalcum."*

Orichalcum disappeared from existence after Atlantis subsided. A few rare coins and jewelry, which collectors pay enormous prices for, have been recovered. *"Orichalcum"* translates to *"mountain copper."* Copper is plentiful in Crimea and Ukraine, however there is a difference in the existing copper and the ancient orichalcum. Native copper oxidizes when exposed to atmosphere. It turns a dull color or green from oxidazation. Orichalcum does not oxidize, it *"flashes the red light of orichalcum."* The above pieces of orichalcum were salvaged from core drill samples while drilling for thermal energy near Kerch. They show evidence of an ancient smelting process. They have been unearthed for 15 years and exposed to air and have not oxidized. They *"flash with the red light of orichalcum."* A spectrographic analysis, of these specimens, revealed the mystery of orichalcum. It is native copper containing traces of silver, zinc and a small amount of gold, which prevents oxidization. Geologically the only orichalcum deposit possibly lies beneath the Sea of Azov.

LEGENDS, MYTHS & HISTORY, in many places on Earth, contain knowledge of Atlantis and Xylanthia.

The Kayapo Indians in Brazil, build circular cities resembling Atlantis. Their legend is, *"their ancestors came form the sky, from a land where there was no night (Xylanthia)."*

Friendship Island, off the coast of Chili; the inhabitants are all tall, blond, blue-eyed, people with miraculous healing powers *(recessive genes)*.

When the military oppression in Atlantis increased, the Xylanthian beings migrated in every direction. One group moved southward and established a kingdom on the Island of Lesbos. Due to the inability of comprehending androgyny, the inhabitants of Lesbos were assumed to be females. This is where the concept of Lesbianism originated.

The Atlantis military destroyed the Xylanthian Alpha Processor contact mechanism in Xoah's temple. The emerald antenna was vital to the Xylanthians. They secretly salvaged the emerald pillar and with great difficulty transported it to the Island of Lesbos. Without the technical components, the major contact with the Alpha Processor was lost. However, to this present time, neuro-biological receptor-transmitter contact with the Alpha Processor is possible if the recessive genetic constituency, of an individual, supersedes the dominant genes. Therein is the abundance of technological knowledge and the intelligence to use it to form a survival cultural superstructure.

A marauding horde of Persians invaded the Island of Lesbos destroying the entire population. The Xylanthians, foreseeing this invasion, transported the Emerald pillar to Tyre in Phoenicia.

HERODOTUS: *"I made a voyage to Tyre in Phoenicia, hearing there was a temple of Heracles at that place, very highly venerated. I visited the temple, and found it richly adorned with a number of offerings, among which were two pillars, one of pure gold, the other of emerald, shining with great brilliancy at night."*

Xylanthian genetics are the greatest gift to Blue Planet. These genes are spread thru-out humanity. They will vacillate from dormancy to activity as time unfolds. Surges of technology and regression of reasoning is natural. The impossibility of calculating the reason for a gene to lie dormant and suddenly awaken, is due to the infinity of the origin of all that exists. All that exists is directly relative to all that exists. True Monism taxes the ability of human understanding. Fully comprehending the universal law of Holism, exceeds the contemporary ability of the human mind. To completely perceive these two principles, it would be necessary to know the exact number of stars and their planets, to know the mineral constituencies of each, to be aware of the exact cosmic influences and emissions of each and to calculate the infinite number of components relative to all of these entities.

The Xylanthians were androgynous, they had six fingers and toes on each hand and foot, they were hairless, blue-eyed and super intelligent. The evolution of their recessive genes and the degree of the admixture of Primitive dominant genes, regulates physical and psychological differences in the characteristics of all humans. Prejudice regarding these differences originated in Atlantis society and continues worldwide. Prejudice regarding skin color, economic status, political differences, boundary disputes and religious conflicts are the offspring of the gross ignorance of the natural various compositions of DNA, genes, and X-Y chromosomes mixtures.

The deterrent to this prejudice and the propellant of understanding and tolerance, of diverse characteristics and cultures, can be achieved by delving deeply into the fine print of DNA, and realizing that every human on Earth is androgynous, to variable degrees. Over three hundred androgynous (hermaphrodite) humans are born everyday.

There are thousands of blue-eyed humans born, on Earth, everyday. Three hundred and forty hairless humans are born daily. Judo-Christian history refers to "Sons of God" and "Daughters of Man" bearing children who became the Giants of Gath, having 12 fingers and 12 toes. Everyday 288 babies are born with 6 fingers on one or both hands, or 6 toes on one or both feet, or any combination thereof.

In November, 2003, a beautiful, happy, healthy baby girl was born with 6 toes on her left foot. Her name is Mana. Many special thanks and blessings to her parents for offering these special photos as a precious gift to help humanity better understand their heritage.

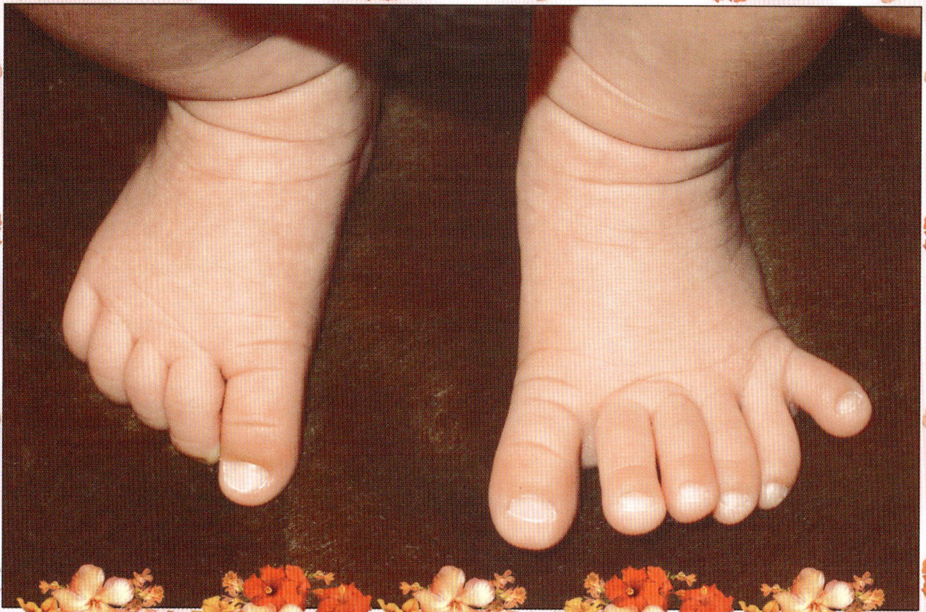

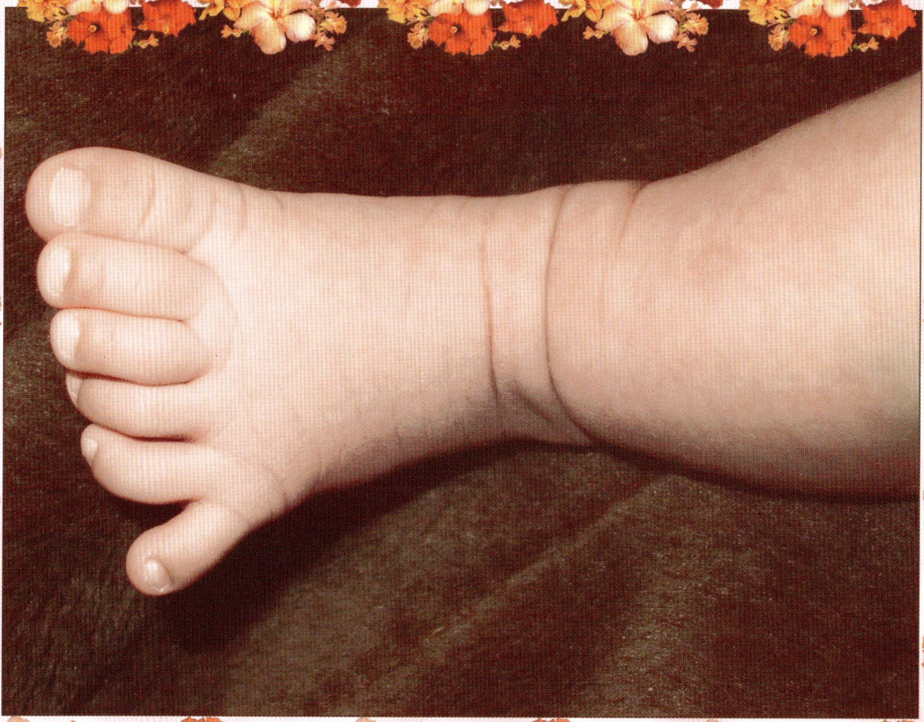

Besides a comparative small number of aborigines, every human being on Earth is a descendant of Xylanthian and Primitive Being interbreeding. For millennia the secrets of our origin in Atlantis has been past down through Medicine men and Shamans.

The Hopi American Indian Tribe in Northern Arizona contains several Clans. The Snake Clan is the spiritual leader of the Tribe. The Chief medicine-man of the Snake Clan was Grandfather Jack, he was 110 years of age when his life spirit left his body, on January 1, 1993. Flying Eagle and Grandfather Jack were very dear friends. When Grandfather Jack performed a ceremonial medicine dance, he would hold a live venomous rattle snake in each hand or a snake in one hand and a sacred meteorite in the other. His rhythmic chant and the beat of the Kachina's drums would completely mesmerize the snakes. The symbolism of the dances was to bring the life spirit of the Earth and the Spirit of the Heavens into harmony, thereby contacting the GREAT SPIRIT OF LIFE. Grandfather Jack possessed an endless knowledge of the history and legends of the Southwestern United States American Indians.

Twenty-five thousand years ago a massive metallic meteor exploded over Northern Arizona, scattering meteorites over a vast area, approximately 100 miles south of Hopi Land.

"Sky-Stone"

Whispering Wind and I (Flying Eagle) had completed our research at the ancient ruins of the lost Tuzigoot Indian tribe, which was 150 miles southwest of the Snake Clan of the Hopi Indians. Absolutely no one knew where we were, or our plans to leave the next day. We were extremely surprised when an old Volkswagen, that had the appearance of being recently salvaged from a wrecking yard, stopped near our camp. A young Hopi male was driving and two young males were in the back seat. Grandfather Jack sat next to the driver. It would have been an insult to ask the Medicine Man, how he knew where we were. Then the second surprise, when Grandfather said, *"you are leaving tomorrow."* After ceremonial greetings blanketed with tears, Grandfather said, *"I bring you two of my Medicine Pieces. One is the Sky-Stone, the other is the Talking-Stone. You will make medicine with the Sky-Stone and the Talking-Stone will tell you where the land of our ancestors is."* I started to venture into the taboo of questioning a Medicine Man, as to why these sacred objects were not placed in the Kiva. He perceived my question and saved my embarrassment. *"The White man's poison is spreading thru our tribe, they are paying big wampum to the young braves for stealing the sacred objects from the Kivas. I have lived in this land for 106 years. My eyes cannot see and my legs are tired. I will be going into the Great Spirit soon. You and Whispering Wind have many years to make Medicine. I leave you now with a Hopi blessing. Distant lands will keep us apart but our spirits will always be close together. Take care of our people."*

The Sky-Stone is a seven pound crystallized metallic meteorite which is composed generally of nickel-iron. It contains several other Earth minerals. This rare and unusual Medicine Piece also contains four minerals not native to Earth and small diamonds that radio carbon date older than Earth's Sun. This places the origin of this meteor, outside our solar system.

The Talking-Stone was found in the 19th century, in an Anasazi cave dwelling in the San Juan Mountains of southwestern Colorado. It was buried in red iron oxide earth with some exotic pottery and the mummy of an ancient Medicine Man. This magic stone is 9.5 inches long, 4.5 inches high and 2 inches thick. Scientific analysis determines the stone is basaltic volcanic origin. There is no natural stone of this type in this region. This indicates the stone was transported from another location on Earth. Microscopic bits of quartz crystal, embedded in the carvings, suggest the carving was done with a quartz crystal point. Evidence indicates sheep fat in the original stone.

An eastern United States cave explorer who found the Talking-Stone, became aware of the legendary curse for disturbing a sacred Indian burial site. He consulted a Ute Indian Medicine Man, 50 miles to the south, to prevent misfortune to himself. The Medicine Man done ceremony. He told the explorer; "there will be no curse, the Great Spirit sent you to find the Talking-Stone. It has been lost for 200 years, it speaks of the land of our ancestors. You must take the Mummy and the pottery back to the cave. You must leave this region and never come back."

The Ute Indian Medicine man kept the Talking-Stone for many years. It would not speak to him. He sent it 100 miles distant to the Navajo Indian Medicine council. After many years, they held peyote council. The Great Spirit advised them that the language of the Talking-Stone was Anasazi, the mysterious Anasazi vanished from this region. The Hopi and Comanche Indians are the only tribes that fully understood their language. The Navajo Indian medicine council had great respect for the young Grandfather Jack's wisdom and knowledge. They gave the Talking-Stone to him in 1920, the year Flying Eagle was born.

ANASAZI is a Navajo Indian word which translates to, ANCIENT ONES. In southwestern United States of America, there is a geographical location called "The Four Corners." This is where the corners of the states of Utah, Colorado, New Mexico and Arizona, join. If a compass point was placed there and a thousand mile diameter circle was drawn, hundreds of ancient American Indian ruins would be encompassed. Some of the most ancient of these are referred to as Anasazi territory. Humans spread thru-out the Earth as they migrated from Atlantis Motherland. In the Four Corners area there is strong evidence of two major migrations. One from the Northern Bering Strait migration from Mongolia and one from South America via Central America and Mexico. It is interesting to note that the Four Corners Area is equidistant from both migration origins in the Western Hemisphere. Mystery shrouds the apparent extinction of these ancient civilizations. Extinction leaves no offspring. If the Anasazi became extinct, there would be no Indians in this area. As these two migrations came together, they found a common heritage and established communication. Interbreeding gave birth to a branching effect. The natural nomadic trait of all Humans, instigated the formation of the numerous present day tribes of Indians in this area. An interesting example is, the Hopi Nation is in the center of the Navajo Nation. The Navajo genetics are from the northern migration and Hopi genetics are from the southern migration. They respect each other and peacefully co-exist.

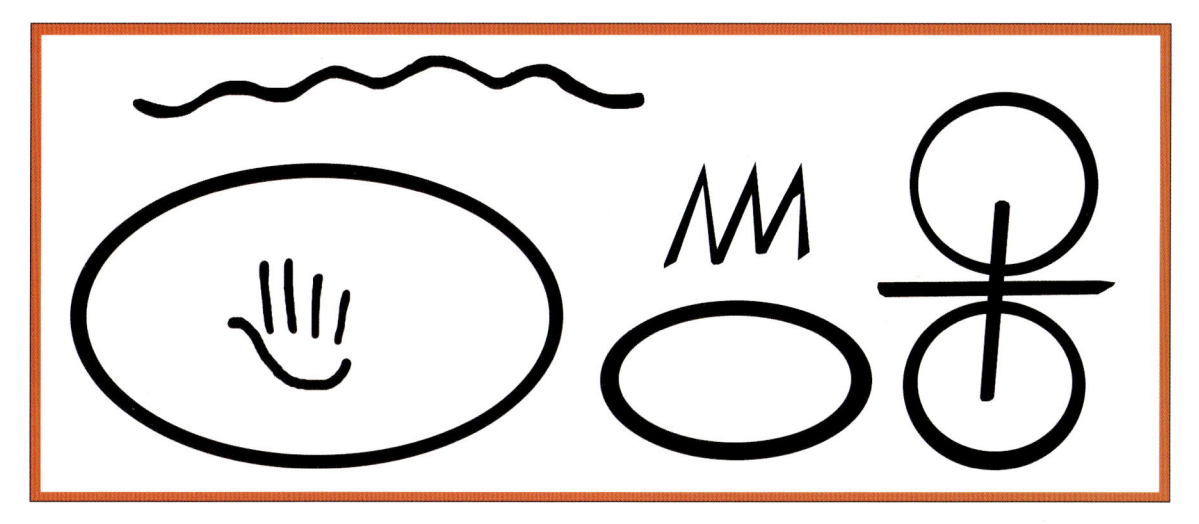

Flying Eagle's ancestry is Comanche Indian. Comanche and Hopi legend speaks of identical ancestry: *"Our People came from a Beautiful Land across the Great Water."* Grandfather Jack and Flying Eagle contemplated the Talking Stone, dozens of times, during the 20 years preceding Flying Eagle's marriage to Whispering Wind. Comparing the petroglyphs of the Anasazi, the hidden knowledge of the Talking Stone becomes obvious.

One hand of waters (five waters). *Father-Sky-Water came into Mother-Great-Water and the top of the mountains. Sky-Water from mountains gave drink to Big-Sister-Water and two Little-Sister-Waters. Little-Sister-Waters provided nourishment to our beloved Ancestors in their far away Motherland. Our Ancestors traveled on the four winds, across many lands and many great waters, searching for their home in the sky.*

153

Whispering Wind and I (Flying Eagle) traveled tens of thousands of miles. We contemplated hundreds of ancient records and maps. We researched the entire surface of the ocean floors and the Earth land mass. We explored innumerable geological and archeological locations to find a place that would correspond with every single detail in the Transcript of Sonchis.

During our extensive research, I became aware of Whispering Wind's intuitive powers. We were slightly frustrated, when I spread out a large map of the entire world. I coaxed Whispering Wind, to permit me to securely blindfold her. I gave her a long pointer stick and asked her to point to Atlantis. Without any hesitation she pointed to the location where Atlantis exists. We then channeled our entire research energies to this one area.

One late night, we were deeply involved in reviewing our abundance of research data. Suddenly there was a very loud thunder clap, followed by a brilliant flash of lightening. We had almost forgotten the Talking Stone which was sitting on a window sill, next to a large quartz crystal which was given to us by a Ute Indian Medicine Man. The brilliant lightening flash refracted a light beam thru the quartz crystal. For a brief instant, the light beam illuminated the Talking Stone, causing it to look like liquid gold. We both simultaneously loudly yelled, "IT"S TALKING TO US!" We quickly placed the Talking Stone on our desk, where it immediately began talking. It's spoken words are recorded on the graphic, herein below.

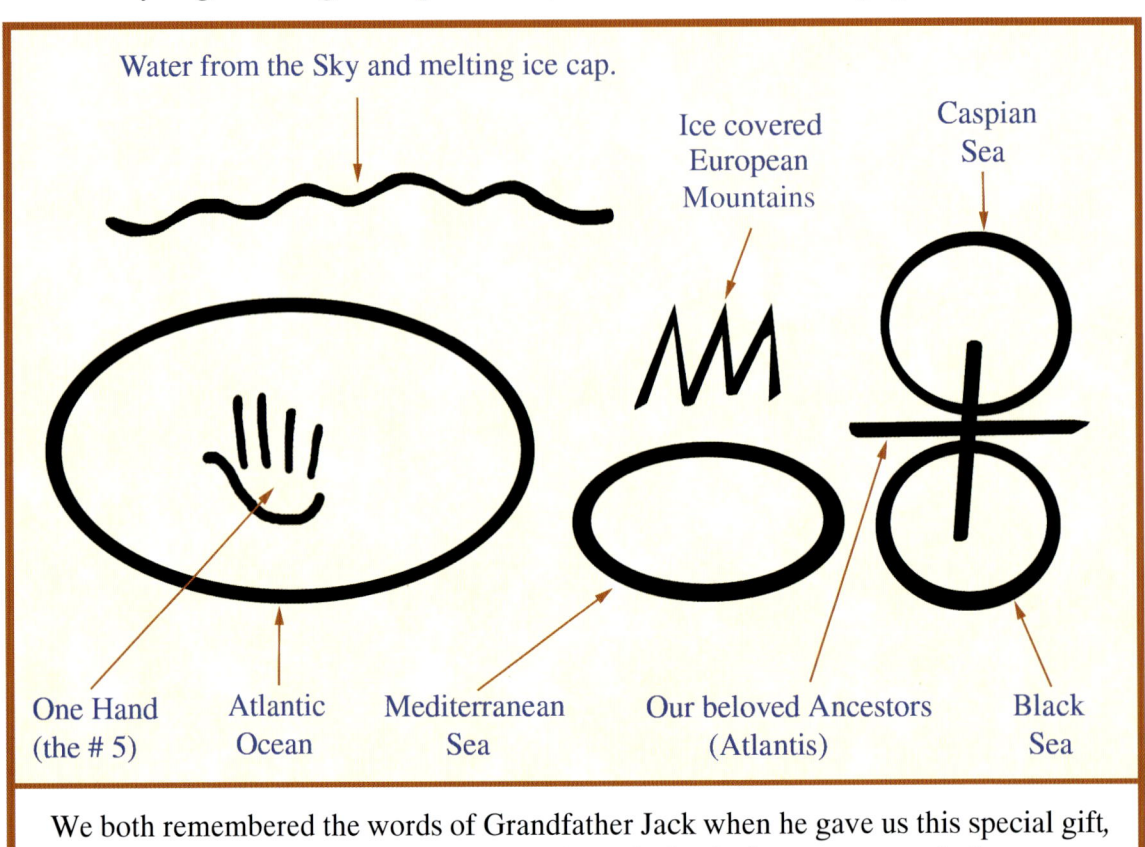

Water from the Sky and melting ice cap.	
Ice covered European Mountains	
Caspian Sea	
One Hand (the # 5)	
Atlantic Ocean	
Mediterranean Sea	
Our beloved Ancestors (Atlantis)	
Black Sea	

We both remembered the words of Grandfather Jack when he gave us this special gift, *"the Talking- Stone will tell you where the land of our ancestors is."*

Photo by: Robert Collins,"Hawkeye"

Knowledge of Atlantis and the Bull has passed from generation to generation, over thousands of years, to be implanted on the stone wall of an Anasazi dwelling. It's exact location is classified by request of the local tribal Leaders, to ensure it's preservation.

The Tuzigoot Indians, near Cottonwood, Arizona, "mysteriously vanished." What did not vanish from the same area is iron cannon balls, which were unearthed along side ancient skeletal remains of infants and their Mothers.

The Tuzigoot ruins are the replica of a miniature Atlantis. Their dwellings were located on a rounded hill surrounded by a plain where they farmed. The plain is laced with irrigation canals, which are visible to this present time. Their main sustenance was pumpkin squash which still reproduces itself after hundreds of years. The Tuzigoot was one of the rare American Indian tribes to utilize irrigation for farming, instead of relying on the nature weather. The petroglyph below portrays psycho-genetic memories of Atlantis and it's farming lots.

Photo by: Robert Collins, "Hawkeye"

These petroglyphs, photographed by "Hawkeye" in the southwestern Unied States, contain the history of Atlantis, it's canals, it's abundance of antelope and it's respect for the bull.

157

Petroglyphs and legends in the Hawaiian Islands, tell the story of an ancient Lizard Clan whose ancestors came from the Lizard Planet. Xylanthian ancestors evolved from Lizards.

The Dogon People, in West Africa, are descendants of Atlantis. They had a complete knowledge of the configuration of the Sirius Star Complex, thousands of years before Alan Clark discovered it in 1862. Preceding this date, Earth astronomers assumed Sirius was a pulsating star instead of two stars orbiting around a common center of gravity. The Dogon People were aware of three stars, Sirius A, B and C. They referred to Sirius C as the "Woman Planet", where their ancestors originated. (Xylanthian androgyny).

One thousand pages in a book would not contain the myths, legends, memories and history of Atlantis, thru-out the Earth. The subliminal awareness of a dual ancestry, regulates the behavior of humans. Dual ancestry generates a conflict of reasoning. Primitive genetics lean toward isolationism and basic survival. Extra-terrestrial genetics, contain a natural wanderlust and a desire for the peaceful environment of Xylanthia. To cope with the Primitive needs the Human builds fences and locked gates surrounding their dwellings and periodically escape to a cabin in the wilderness. The Xylanthian wanders thru the heavens with telescopes and space-crafts, subliminally searching for a new world and the ultimate technology, to find their way back home to Xylanthia.

A DORMANT PSYCHO-GENETIC MEMORY AWAKENED WHEN A SPACE SHUTTLE WAS NAMED, **ATLANTIS**.

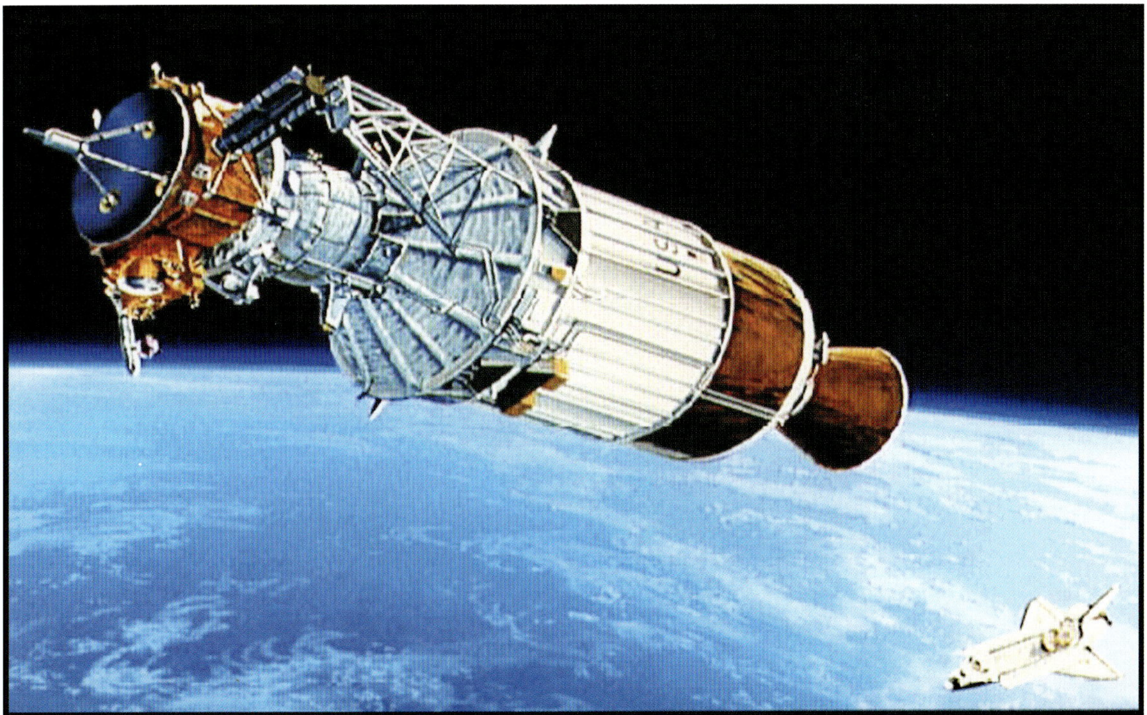

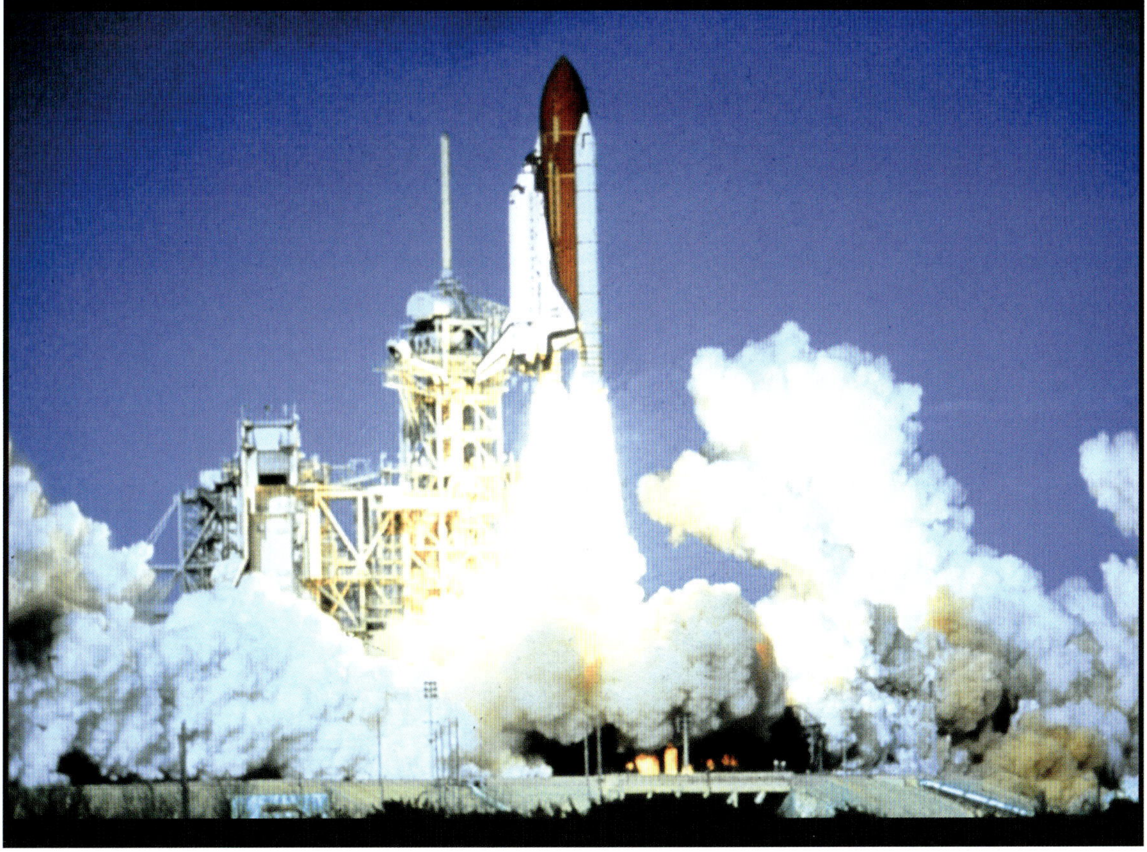

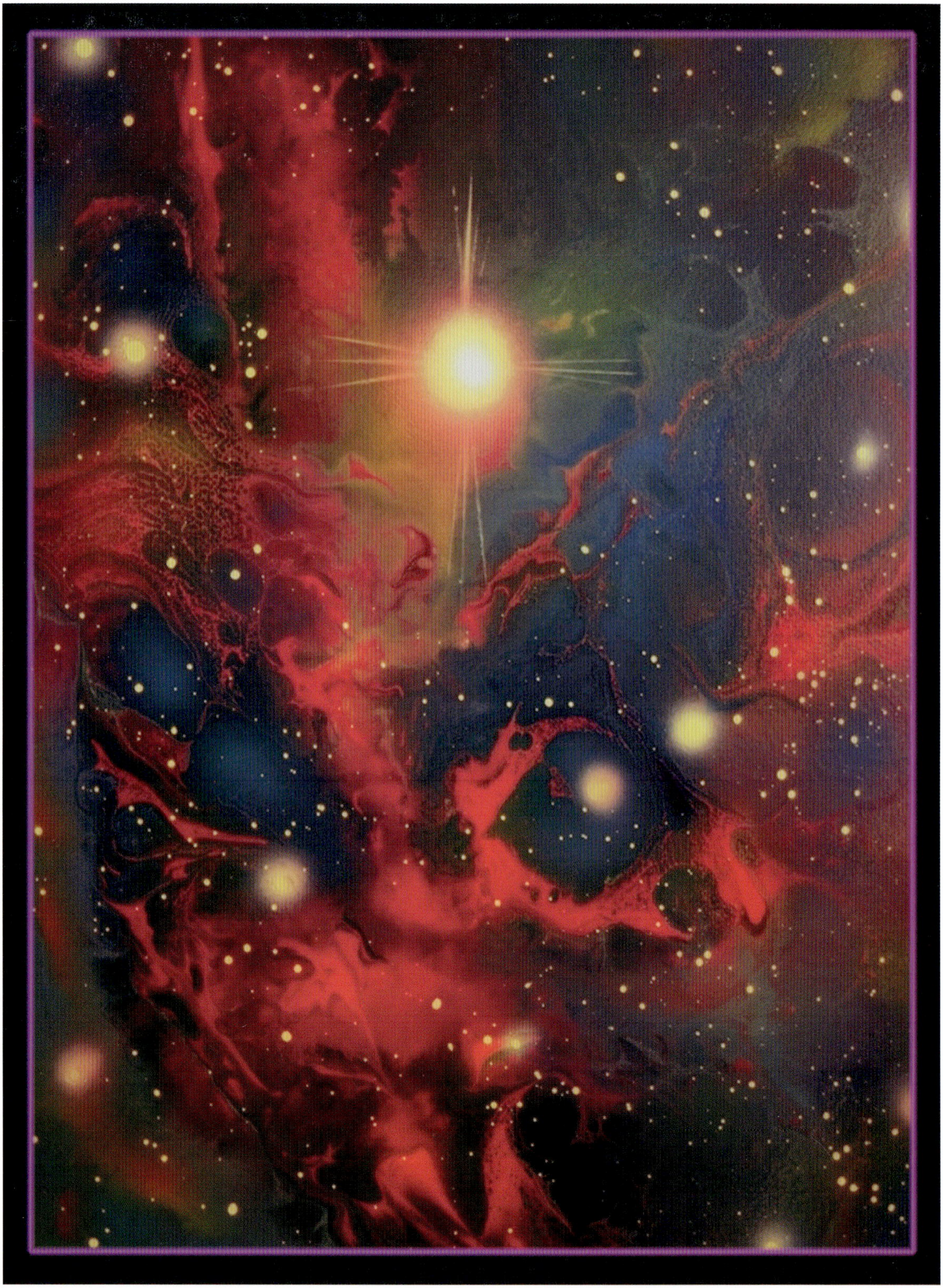

Humans reach for the stars and explore the unknown universe. In this present age of technical evolution, priority should be granted to exploring the unknown dormant powers of the human mind.

A sadomasochistic subservient trait of all Humans, is inextricably intertwined with a benevolent loving nature. A presently existing behavioral imbalance of these two natures, gives birth to confusion. It is very important to note that this conflict is not only prevalent between factions, it resides within the constitution of each individual. Every person possesses these two qualities. Every person, also possesses a free will to determine the degree of anomaly.

Everything in existence, functions by relative influences. The light of the dawn, influences birds to awaken and begin to sing. On the horizon of Human existence, the faint light of the Dawn of a New Age is appearing. WAKE UP, LITTLE BIRD and sing a song of joy and hope. SING YOUR OWN SONG. If it comes from your heart and soul, it will blend harmoniously with the songs of many. Your song will encourage others, that do not realize they have a voice, to sing their song.

Dear Reader, there is no other being in the endless universe, exactly as you are. This is the foundation of your true identity. Built upon this base is the total grandeur of ALL that you are, one rare treasure among uncountable multitudes. All entities in existence are purposeful. ONLY YOU, in the depths of your inmost being, know your true purpose for being on this Earth. Everyone's BASIC purpose is to survive and procreate. Procreation is not only producing offspring of your species, it includes creating ways and means to survive. Each human is born with predestined talents and abilities that differ in each person. A recent survey shows over 85% of all people are culturally channeled into subsisting in a manner that is contrary to their natural desires and abilities. This instigates a psychological deterrent to progressive evolution and produces an infirm society. Continued infirmity leads to depression. Extended depression incites genocide. Guilt is the assassin of self-respect. The lack of self-respect, inhibits the desire to search for true identity. Perennial guilt develops into self-hatred which breeds hatred for others.

Humans are genetic templates of their ancestors. Guilt began in Atlantis, with the mixture of dominant and recessive genes. This blending of genes is responsible for the psychological paradox in Human cognisance. Xylanthian nature is total equality, with self-respect and respect for others. Primitive nature is strong tribal leaders dominance. These two traits are opposing energy forces. Human Xylanthian genetics are guilty for being forced to use primitive violence to survive. The Primitive genetics are guilty for not using Xylanthian equality to survive. This double dose of guilt is the building blocks for inner psychological turmoil, which radiates thru-out the entire species.

The opposing force of guilt is innocence. The monarch of the powerful Human mind is free choice, to wallow in the guilt of ancestors, or walk into a new age with innocence. Condemn evolution, or be thankful for the genetic transfer of the intelligence and ability to change. The greatest gift in existence is life, procreated by ancestry. These brave pioneers launched into the unknown. They were adventurers. All Humans have inherited this trait. Now is the time to utilize this spirit of adventure. Join hands and sing the song of freedom to herald the DAWN of a NEW AGE.

Dear Reader, I am Xoth. The Greeks called me Zeus. My tactful talents are now, a hereditary part of you. There is a locked door into an endless kingdom inside the omnipotent powers of your mind. The key to open that door is desire and dedication. Dedication is hampered by complacency. Desire supersedes complacency. Tact will guide you on the endless journey into your true being. Cherish the past, it is a stepping stone to your NOW. Unreasonable contemplation of endlessness, prevents concentration of each ever-changing NOW. Tactfully respect yourself for ALL that you truly are. You are a vital part of all existence. Your endless MIND POWER, combined with millions of others, will complete the Xylanthian Mission to preserve this Blue Planet paradise. Xylanthian genetic evolution has enabled many Human neuro-receptor-transmitters to begin reviving communication with the ALPHA PROCESSOR.

I am Xona, the Greeks gave me the name Hestia. After E-Gu transcended to the cosmos, I discovered we had corrected his infertility. I was pregnant with his child which was a healthy heterosexual male. I gave birth to several children, some were heterosexual females and males, others were androgynous. Xylanthians extremely enjoy sex. On Xylanthia we had great respect for each other in our sexual encounters, without any possessive attachment. I discovered a new wonderful emotion, LOVE. I know E-Gu would have been very proud of our beautiful son. I was an obstetrician, my genes are within each of you. This is why Humans are attracted to infants, whether they be a baby Human, a kitten, a bunny, a chick or any other new born. Cherish your young, they are tomorrows intelligence. Do not place sexual restrictions or prejudice on them. LET THEM BE FREE OF ARCHAIC CULTURAL PROGRAMMING.

I am Xiza, my Greek name was Demeter. I am contacting you thru the sophistication of the data base of the bio-function of the ALPHA PROCESSOR. I am a Botanist. My genes infiltrate the Human populace. I have given you a heritage of communication with the flora of Earth. If you visit Crimea, where ATLANTIS existed, you will find more varieties of exotic flora than any other place on Earth. Six billion Humans and billions of life forms are in contact with flora, everyday. No one will pass by a flower without communicating with it. Flowers speak a language of love and friendship. They provide essences for thousands of cosmetics, to attract friends. Forests are a major weather influence, extreme replenishing methods are necessary to preserve balance. When genetically altering flora for Human necessities, also provide flora needs for insects, this protects the food chain for birds, fish and reptiles.

I am Xeti, Greek name Hades. I am a Geologist and by gene transference, so are you. As we walk on the surface of Blue Planet, we stop and pick up a beautiful pebble. As we search beneath the surface, we encounter a vast crystalline wonderland of astounding glory. Crystals are every shape and color, they are living beings. The layers of the earth are pages in an ancient history book, dating back millions of years. The building of Atlantis and the entire Human evolution depended on minerals. The present electronic and machine age requires minerals. The use of some minerals is purposeful, in teaching Humans to advance into discovering different energy sources. Anti-gravity, magnetism, solar, stellar, tidal, geothermal, atomic transformation and other clean methods, will be the future energy supply. The emissions of energies from various minerals and crystals will be the medicines of tomorrow.

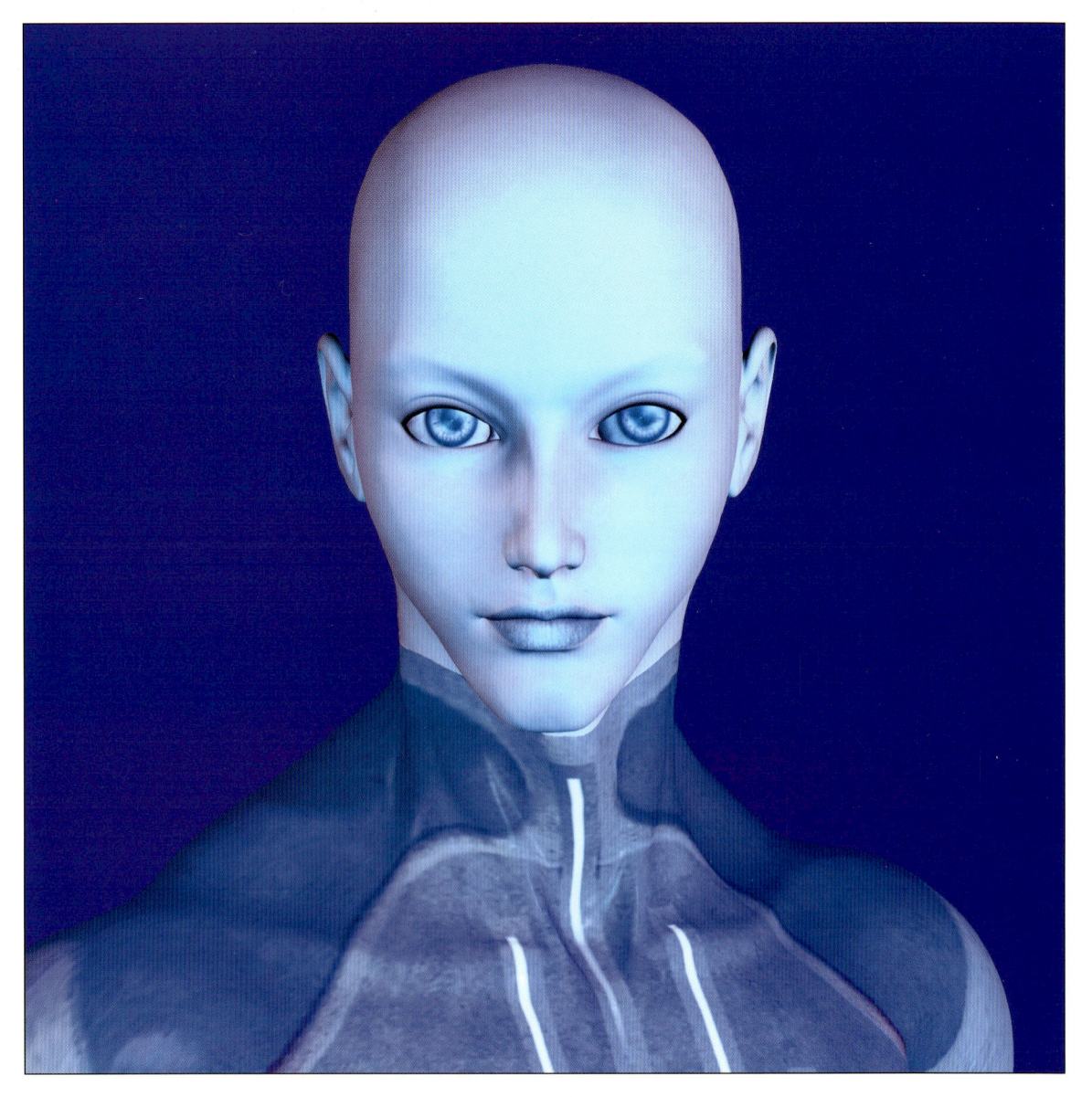

I am Xaah, Greek name Hera. I am a psychologist, you possess my genes, this makes you a psychologist. The Human Mind is the nucleus of Human behavior. The mind is not the brain. It is the function of the brain. If we compare the potential of the Human mind, with the contemporary use of the Human mind, we are encouraged to explore this unknown realm of fantastic ecstasy. The difference in the Human brain and a computer is consciousness, a computer can not love. A computer can only access applied knowledge. The brain has access to all knowledge. I adventured far, to explore Blue Planet. You have my pioneer genes. Explore your mind. THINK. Thought is the ultimate speed of existence. Thought frequency is a conductor for other frequencies. You have a bio-transmitter-receiver in your brain. I am an androgenous Xylanthian, I enjoy sex. Access the Alpha Processor, I will meet you anywhere you choose.

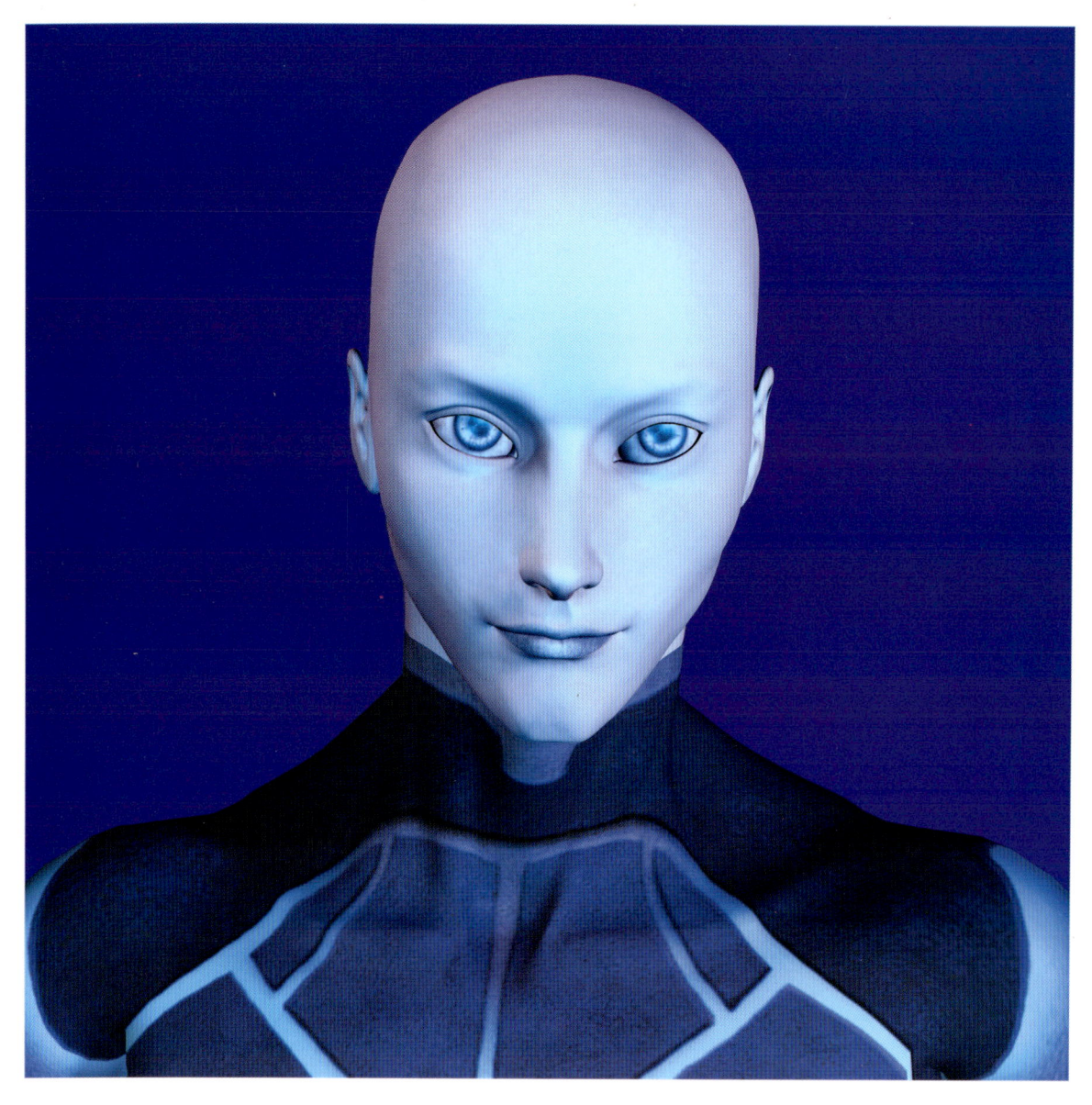

I am Xoah, the Greeks fantasized me as Poseidon. My genetics and your genetics are immortalized in the bio-memory of the Alpha Processor. We all live forever. My intense sensual desire for Tua, the paradise of Blue Planet and apparent extinction of Primitive Beings, beckoned me to Earth. Tua, in all her glory, was a wild animal. My ancient ancestors were violent reptilian beasts. TOGETHER, we changed our behavior and arbitrated with our counterparts, therein is the key to change. Togetherness is the key to change a confused species into peaceful society. Protest and condemnation creates confusion. IT IS BETTER TO LIGHT A CANDLE THAN COMPLAIN ABOUT THE DARKNESS. YOU ARE A CANDLE. Join hands and light millions of candles. Enjoy life, beat millions of drums and chant the songs of Freedom and LOVE. Your psychogenetic-memory is awakening. LOVE ONE ANOTHER.

GRATUITIES

Special Acknowledgment:

Japan Cosmic Vortex Family

Reverend Zuiko Tokunaga

Shoko Umehara, President, Cosmic Vortex Japan

The parents of Mana

Robert Collins "Hawkeye" for petroglyph photos (email: oldcowboy44@aol.com)

Special thanks for the considerations extended by the Kerch Police Department.

Hollywood Trident Network

RomyLeah, Maui, Hawaii.

Archeological Research:

Institute of Archaeology NAS of Ukraine

Ukrainian Academy of Sciences

Catahoyuk Project

Info on Atlantis Motherland:

Center for the Study of Historical Monuments at the Academy of Sciences of Ukraine.

The Ukrainian Society for the Preservation of Historical and Cultural Heritage.

Ivan Nechui-Levytski, Renate Rolle, & Jeannine Davis-Kimball, Dokia Humenna Foundation

St. Petersburg Museum

The Golden Plow, Yuri Chopivskyi

Ancient Inventions, by Peter James & Nick Thorpe

Ministry of Health Resorts and Tourism of the Autonomous Republic of Crimea.

The Ukrainian Museum in New York

Photographs, Images & Cartography:

Cherilyn Smouse, artist, Oregon, USA

Aleksei Korsakov, www.korsakov.ru

Visipix.com, BigFoto.com, pdphoto.org

Brooke McDonald, seashepard.com

animalsvoice.com and FreeStockPhotos.com

Research Information:

Mauna Kea Astronomical Observatory, Science City, Hawaii

Oxford University

Mamma Haidara Commemorative Library, Timbuktu, Mali

Kenneth Smouse, Oregon

Istanbul Koprulu Library

Geologic and Hydrologic Research:

United Nations

Black Sea Environmental Programme

Black Sea Geographic Information System

Depart. of Cartography and Geoinformatics, Moscow University

Kiev University, Institute of Nautical Archaeology, Underwater Archeology and Training Center

Woods Hole Oceanographic Institute

MIT DEEPArch Research Group

Special thanks to the people of the United States for creating a public domain database of research information, photographs and graphic images accessible to the world. Special acknowledgment to: NASA, JPL, NURP, NOAA, BLM. USGS, USDA, DOE, NIL, NIX, FWS, DOD, FBI & LOC.

For additional information visit: atlantis-motherland.com